ARRANGED VACANCY

IRENE BAHRD

Formatted with Vellum

To every overachiever
who struggles with self-doubt...

Alex believes in you.

CONTENT WARNINGS

By reading this book, there is a good chance you will experience the following side effects:

- Wet panties.
- Sudden urge to register to vote
- Realizing a fictional morally light gray character would be a better option than most of the people in government
- Considering a vibrating butt plug, but after the epilogue, think better of it

You're welcome.

All jokes aside, this is a slow-to-medium burn, **low-medium spice** novel, with on-page explicit content. It's a bit more vanilla than my other books, but is still intended for mature audiences. Also, because it's lower on the spice side for my books, only expect this sexy read to have your hands in your pants maybe twice before it's over.

Additionally, there are scenes with:

- Love triangle-ish that includes cheating/revenge cheating
- Oral sexytime — it's an Irene Bahrd trademark, you knew it was coming
- Sexytime during that time of the month
- Vanilla sexytime — sorry
- Butt stuff in the epilogue
- On-page death (Chapter 40 and Bonus Epilogue)
- Mention of infertility (Epilogue)

If you are triggered by anything in this book, do us both a favor and don't read anything else in my backlist. The rest of my books are equally (or more) unhinged.

Finally, this book is <u>NOT</u> a how-to guide. There is no use of birth control in this book. Please be safe and talk to your doctor about what works best for you and/or your sexual partners regarding birth control and STI protection. Jaclyn, Alex, and Chris are fictional, you are not.

CHAPTER 1

JACLYN

"**A**ll right, Jackie, we'll begin once Christopher is ready," Lisa quips, studying her clipboard and adjusting her glasses.

I purse my lips, not daring to correct her for calling me Jackie, even though I detest it. The last thing I need is someone leaking to the press that I'm a 'bridezilla.' Instead, I admire my A-line satin gown in the mirror, swiping at my non-existent wrinkles and nod once.

Poised. Pleasant. Polished.

"Thank you, Lisa. You've been a tremendous help today." She offers a genuine smile in response and steps out.

My entire life has been curated to bring me to this moment. Growing up in the White House, society and the media have dictated each facet of my life. Today is no different. Except, my wedding coordinator has given me more stress than the planning itself.

As for my fiancé, Christopher will be the perfect husband. Or, rather, he's a good political match; we have plenty in common. Perhaps plenty isn't the proper term. Enough. We have *enough* in common.

Who needs love? Friendship and respect are more important.

Or at least friendship.

Friendship is essential... Right?

Chris and I come from political families who have the highest expectations of us, and he understands the microscope I've been under since I was a child. Chris and his twin brother, Alex, are Senators, and their father was the President before mine. Despite my father's political career being over three years ago, as a soon-to-be Senator's wife, I'm still in the limelight.

State Assembly, Governor, Congressman, and two terms as President... I don't remember the last time I wasn't supporting my father. The next decade will be more of the same, this time for Chris.

Inspecting the last few details of my appearance, I can't help my sigh. It may be a loveless arrangement, but it's advantageous for both of us. As one of the youngest of the party, Chris' chances of being the presidential nominee increase exponentially when he's no longer a bachelor—especially marrying a Taylor. If everything goes to plan, he should be able to announce his candidacy shortly after our honeymoon.

The perfect Washington power couple.

I check my phone for what must be the tenth time in the past hour, and there are only twenty minutes before I'm supposed to begin the next chapter in my life. My attention is pulled away from it when, without looking up from her own phone, one of my bridesmaids robotically tells me, "You look beautiful."

Glancing around the bridal suite, my bridesmaids are three women I hardly know. None of them appear anxious, though given we're practically strangers, I shouldn't expect them to be. With nothing going the way I envisioned it would on my wedding day, my nerves are slowly getting the best of me, and I'm starting to regret my decision to not have my real girlfriends stand up with me.

I wouldn't want Ileah or Evelyn to be part of this charade —today is more for the country, the party, and the press, than it is for me. Though, I suppose my stand-in bridesmaids and I have more in common than I'd like to admit. We've all been meticulous about our public personas to ensure we'd be the picturesque wives to Senators and Governors.

Educated, but not opinionated. Feminine, but not too delicate. Social, but always keeping secrets guarded. First Lady is in my future if I marry Chris; I have to play the part.

Despite having political aspirations of my own, being an unmarried woman in my father's party, my career would fail miserably if I ran. While the Taylor name opens *some* doors, those doors are only a crack you can slip a hand through, and after today, the name will no longer be mine. My best chance at being anything other than a political trophy wife is to help my husband's career flourish. If luck is on my side, in a few years—and after birthing a few obligatory children—I'll have my shot at stepping into the political ring. I just need to bide my time.

Five more minutes pass before Lisa breathlessly rushes in. One hand presses her headset closer to her ear, and she gasps, "You need to speak with Former President Taylor."

My shoulders sag with a sigh. "What does my father need?"

"He didn't say, but he's in room seven down the hall."

She's as utterly useless as my bridesmaids.

With a last look around the room, I lift the skirt of my dress enough not to trip over it, and briskly walk to room seven. Hand poised to knock, I pause. There's shouting coming from inside, and I rest my ear on the ornate wooden door.

"We have to cancel," Father grits out.

"No, Jerry! That's not what we discussed. In no world will I allow my daughter—*our family*—to be disgraced because of *his* mistakes!" Mother snaps back. "She's worked too hard for this. *I've* worked too hard for this. I don't care about him saving face; we find another way. Isn't there some crisis we can make up and toss to the media sharks? Something to distract them?"

What the hell is happening?

I finally knock, and to my surprise, Christopher answers —wearing a navy suit, not his tuxedo. "Chris, what are you doing here? Shouldn't you be—" My breath is stolen from me; the blue in Chris' hazel eyes is more brown. We haven't talked in years, yet he still makes my heart stop and my stomach twist. As the air returns to my lungs, I exhale, "*Alex.*"

"Well, don't you clean up nicely?" His heated gaze slowly takes in every inch of me, sending shivers down my spine. While they may be identical in appearance, they couldn't be more different. Alex's irises flare, looking at me with a hint of longing; something Chris has never done. When Alex eventually meets my eyes again, he smirks. "Seems you don't know my brother all that well, if you're confusing me for him. Maybe it's best you're calling it off."

"No one is calling anything off. What are you doing here?" Shouldering past him into the room, I don't wait for his response and address my father, "You summoned me?"

"Yes. Christopher was in an *accident.*"

Looking back at Alex, I gulp. "Is he okay?" *He better be, my plans depend on it.*

Father pauses and lets out a long, almost exaggerated breath, pulling my attention back to him. He lowers his head for a moment before his stoic expression and stiff posture returns. "I'm sorry. He's not coming."

Mother rushes to me, pulling me into a tight embrace as she whispers, "Don't let him cancel it. We have to find a way to fix this."

Quickly stepping out of her hold, my brows pinch. "If he was in an accident, why don't we just postpone?"

"Because we can't disclose how my brother got into said accident. The story will be that he stood you up," Alex replies, though he's less smug about his suggestion than I expect. He actually sounds... *sorry?* Hell must've frozen over; this man has been nothing but a thorn in everyone's side since he took office. Not only does he not vote with his brother on a single policy issue, but based on his approval rating, it's blatant to all of us that he's making his own moves for the executive branch. He should be elated by a chance to take Chris down; none of this makes sense.

Also, how can those golden flecks in his hazel eyes still draw me in after well over a decade?

I'm still unsure why he's here and not his father. Even more curious is why he can't keep his eyes off me. My skin is on fire under his gaze, and I can't seem to keep mine to myself, either.

With my jaw tight, I bite back my words and keep my composure. Mother is right. It would ruin me if the story is that Chris stood me up—it's bad enough some tabloids have dubbed me an ice queen. The safest route is to echo her sentiment. "If you need to sweep the accident under the rug, we need to find another way."

Alex's lips tilt up in a half-smile, and my eyes briefly fall to them before I catch myself. There is absolutely nothing humorous about any of it, and I hate that he's enjoying this. He briefly hums and asks, "Do you actually want to marry my brother?"

His tone isn't accusatory, but I still pierce him with a cold glare and dramatic scoff. "Of course." I have no desire to participate in whatever game he's playing.

He nods thoughtfully. "Then, marry *me?*" His words steal my breath yet again. The suggestion is absurd, but somehow Alex's odd proposal feels more honest than Chris'. A public relations company staged our engagement—the time, the location... all of it. Unlike today, everything was executed with precision.

"What?" Mother laughs. "*You?* Don't be ridiculous, Alexander. It would be a bigger scandal than your brother's accident. Absolutely not."

"She's right. You're a damn playboy, not to mention the wrong side of the aisle. You'd ruin her life," Father seethes.

"Just as a stand-in for Chris. No one would know it's me," Alex explains, raising his hands in surrender. "Jaclyn briefly thought I was him when I opened the door; it's not a stretch. So, I marry her in the ceremony. Everyone thinks I'm Chris, and we say 'Alex' had an emergency. The only one who saw me here was your secret service detail, so as far as everyone else is concerned, I'm not here."

My plans are in flames. After all these years of avoiding each other, why would Alex do this? I can't marry him, even if he's only pretending to be Chris. I'll have to lie to my friends, our families... to God. We were both brought up in the church; he has to know vows aren't empty words.

No, I can't do this.

"Their marriage certificate is already signed," he continues, "except for the officiant and witnesses, correct? So, she'll be married to Christopher, his accident remains a secret, and you—" He pivots to face me, and arrogance drips off him as he purrs, "*You,* princess, will get your happily ever after." His words are a twisted knife to my heart. He has to know this is just an arrangement, not a happily ever after for me.

I thought agreeing to marry Chris would be like marrying someone like Alex, but the twins share no emotional similarities. It's been years since Alex and I were friends—though I secretly wanted more. Even now, he's one of only a few people who really understands me. My childhood was spent on campaign trails, making it difficult to be able to maintain true friendships. It was lonely—still is. If only Alex and I could've remained close, perhaps he wouldn't be so aloof about this?

Perhaps if I hadn't listened to my family, Chris wouldn't be in the picture, and I would be marrying Alex instead...

"That's... actually brilliant. It'll smother the scandal for now. She'll do it," Mother accepts before I even have a moment to register what she's agreed to.

"It could work," Father adds, void of emotion and smoothing his beard. "As long as it's temporary."

Small laugh lines appear at the corner of Alex's eyes; he's enjoying this far too much.

"We don't have much time. Alex, go find Lisa. For it to work, none of us breathes a word of this... or the accident," Mother announces indignantly.

"Will anyone tell me what's going on? Where is Chris? Where was the accident? Was he hurt?" My questions come out in rapid succession, glancing between the three of them. Father gives me a knowing look—he'll never tell me. My gaze lowers in submission.

Unfortunately, given my current predicament, marrying Alex appears to be the only viable option for a chance at creating my own happiness. It isn't as if it matters what I want; if it's my father's wish, I'll be marrying Alex within the hour.

"From this moment forward," Mother tells Alex, "you're Christopher Blake. At least until Jerry and your father say otherwise. Is that understood?"

"Hold on," I shout at the same time as Alex replies, "Yes, ma'am."

Everyone is talking, and my ears are ringing; all I see are lips moving. My whole body silently vibrates, my heart racing to escape my chest, as I pray this is all just a bad dream.

No, this is my reality, and I'll be damned if they destroy everything I've worked for by being careless—they are all rushing into something without considering the small details.

"Stop!" My raised voice is enough for everyone to cease speaking over each other, and face me. "I'll do it, but we need to make sure our stories are straight. Alex—*Chris*—was in traffic, to account for him being late." I close the distance and grasp his tie with one hand, loosening it with my other. After popping his collar, I slip it over his head and hand it to Mother. "You can't go out there looking like Alex. Take off your jacket." He does as I ask, and I smooth his collar down. My fingers linger longer than they should, and my cheeks heat as I quickly pull away. Mother takes out a small comb from her purse, handing it to me. "Thank you."

I reach up to comb Alex's hair, but he snatches my wrist. "I don't think so."

"You're impossible." Jerking out of his hold, he reluctantly lets me part his hair the same way Chris does. "We don't have any styling gel or pomade, but you need to appear unprepared. It works."

"I'm *never* unprepared."

"There's no time for this," Mother grumbles, taking the comb back. "Go find Lisa. While she's not the best event coordinator in the world, she'll at least be able to find you a hairstylist, and whoever has Chris' tux."

"Why did you hire her if she's not good at her job?" he asks with a light chuckle.

"No time, Alex," Mother snaps. "Go!" Then she tells me with less fire, "You too, Jaclyn. It's almost time." I nod, and as Alex begins to walk me out, my father's voice pierces the air. "Jaclyn, you know what's at stake."

Heat creeps up my neck; if steam could come out of my ears, it would. I do *not*, in fact, know what's at stake, only that my marriage to Chris is part of some elaborate plan of my father's. With a deep sigh, I straighten my posture and paint on a smile. "Of course."

Alex leans in to whisper, "You know, anger looks good on you, *wife*."

CHAPTER 2
ALEX

Marrying Jaclyn, albeit for show, was not on my election cycle bingo card.

I suppose my life could be worse. I'm not sure how, but it absolutely could.

Undrinkable water for millions, even in my home state...

Broken systems I'll never be able to fix...

Hungry children all over the United States...

Yes, life could be worse. Not worse than Jaclyn's if she doesn't marry my brother. She's right, the story of her being stood up would ruin her.

I'm putting my ass on the line, and with one wrong move, the truth will get out. My family will ensure my brother's indiscretions are covered up. I'll be seen as the power-hungry son who turned his back on his father's party, leaped across the aisle, and stole his brother's wife. I can almost taste the bitterness of the headlines now.

When I saw Jaclyn in her white satin gown, the way her breath hitched when she saw me... my heart squeezed in a way it hasn't in years. We've hardly spoken since college, but I'm having flashbacks of her laughing at my stupid jokes while cramming for finals, our late nights researching in the library, and how she would always insist on buying me a drink if she did better than I did on a midterm. Then one day, she distanced herself—stopped sitting next to me in our shared classes, and avoided me in every social situation we were presented with.

I never asked why, and she never explained.

But Jaclyn doesn't deserve to have her social and political reputation tarnished or destroyed because of my errant brother. She's stuck between a rock and a hard place, and now I'm right there with her. Except, it's all a game of chess and she's two moves away from checkmate. There are big players lurking in the background, pulling the strings. And I can't believe for one moment that Chris loves her; he can't, considering what he did. Does she love him? After today, I fucking hope not.

She deserves better, even if she chose this... chose *him*.

Once the door shuts behind us, I glance in either direction to ensure no one is within earshot and, with my hand on her hip, press her against the wall beside the door. "Before you go back, we have to practice."

"Are you insane?" she whisper-shouts, eyes molten, and I'm drawn to the heat.

As Jaclyn attempts to push me back, I hold my ground. "I'm serious. Does my brother go to the left or the right?"

"Alex," she sighs, "stop." I take a step back, and she takes a couple of deep breaths. Being the smart girl she is, she also checks the hallway before adding, "I don't need to kiss you to marry you."

I shake my head and close the distance again, placing my hand on the wall above her head. "Have you forgotten the very last thing the officiant says, princess?"

"He's a pastor, not an officiant," Jaclyn corrects, her dark blue eyes narrowing, and I can't help but admire the fight in her.

Her rebuttal does little to deter me from continuing, "The *pastor* will say, 'You may kiss the bride,' and we'll be forced into it. We both know what the paps and the media expect, and I don't want to blow my cover here. So, does he go left or right?"

Jaclyn shuts her eyes tightly, lowering her head slightly as she exhales in defeat. "I'm sorry. I forgot I'm not the only one trapped; we're in this together."

"Keep your eyes closed," I whisper, and press a soft kiss to her cheek. She doesn't stiffen as I expect her to, instead letting out a relieved sigh. "I can fake a kiss. Closed-lipped. A few seconds too long. We can fool them into feeling like it's real. When we have to do it during the reception, wrap your arms around my neck, I'll hold you close to me, and kiss your cheek, just like that. The media will eat it up."

Jaclyn's posture remains perfectly straight, but her shoulders slightly relax. "Thank you."

"Despite what your father may think of me, I respect the sanctity of marriage." Jaclyn scoffs, but I continue whispering beside her ear, "You and I will share *one* kiss. The rest will be a game of how to fool them into believing we're in love. So, we need to get the details right. Does he go left or right?"

"Right." We both swallow thickly, and as I pull back, her eyes flutter open. The moment her blue eyes find mine, I'm lost in them, so entranced that I nearly forget her soft reply.

I'm unable to hide my smile, though I have a pang of jealousy that my brother is marrying her, despite his absence today. She never asked for this—she's more than a prize to be won, especially since she graduated first in her class from college, rightfully stealing valedictorian from me.

There's a chance I'm very wrong about her. She could be playing her own game, one where she's not the pawn, I am.

Leaning in once more, I brush the left of my nose to hers. "We'll get through this. It should only be for the night."

Our lips a hair's breadth apart, it takes everything in me to not kiss her; I can almost taste the strawberry and champagne on her. But... she's not mine, and she doesn't want me. If she did, I'd already have her dress hiked up around her waist, kissing a hell of a lot more than her cheek.

"Chris!" a woman shrieks behind us, making Jaclyn chuckle softly; we've already fooled someone. "You're needed in the groom's suite, and you know you're not supposed to see the bride before the ceremony!"

I pull back an inch, mesmerized by Jaclyn and her deep blue eyes. They aren't just cerulean, there are streaks of dark navy around the edge of her irises. I'm not sure how my brother got so lucky with such a beautiful and intelligent bride, but those eyes have haunted me, and will continue to forever. She doesn't tear away, doesn't flinch, keeping her gaze locked on me.

"Chris will be there in a moment. There was horrible traffic. He'll be ready in a few minutes," she replies on my behalf.

"We're down the aisle in a *few minutes*, Jackie!" A flash of anger appears in her eyes at the name, a small recoil, but she is otherwise unmoved.

"*Jaclyn*," I correct, not wanting to leave the magnificent creature in front of me, "will be in her suite momentarily. I'll get changed and will need someone to adjust my hair before I'm at the altar. Want to look my best for my future wife."

Jaclyn's lips part and she sucks in a sharp breath, drawing my attention to them. If I leaned in, would she let me kiss her?

For practice, of course.

No. She isn't mine.

"Right this way, Mr. Blake," the insufferable woman sings as she attempts to pull me from Jaclyn.

I shouldn't be the least bit attracted to my brother's fiancée. Coupled by the fact that she's a Taylor, in no world could she be mine.

Resisting temptation, I willingly follow the woman, and she finally introduces herself as we walk away from Jaclyn. "I'm not sure if you remember me. I'm Lisa, your event coordinator, here to elevate your wedding experience. We've had a few bumps, but everything is going according to plan now."

Everything is not going to plan, Lisa. It's a fucking shit show.

We continue down the hall to the groom's suite. As she opens the heavy wooden door, she asks with a sickeningly sweet voice, "Is there anything else I can assist you with? The groomsmen are staged."

Chris would bark at her, and I'm no longer Alex. I take a quick breath and growl, "No. I need hair and makeup in here immediately. I'll be changed in three minutes." I walk in and shut the door in her face, hating every part of that interaction.

I swiftly change into a tuxedo that fits too snugly, and with things no longer going as they were supposed to, I message the one man who could ruin my political career at the snap of his fingers.

I'm standing in for Chris.

The Taylors have been briefed.

As I stuff my phone in my pocket, Lisa is knocking on my door precisely three minutes after I walked in here. I wouldn't be surprised if I opened the door and found her with a stopwatch.

"Everything all right in there?"

"You're late," I grit out, fastening my lavender snap-dragon boutonniere to my jacket.

Lisa rushes into the room with two other people—both have short, black half-aprons. One has a variety of brushes and combs, the other with fluffy makeup brushes peeking out.

"Your brother, Alexander, appears not to be in attendance," Lisa hesitantly admits.

I do my best to school an indifferent expression. "Yes, he had an emergency." My father will likely ask where I am, since I should be seated behind him. I hate lies, particularly when it comes to family, but there's no way around this—Alex is missing, not Chris. I'll have to fill him in after the ceremony, if the fixer, Ned, hasn't beaten me to it.

With a curt nod, Lisa looks at the women. "Okay, girls, work your magic!"

CHAPTER 3
CHRIS

I wake to a swirl of obnoxious noise: Beeping that sounds like a truck backing up, women whispering... And there's a strong medicinal scent I can't quite place. My entire body is sore with a dull ache, and I carefully open one eye, then the other.

A hospital?

The last thing I remember is driving to the wedding venue. I take a quick survey of the room—no family, only two nurses talking in hushed tones next to a computer. As I attempt to sit up, one of them hears me struggling and rushes over.

"Sir, you need to lie down. You were in a very serious accident. Penny, page the doctor!" The other woman clicks a button on a device and summons an entire team of people in white coats who enter the room seconds later.

All of them scurry around me like leaves on a blustery day. *Am I drunk?*

After a battery of tests, no one can tell me why I'm here, what day it is, if I missed my wedding, or what happened to my aide who was in the passenger seat.

"Has anyone spoken to my father?" I ask, my voice raspy.

"Please rest. Former President Blake will be here as soon as he can," a woman replies.

"With all due respect, can you find me a *doctor?*" I don't need a nurse placating me, I need a fucking doctor to tell me what's going on.

She huffs an unamused laugh. "Mr. Blake, I'm your cardiologist. If you'd prefer, I can find a doctor who doesn't specialize in cardiac events to discuss why you had a heart attack while driving."

Heart attack?

"I was on my way to the venue when—"

"Sir, as much as this pains me to say this, I'd avoid discussing who was in the car with you and what transpired prior to the accident—at least until you have a lawyer present."

"It's not what it looks like," I hiss as I attempt to sit up straighter in bed.

Keeping her tone even, she repeats, "Do *not* discuss anything with anyone, until you have representation." I nod and her posture slacks. "Now, would you prefer a different cardiologist?"

"No. I apologize. I assumed you were a nurse." She purses her lips, but I don't have time to stroke her ego. "What is happening with my heart?"

"Based on your records, you've met with a pulmonologist for your sleep apnea in the past. You haven't seen them in over a year. In the notes, it states they have discussed with you at *great length* how our lungs and heart are very much connected, and that it's recommended that you see a cardiologist regularly due to an increased risk of heart failure. Sometimes strenuous activities can aggravate this."

"I wasn't doing any strenuous—"

"Mr. Blake, I cannot stress enough that you wait for representation before discussing the accident. While everyone in this room has signed an NDA, the walls always have ears."

"Fine." *So help me, if this woman cuts me off again.* "Where's my father?"

"He's likely still there," a woman in blue scrubs says and turns on the television. The headline ticker reads: *Presidential Hopeful Christopher Blake Marries Washington Darling Jaclyn Taylor*. The entire room turns, all eyes on me. Then, the only thing I hear is the sound of the beeping of the monitor quickening as the room goes black.

CHAPTER 4
JACLYN

Walking down the aisle with Alex at the end has my stomach in knots. Putting one foot in front of the other, my father keeps a firm grip on my hand in the crook of his elbow. I wouldn't run; this isn't some movie or book where the bride runs from her own wedding. Alex standing in for Chris is a quick fix, but only a bandage on a bullet wound.

I will have my work cut out for me once this is over.

The aisle is adorned with lavender roses bundled in white satin bows adorning the end of each pew, and matching petals are placed along the edges of the runner. If it were up to me, they would be cornflower blue, not lavender. The music selected is a slow rendition of Wedding March, despite me suggesting Canon in D on violin with piano accompaniment. I would've preferred live music over recorded, but everyone insisted it had to do with the acoustics of the space. On the Tuesday following our meeting here, I brought a violinist with me, and it sounded incredible. Why they wouldn't allow it is beyond me.

As we continue toward Alex, I'm struggling with the reminder that as soon as Chris is back from wherever he is recovering from his secret accident, we'll begin our life of carefully planned social engagements, starting with our professionally photographed honeymoon. A two-week-long honeymoon is excessive, but with Congress being out for the majority of August, it's the perfect time to get to know each other better. Despite the fact that we have been dating for years, we're still strangers. For all I know, he could sleep with the concierge on the first day. Even through the prospective infidelity, it's the one aspect of the wedding traditions I've been looking forward to, when I won't need to be 'on' all of the time.

"Focus, Jaclyn," Father tuts as we take our final steps to the altar. When we reach it, he takes both of my hands, kissing my knuckles, then presses a chaste kiss to my cheek, and whispers, "If he tries anything unsavory, I can make him disappear."

Though he means it as a joke, I can't help the small laugh that escapes me—my father would most definitely make good on the promise. Alex offers his arm to help me up the final four steps to the pastor. Even though Chris and I went through this in rehearsal, the real thing is an entirely different experience when the seats are full and I'm up here on display... with *Alex*.

Checking my posture and position before ensuring my dress is fluffed out enough for pictures, I'm more nervous than I thought I would be. The downside of politically elite wives as bridesmaids is they don't care about you—my friends would've made sure I look my best.

Alex takes my hands, and I glance out into the sea of attendees. My pulse eases when I find Ileah, my friend from college, seated next to her husband, Tim—a representative from Delaware. I love that she's close to D.C., but being that Tim isn't the same party as Chris, I can't have her standing up with me; it would be bad for both of us. The only way I was able to invite her without raising suspicion was by inviting nearly all of Washington. What was supposed to be a small, intimate wedding is now one of the biggest political events of the year.

Tim is friends with Alex, so if Chris isn't back, maybe there's a chance the four of us can have lunch tomorrow...

No, damn it, I'll have to tell them Alex is pretending to be Chris.

Without a moment to entertain the idea further, the pastor begins with the ceremony. For the first time since I took Alex's hands, my eyes find his. Now in a tuxedo, with his hair styled like Chris, it's almost as if I'm marrying the man I'm supposed to. I still don't understand what Alex has to gain by helping me today, especially since conflict is written all over his face. He had the same look at our graduation when I took the stage—a swirl of sadness and disappointment, with a dash of respect and pride.

The pastor drones on stiltedly about love and finding your soulmate. I cast my gaze away from Alex's and he squeezes my hands, bringing my attention back to his golden hazel eyes. They are the first tell that he's not Chris. The second tell is that his shoulders are testing the confines of the ill-fitting jacket; Alex must work out significantly more than Chris does.

Shame washes over me, admitting Alex is the more attractive of the twins as I drink in the man before me. Goosebumps prickle down my limbs, and my breath picks up ever so slightly, enough for Alex to notice.

"You're doing great, Jaclyn. Keep breathing. It's almost over," he whispers, leaning in to brush his lips to my cheek. His sweet gesture and his smooth voice calm me more than I thought they would. My heart slows, and I'm able to focus on the pastor again.

We begin the unity ceremony, and as we pour the sand into the larger vase, I feel like a damn hypocrite. This is supposed to represent the joining of our families, but also of our hopes and dreams. Meanwhile, mine are dependent upon a man who isn't even here. There is nothing *unifying* about any of this.

The pastor leads us in a prayer, and my stomach falls— not only am I lying to everyone in attendance and the country, I'm lying to God. This whole ceremony goes against every fiber of my being, everything I've been taught, everything I believe in. On paper, I'm marrying Chris, but in the eyes of God, I'm marrying Alex.

Oh, shit. Am I adding polygamy to my list of sins? Coveting my fiancé's brother is likely at the top.

It's time for the part of the ceremony I've been dreading, and I hand my bouquet to my maid of honor. She gives me the ring to slip onto Alex's finger; his best man, Phillip, does the same. The fact that Phil hasn't noticed that Alex isn't Chris gives me pause.

Alex and Chris couldn't be more different, how am I the only one that notices?

We exchange rings and vows, all meaningless to Alex. "With this ring, I thee wed, and pledge you my love and devotion, now and forever," I proclaim.

He then repeats, "With this ring, I thee wed, and pledge to love, cherish, protect, and be devoted to you, now and forever."

Those are not the vows, Alex!

The pastor then ends the ceremony with, "By the authority vested in me by God, and by the District of Columbia, I now pronounce you husband and wife. You may kiss the bride."

Oh no...

A small smirk tugs at Alex's lips as he leans in, tilts his head to the right, and kisses me softly. It's chaste, as promised, but I can't help noticing the difference kissing him—his lips are fuller, he's gentler, and a quiet hum escapes me the moment our lips touch. My cheeks warm in embarrassment as I find myself a bit curious what he tastes like.

If I part my lips slightly...

No! What am I doing?

I brush the thought away as we pull back. It's the first *and last* kiss we'll share.

Cheers erupt all around us, and Alex quietly asks, "Are you ready?" I nod, and he guides me down the aisle as we're showered with lavender and white rose petals.

If I never see another lavender flower again, it'll be too soon.

When we reach the end, we're ushered away by Lisa for photographs. My stomach sinks at the prospect of staged pictures of us embracing or...

The blood drains from my face. That wasn't our last kiss, we have no less than twenty more.

"Lisa, my wife isn't feeling well. In order for us to continue with the reception, we'll need to reschedule our wedding photos for a later date." His tone has a bite to it that I didn't expect, only adding to my confusion.

"Mr. Blake, I can't just—"

"Yes, you can," he barks. "I want to make sure Alex is here for photos, as well. We may not get along, but he's family. You will reschedule the photographer, a makeup artist, and her hairstylist for another date when Jaclyn has recovered. One of my aides or Jaclyn's assistant will reach out with dates that suit."

Lisa looks to me, eyes full of hope that I'll disagree with him. I have no intention of saving her. "Thank you for being so amenable, Lisa." Her face falls, but she should know better than to argue with a Blake. "We'll start the reception shortly. I want to speak to my husband first."

"Of course, let me find you an acceptable space." She leads us down the hall to the same room that we were in earlier when Father broke the news to me. "Will this do?"

Seven is not a lucky number...

"Yes, thank you," Alex growls. While I knew him when we were younger, I don't know him now. Yet, the way he's treating Lisa feels out of character for him. She scurries away, and once the door closes, he takes out his phone and pulls up an application that checks your surroundings for microphones and cameras. None are found, so he speaks freely. "Was that all right?"

"No," I huff. "You bit her head off for helping us. It was too much. She'll figure out you aren't Chris!"

Alex rakes his hand through his hair, messing up his part and making him look more like himself again. "I'm sorry. I may have gone overboard."

"May? You were awful to her." I cross my arms over my chest. "What's going on with Chris? Where is he?"

His eyes widen at his brother's name and he lets out a long sigh. "I can't tell you. It isn't my place. He'll tell you himself when he's... I'm sorry, all I can say is Chris is doing better than expected, given the circumstances."

The door bursts open, and his father storms in. He doesn't stop until he's fisting Alex's tuxedo lapels, growling, "Where. Is. Chris?"

CHAPTER 5
ALEX

"This isn't his fault," Jaclyn defends, standing between me and my father. "Chris was in an accident. Alex was only stepping in for him."

His shoulders relax, and the creases between his brows soften. "Where is my son, Jaclyn?"

Jaclyn looks back at me for the answer I can't divulge in front of her. My gaze bounces between them. "She's correct; he was in an accident. I got a call and hired someone to... *take care of it*," I carefully reply. Hopefully, he's picking up in my tone that the Gallaghers were the ones who called me. Dad shakes his head in disappointment, and I continue to placate him. "They're moving him off the grid for medical treatment, but I was told he's in good condition. I warned Jerry—" He gives me his 'disappointed in you' expression that he's mastered over the years. "Sorry, I meant *Former President Taylor*, about the accident before the wedding so they could decide next steps. The hired fixer recommended the wedding should be canceled."

"Fixer?" Jaclyn whispers.

"Well, there *was* a wedding," my father snaps. "She married *you*. Do you know how this will look if it gets out?"

"If I may," Jaclyn interrupts with a firm but gentle tone, "Alex was only trying to protect both of our families. Chris and I signed the wedding certificate last week, it only needs the pastor and witness signatures. I'll legally be married to Christopher, not Alex. This is only temporary."

"No one knows what happened to him, except her parents," I add to calm his rage.

"What about...?" His eyes fall on Jaclyn.

I hate answering as if she's not standing right here, but I'm left with no choice. "She's not privy to *all* of the details at the moment."

Hurt paints her features, and I instinctively want to reach for her. I ball my hands into fists at my sides to keep them to myself. My father blows out a long breath. "So, what now? When can I see him?"

"I canceled the rest of the wedding photos, so Jaclyn can reschedule them with Chris when he's up to it. We only need to get through the reception. You, Mom, and Jaclyn can see him later tonight, if you'd like."

"Should I cancel the honeymoon?" Jaclyn asks, chewing on her lip. "Or at least postpone it?"

My father shakes his head. "Not yet. It'll be suspicious. Let's wait and get through the next few hours." His eyes narrow on me as he insists, "And keep your hands off your brother's wife."

"A little hard when I'm supposed to pretend I'm married to her," I chuckle, cocking an eyebrow. Though he finds no humor in this, he knows I'm right. "But, yes, in a few hours, it'll all be over."

There's a pounding at the door, making Jaclyn jump. I answer it, finding secret service side-eyeing Lisa on the other side while one of their hands is aloft to knock again.

"The wedding, uh, person is here to see you," he announces. Something about him feels off; I can't quite put my finger on it.

While there is a small chance Lisa caught the tail end of the exchange, based on her genuine smile, we should be in the clear. "We'd like to begin the reception, whenever you're ready." Her sweet demeanor calms everyone, except Jaclyn.

"We're ready." Jaclyn slides her hand into mine, and an unfamiliar warmth fills my chest. Her voice is delicate and demure—not the Jaclyn I knew in college.

"Perfect. Let's begin, shall we?" Lisa turns on her heel, and the three of us follow her to the outdoor reception with my father's secret service in tow behind us.

It's entirely too warm to hold this outside, but it's still beautiful—lavender flower arrangements and crisp white linens adorn each table, strings of soft lights illuminate the ivy climbing the walls, and a four-piece orchestra plays quietly in the corner.

It would've been nice to have them play during the ceremony, and the lavender doesn't feel like Jaclyn.

This whole wedding feels like something my mother put together. If it were up to me, it'd be on the beach, just the two of us, the fragrant gusts of ocean air, and...

Fuck, I need to stop thinking about this.

Jaclyn stiffens as we're announced. I keep her hand firmly in mine, squeezing once as I tell her softly, "You're perfect. Just follow my lead."

Everyone stands, and polite applause muffles the music. I lead her onto the dance floor and she whispers, "We're not supposed to do the first dance yet."

I lift Jaclyn's hand above her head to spin her, and she lets out a small laugh, her dress twirling a second longer than she does. She moves with grace, practically floating. Snaking my hand to her lower back, I splay my fingers on the smooth satin and bring her close—avoiding keeping her flush with me. As she rests her free hand on my shoulder, I can't seem to look anywhere except her captivating blue eyes, completely entranced.

"We shouldn't be dancing, Alex," she warns.

With a light laugh, I pull her an inch closer. "Who the hell cares? Why not have a bit of fun?"

Swaying her in a small box-step, I overhear someone saying, "I didn't know Chris could dance."

Jaclyn looks up at me, stifling a giggle, and my eyes widen. "He doesn't know how?"

"Chris is a horrible dancer." A playful smile dances on her lips. "I was really worried about our first as husband and wife, especially with everyone watching." Cupping my neck, she pulls me closer, her cheek brushing mine. I love and hate how good it feels to have her in my arms.

Camera flashes come from all directions, and I press a gentle kiss to her cheek. She hums in response; my heart squeezing at the sound. I shouldn't enjoy having her pressed against me, the scent of her citrusy perfume, how her hand fits perfectly in mine...

"I'm sorry. For all of this," she sighs, pulling me from thoughts I absolutely should *not* be having about my brother's wife.

Is she his wife? Or is she mine?

I could tell her, 'It's fine,' but none of this is. I'm caught up in a fantasy that can never be. I need to remind myself over and fucking over that even if she weren't married to my brother, we would never work.

When we were younger, I wanted to end regulations on rainwater collection, while Jaclyn was focused on how to create additional tax breaks for oil companies and billionaires in the name of trickle down economics. We're quite literally oil and water. If she's elected to office, I can only hope she won't cling to her father's policies and will listen to both sides of the aisle to unite the country.

If we're so wrong for each other, why am I still so drawn to her after all these years?

The song ends and I close my eyes, resting my forehead on hers to give the photographers the perfect shot. After a few brief moments, I tilt my chin and press a kiss to her forehead, and that damn sighed hum of hers seeps into my heart again.

Needing to be out of her personal space immediately, I take her hand and lead her to the sweetheart table set for us. As I pull her chair out, I resist the urge to kiss her exposed neck when I push it in. I hate that I'm desperate to know how she tastes and how, if it was just the two of us, I'd be on my knees in an instant.

No.

She's. Not. Mine.

CHAPTER 6
JACLYN

I gasp as I feel a ghost of a kiss on the side of my neck. When I glance behind me, Alex isn't touching me. No one is. He takes a seat next to me, and I'm grateful that the small round table allows for extra and much needed space between us.

My bouquet is displayed in the middle of our table, and it's truly the most uninspired arrangement I've ever seen —white and lavender roses bundled with satin ribbon, not a single sprig of green to be seen. Small tealights flicker on the table, highlighting the polished silverware and pewter charger. I would have preferred a simpler place setting with no charger. Sadly, I was outvoted by my mother and Mrs. Blake. More reminders of how this isn't truly my wedding.

A server sets two glasses of water in front of us, and I anticipate Alex to launch straight into ordering a stout— just like his brother. Instead, he thanks the server and gestures to me. I'm caught off-guard, taking a moment too long to respond.

Leaning in, Alex asks with a hint of flirtation, "Would you like something to drink?"

"Yes, sorry. A glass of Pinot Grigio. Please," I reply directly to the server.

He nods and takes Alex's order—an Old Fashioned with an extra cherry—then scurries off to retrieve them.

"Is that your usual?" *Really, Jaclyn?* We'll likely never share a meal together again after tonight; there's no reason for small talk.

"Sort of. I don't drink often, but when I do, that's what I order. It is a special occasion, after all." His smile meets his eyes, and they don't leave mine as he takes a drink of water. I'm staring too long and quickly glance away into the sea of people seated for dinner. "He's a lucky man."

My gaze snaps back to him. "Excuse me?"

"He's a lucky man," Alex repeats, with a tinge of sadness in his tone. "I'm sure you two will be very—"

A server appears with our dinner, unfortunately without our drinks. Mine is chicken that's seen better days, and Alex has the steak Chris requested; although it also appears to be less than desirable and could feed a small toddler at best. Considering how much our families paid for this, I'm genuinely surprised by the quality. Or rather, lack thereof.

Once they are out of earshot, Alex shakes his head with a soft laugh, muttering to himself, "Of course he'd order the steak."

"Oh, I'm sorry. Are you vegetarian?"

"Hardly." He places his napkin on his lap with a huff, and slices into the meat with his dull steak knife. "I suppose you don't follow what your husband supports."

Of course he had to ruin the evening by turning it into a political pissing match over cattle.

I fold my napkin in half and drape it across my lap. "I'm well aware of what Chris supports. A good wife stands by her husband's policies and beliefs. Why do you have an issue with him asking for additional tax incentives on the Livestock Health and Wellness Act?" I fork a small piece of broccoli a little too forcefully, and it flies off my plate and onto Alex's. "*Shit.* I'm so sorry!"

Mid-chew, he still manages to let out a full laugh. He pierces the broccoli and brings it to his mouth, about to take a bite. After a long pause, he doesn't and sets it down on his plate, lifting his napkin to wipe the corner of his mouth. "First of all, I love that you said 'shit.' But your *husband* is worried about the price of beef when the farmers and ranchers want to create regulations to ensure the wellbeing of their livestock."

"I'm aware." I reach over and take his fork, eating my rogue broccoli off it and setting it back down on his plate.

"You support that?"

"I support my husband."

The server delivers our drinks and Alex thanks him, sliding a bill into the man's hand. He stammers, "Gratuity is included, sir."

"I won't tell, if you won't." Alex winks with an adorable smirk. "Keep 'em coming."

The man slips away, and I can't help asking, "Why are you being so difficult?"

"You only get married once." He shrugs and takes a long sip of his drink. "So, based on your logic, if the two of us were married, you would support the ranchers in creating safe environments for their livestock?"

I take a quick survey of our surroundings to ensure no one could be listening in. "Yes, I would."

"And if you weren't married?"

I drink a third of my wine quickly, annoyed to admit, "Yes."

"Yes, what?"

"Yes, I would support the ranchers," I huff, but quickly adjust my posture and ensure my soft smile is in place in case someone photographs a candid shot. "It doesn't matter what I want."

"It matters. Your opinion matters... *You* matter, Jaclyn." Alex bites his lip and chuckles softly, "It's a shame we're not married. I could've used your wifely support in committee."

With my jaw tight, my painted-on smile remains intact as I lift my chin. "Truly a shame," I reply sarcastically, but my rehearsed smile becomes more real by the second.

A small dimple appears as he continues eating without another word. I've lost my appetite, only taking a few bites of my overcooked chicken and under-seasoned vegetables before setting my napkin on the table. Alex cuts off a small piece of his steak that's perfectly pink in the middle and offers it to me. With a few sets of eyes on me, I reluctantly lean in and take a bite. It's surprisingly flavorful, though my stomach is still in knots and I don't think I could eat any more.

"Would you like to finish mine?" he asks. His brows are pinched with genuine concern, and I reply with a shake of my head, taking a sip of my wine. "Are you sure? You've barely touched your dinner."

"I'm sure," I sigh. My heart is twisted over all of this. "Thank you, though."

Alex offers me another small smile, and the longer I'm sitting here with him, the more I wonder if we could maybe be friends again one day. While we may not agree on everything, he's not the man Chris and their father have made him out to be. Except I'm not sure how that would work, being friends with someone who actively votes against everything my family stands for. With pressure from my father, I've had enough trouble remaining friends with Ileah all these years; there's no need to rock the boat further.

He's about to say something when he spots Lisa rushing over. "How was everything?"

Alex's tone is gruff in comparison to her overly bright tone when he replies, "Great." I hate to admit that it's not an exaggerated mocking of Chris—it's spot on, playing the part perfectly and reminding me once again that this is all just for show.

"Wonderful," I lie, keeping my tone light to mirror hers.

"I know you already had your first dance." She glares at Alex, then softens her expression before looking at me. "What would you like to do?"

Alex stands, pushes in his chair, and offers me his hand. "My wife and I would like to dance again."

CHAPTER 7

ALEX

Proposing a wedding activity that requires me to be close to Jaclyn is by far the worst idea I've had all night. But messing with the event coordinator is far too much fun. The mere suggestion of skipping cutting the cake to dance with Jaclyn had Lisa fuming. Despite my fake wife being one of the most rigid women I've ever met, she seems to welcome the chaos. It feels like college all over again. This time, the stakes are higher than failing an accounting class.

Maybe it's the whiskey, or the whirlwind that was today, but I take a risk going off script once more. Spinning Jaclyn out and back into my arms, I dip her at the end of the song. She throws her head back, letting out a full laugh; it's music to my ears. When I pull her upright, her laughter ceases almost immediately, now acutely aware of what's expected of us.

I'm a man of my word, so I give her a discreet, curt nod. Catching on, she wraps her arms around my neck, and I kiss the side of her mouth—enough to appear to be a real kiss.

Fuck, why do I want more than a fake kiss with her?

I pull back, but she moves closer, pressing her soft cheek to mine and whispers, "Thank you." Her warm breath fans my ear, making the hair on the back of my neck stand up.

There isn't a moment to enjoy having her in my arms because a hand clamps on my shoulder. "May I cut in?" I stiffen and abruptly pull back from Jaclyn at her father's deep, commanding voice.

"Of course, Former President Taylor."

"I'm pretty sure that you're supposed to call me 'Dad.'" He winks and I step to the side, finding Jaclyn's eyes full of fear. Neither of us have done anything wrong, but I feel the same worry she's exuding. Her eyes soften as quickly as they widened, and her well-rehearsed smile appears, leaving me to awkwardly move away from them to enjoy their father-daughter dance.

The music begins, and they start swaying side-to-side. Standing next to my father, he grumbles, "She's not yours, Alexander." Thankfully, he's quiet enough that no one can hear him as we watch Jaclyn dance with her dad. Despite my father's warning, I can't seem to take my eyes off her.

"I know. But I had to do it," I whisper back. "She deserves

the perfect wedding. Especially once she finds out what happened."

"I was briefed by the Gallaghers; we can never tell her. Mickey's not happy with the turn of events. He didn't go into details, but we'll deal with it another time. After the wedding, we'll go see Chr—" He looks behind him. "*Your brother.* Then, you'll take Jaclyn home." My eyes fix on him as he continues looking out at the dance floor. "You need to keep up appearances. *Alex* had an accident. Hit by a drunk driver on his way to the wedding." I nod in understanding. With prying eyes everywhere, I do my best to keep my expression neutral. "We'll cover for you until your brother is home. Thank you for doing this."

He claps me on the back twice, and I can't help the mixture of pride and hurt I feel. The day I told my father I was running for office, I'd never seen him so excited. His enthusiasm died instantaneously when I told him I was running as a moderate in the opposing party. We haven't spoken more than two words to each other in the five years since I won a Senate seat in Texas. Until now.

The song ends, and I take to the dance floor with Mom. We remain eerily quiet for the four minutes, swaying to a classical rendition of a song I've heard before, but can't place. When it ends, she says softly, "You're a good man, Alex."

I am not.

I've spent the afternoon flirting with my brother's now-wife. If there's a hell, I'm certain today has earned me a ticket straight to the gates.

My mother gives me a final hug, and Jaclyn takes my hand to lead us to the cake table. I suspect Lisa has gotten to her about our schedule and the fun is over. Firmly gripping the handle of the flimsy knife, I push down, only to be met with a hard material I can't seem to cut through. While the knife is a thick plastic posing as metal, it shouldn't be an issue. Jaclyn chuckles softly and delicately places her hand over mine. She moves my cut a few inches to the left, where I'm able to slice into the spongy cake.

"The majority of it is for show. There's only a sliver of real cake in this whole thing; the rest is dense styrofoam. It's too warm for a cake to be sitting outside for us to cut," she explains, her fingers lingering on top of mine. "This way, we still get a bit of fact in the fiction."

We plate the piece together, and I break off a small portion to feed it to her. There's no hesitation; our gazes locked as I lift the chocolate and vanilla marble cake to her. My cock twitches in my slacks as she takes a bite, briefly imagining her mouth wrapped around something significantly less innocent than my fingers.

Forget a ticket to hell, I'll be catching the express train.

Jaclyn does the same; feeding me a broken-off part of the slice. Except, when we're done, she sucks her fingers clean of the frosting. She has to be fucking with me at this point, doing this intentionally. I'm transfixed by her until it's announced that we'll be tossing the bouquet and garter, which pulls me from my wicked musings... Only for them to quickly return at the thought of kneeling before her.

And I'll have my hand up her dress...

The single women line up, and she tosses her bouquet over her shoulder. It's always been my understanding that a second bouquet is used, so the bride may keep her original one as a memento, but the one Jaclyn is tossing is from the ceremony.

It isn't until I'm on one knee in front of her to retrieve the garter that I'm able to ask, "Didn't you want to keep it?"

"The bouquet? No. She'll enjoy it more than I will," she replies softly. "I love roses, but hate lavender... and red. Thankfully, I talked them out of red."

I nod at the curious admission, wondering if my family is one of 'them,' as my fingers carefully slide up her smooth leg in search of the pointless fabric. Her breath hitches when I reach her thigh. "I'm so sorry," I quietly apologize. I'm not, but need to behave myself as I tug it down quickly; I'd hate for her to be any more uncomfortable than she already is. The tradition is incredibly awkward —*who wants their wife's garter in the hands of another man?* Flinging it into the crowd of eligible bachelors, cheers erupt when a fellow senator catches it.

For the rest of the evening, Jaclyn and I visit with guests, never speaking with anyone long enough to raise suspicion that I'm not my brother. We share one last dance, and I feel a bit like Cinderella with the clock striking midnight—this will be the last time I'll have her in my arms. Tomorrow, we'll part ways, and there's a fair chance we'll never speak again after tonight. The realization stings more than I ever thought possible.

Our song ends and I can't resist pressing a single kiss to her temple. Her small hum is a punch in the gut. It'll be the last time I hear it...

The last time I kiss her...

I bring my lips next to her ear, keeping my voice low. "When we leave, be careful to not call me Alex, and don't mention the accident. You never know who might be listening in or who we can trust. Even his own doctors. We'll get changed here and drive straight to him."

Jaclyn takes a deep breath and pulls back, searching my eyes for a moment before sighing, "Okay."

"For what it's worth, he doesn't deserve you, princess," I admit, as much as I shouldn't.

And in no lifetime would I deserve you, either.

CHAPTER 8
JACLYN

My father suggested Alex take me to the hospital, instead of a hired driver. *"The fewer people who know about this, the better."*

The ride is quiet as Alex white-knuckles the steering wheel, his jaw tight as he continuously checks the rearview mirror. He saved my reputation today, but he's so on edge that I'm afraid to even properly thank him. If he's anything like Chris, I don't dare say anything, out of fear of upsetting him further.

Pulling up to a high-rise hotel in Alexandria, I can't handle the silence a moment longer, and tread carefully. "Is this where Chris is staying?"

"No, we had a tail." His tone is clipped, unlike the rest of the evening. "I'm going to get us a couple of rooms for the night. We might be able to sneak out in a few hours." The wedding was for show, and I shouldn't read anything into his kind gestures. I have whiplash from the change.

I sigh, though it comes out more like a grouchy whine. "One room."

"What?" he snaps, finally looking at me.

Hoping to defuse the situation, I keep my tone sweet and quiet. "One room. It'll look suspicious if we get two. We didn't come this far to slip up with a simple mistake."

Alex's shoulders tense, and before he can fight me on this, the valet opens my door. He gets out and hands the key to the valet with a tip and asks, "Could you have someone run our luggage up to the room?"

"Of course, sir. What name is the reservation under?"

Alex looks to me and stammers, "N-no reservation... but the room will be under the last name Taylor."

I frown at Alex as the man nods and begins retrieving our luggage. Sliding my hand into Alex's for show, he lets out an annoyed groan. I never expected him to enjoy the charade, but it's still a blow to my ego that it pains him to hold my hand.

So much for being friends...

Once inside, he leans in to whisper, "I only have *my* wallet, we'll have to use your card."

It takes me a second, and he's right; how could I be so stupid? If we use his, we'll leave a paper trail blowing our cover—or worse, someone could think I'm cheating with

Alex on my wedding night. I squeeze his hand and reply, "I'll take care of it."

Alex keeps his voice quiet. "I'll find a way to repay you."

"No, it's okay. But, thank you."

A sweet smile pulls at his lips for a brief moment. And in that split second, I see the man who has been nothing but kind to me the entire day. Doesn't he see that the least I can do is pay for somewhere to stay for a few hours? Alex doesn't need to pay me back, money is no object; he has to know that. My heart, on the other hand, is aching for the small connection I thought we had at the wedding.

When we approach the reception desk, I insist on a king bed—I can build a pillow wall between us with the extra space. Unfortunately, the only room they have available is a presidential suite with two queen beds.

"There has to be a king available. Should we stay somewhere else?" I plead.

Alex wraps his arm around me and kisses the top of my head, speaking into my hair, "It's fine, princess. A queen bed means I'll get to keep you close to me all night."

My stomach drops at his fib, and I struggle to find my voice. Chris is never this affectionate, even for the cameras. A naive part of me thought that tonight I was supposed to be living the fairy tale—enveloped in my husband's arms, making love until the sun rises. Though, if I'm being honest with myself, with Chris the love-making would last seven and a half minutes before he comes. Then, he'd put on his CPAP mask, leaving me alone with my thoughts for hours in the darkness... orgasmless.

Would Alex do the same? Why do I think he'd make sure I came at least once? Maybe twice.

Shit, I shouldn't be thinking about hypothetical sex with Alex... even with Chris' extracurriculars over the years.

'Thou shalt not covet thy husband's brother' should be my new commandment.

I put my card on file, and we make our way up to the room. The moment we're in the elevator, Alex takes his hand back and pulls away from me as if I burned him. I lower my head, mumbling, "I'm sorry," and take a step to the side to give him space.

"No," he growls, more forcefully than I expected. "*I'm* sorry." He rakes his hand through his hair. "I'm exhausted from"—he glances up at the elevator camera—"the *eventful* day."

"Welcome to my life," I laugh humorlessly and he frowns. I don't explain myself, on the off chance he's onto something and someone is listening in. It isn't easy pretending to be someone you're not; I don't blame him for being short with me. "It's been a long day; we should get some sleep."

"We need to see him in a few hours," he regretfully sighs.

"Can you message your father and tell him we had to stop here for the night? Maybe go in the morning, instead?"

Agony is etched in his irises, and I can't figure out why. "Is that what you want?"

I want to stop wondering what it would be like if things were different and I married you instead.

The elevator dings, the doors opening to a dimly lit floor. We step out and find our room; Alex doesn't reach for my hand, and I don't seek his out. I walk behind him, not wanting to address his question because, honestly, I don't know what I want. He stops, waiting for me to walk beside him for the final steps, then swipes the keycard against the sensor. As he opens the door wide for me to step in, my shoulder accidentally brushes his chest, and a rumble comes from him at the innocent touch.

If he hates me so much, why did he agree to this?

The door shuts, and I take in the room. For a presidential suite, it looks more like one of the motels my family stayed at while my father was on the campaign trail. I can't help but smile at the memories—life before I was a President's daughter. There's a small loveseat with matching side chairs, an old wooden coffee table, an undoubtedly neglected kitchenette, and a door separating the living space from the bedroom. As I begin walking toward it, Alex catches me by the wrist. His hold is firm. When I meet his eyes, his voice is strained as he asks, "What do you want, Jaclyn?"

"Why do you care? I already told you, it doesn't matter what I want," I reply breathlessly.

"If you want to see Chris right now, I'll find a way to make it happen. But if you're drained from everything, or not up for it, I can insist we go in the morning. So, what do you want to do?"

It isn't what I thought he would be asking from me. Unfortunately, my loose tongue has a mind of its own. "What I want is to be free of the lies!" My hands fly to my mouth. "Sorry, I didn't mean to shout."

"No, go on." Alex's charming, flirtatious smile from earlier today appears.

I want for you to not disappear when this is all over and... a husband who loves me.

Straightening my posture, I opt for a toned-down version of the truth. "I want this to be over, to have a real wedding. I want..." *Love and respect. I want to be happy.* I lower and shake my head in shame, unable to speak it. In all the ways that truly matter, I'm married to Alex. And the more time I spend with him, the more I wish it was his name on the marriage certificate, not Chris'.

All of this is a mess.

Alex takes a slow step toward me, then another. "A husband who loves and respects you?"

Did I say it out loud?

"How did you...?"

"Because I, too, want a partner who loves and respects me. Who treats me as if I'm the center of their universe, who craves me when I'm not with them. Someone who loves me through all of my flaws... Am I getting close?"

"Are you saying I'm flawed?" I tease, and Alex's eyes darken.

"To Chris?" He shakes his head with anguish in his expression. "No, you're perfect."

"And you?"

He swallows thickly and lets out a huffed sigh. "Your only flaw is that you were born for greatness but are settling for less than you deserve." There isn't a hint of sarcasm. Alex rubs a hand over his face, his voice muffled. "I'm sorry, that was inappropriate."

"You think I'm born for greatness?" I ask carefully, taking a step toward him.

"Your foundation for the protection of cherry blossom trees isn't exactly going to help your chances when you run for office. You're capable of so much more than you're settling for."

"Hey! The cherry blossoms need protecting," I deadpan, failing to hide my smile. He's right; it's a fucking joke.

"They bloom for a month a year!" he chuckles, and it's the lightest I've felt since we stepped into the room. "What are you doing for the other eleven?"

I narrow my eyes playfully at him. "Cherry blossoms are in our hearts year-round... But it's my mother's foundation, I'm just on the board."

73

Alex lets out a hearty laugh, small crinkles forming around his eyes. "We may need to work on your branding when you run for office. Maybe add in a few *more pertinent* issues for you to get behind than pretty trees."

Cocking an eyebrow, I insist, "I'm not running for office."

"I thought you said you want to be free of the lies?" He mirrors my expression, and, *damn it*, he's got me there. I've never felt more seen, stripped bare in a single question.

I reach up and begin unpinning my hair, haphazardly tossing the pins onto a small table one-by-one. "You want the truth? I'll help my husband run for President, bide my time as the perfect First Lady, and campaign for a representative seat in the midterms after his eight years."

"Or, you could let *him* wait and run in the midterm election in three." He shrugs, then gestures for me to turn around to help me pull out the last few dozen bobby pins. I spin, and his warm breath tickles my neck as he whispers, "Congresswoman Taylor has a nice ring to it."

Goosebumps cascade down my arms, though not from his suggestion; the sheer proximity has me on edge. "My experience is lacking, as you so aptly pointed out."

"You're married to a senator, you're the daughter of a former president. And if your last name isn't a foot in the door, you finished valedictorian for undergrad. Rumor has it that you finished top in your class at law school as well." *How does he know about my J.D.?* He lowers his voice slightly as he adds, "You're more than a cherry blossom conservationist, Jaclyn."

Alex pulls a pin from my hair, then traces his finger from my ear to my bare shoulder, and I find myself wishing it was his tongue. My impure thoughts rattle me, and I accidentally elbow him in the ribs. Quickly pivoting to assess the damage I've inflicted, I find him gripping his middle.

"Shit, Alex, I'm so sorry!"

He laughs through the pain, "No, I should've been more careful. I didn't mean to tickle you."

Tickle me? Is that what he thought that was?

"Right, yes, well... I'm very sensitive." I check him over, pulling his arm away and pressing my hand to the middle of his chest. Though with his shirt on, I have no idea what I'm doing—not that I'd know what to look for if he was shirtless. "Are you all right?"

"No, definitely not."

I glance up, finding no hazel in his dark irises, swiftly pulling my hand back. "I think you're right. It's been a long night. It would be best to get some sleep."

There's a knock at the door, making me jump, and as I sigh out a long breath, Alex answers it. I'm grateful for the reprieve as the bellman pulls in our two large suitcases on a dolly and unloads them from the cart. Alex tips him, and once the door closes, he groans to himself. "Here's to hoping my brother's clothes fit me. Why don't you take a shower first and I'll send a message to my father that we'll come by tomorrow?"

I nod and take my suitcase into the bedroom, tossing it onto one of the mattresses. He does the same on the other bed. With his hand poised to unzip it, I lift mine to stop him. "Wait!"

"What's wrong?" He steps back, hands surrendered.

"The housekeepers. They'll notice two unmade beds in the morning. All it'll take is one of them talking and the headlines will read: *Jaclyn and Chris Blake Fail to Consummate Marriage.*"

"Ah, we can't have that, can we?" he laughs. "It's fine, I'll take the couch."

"It's hardly a couch; it'll only fit half your body. We're both adults. We can share a bed."

"No." His jaw tics. "We can't."

"Why the hell not?" I open my suitcase, and after a quick once over, I realize I don't have pajamas to stay the night with him—I typically sleep naked. Pulling out a pair of red lacy underwear, I quickly hide them in black leggings and a heather gray tank top.

I look over at Alex rummaging through Chris' suitcase as he mutters, "Fucking boxers? You have to be kidding me."

"What's wrong with boxers?" I ask curiously, clutching my clothes to my chest. "Don't tell me you have a bill coming up for textiles, too."

"No." He shakes his head, a small smile threatening to appear. "I just prefer boxer briefs. No political agenda items surrounding clothing in the near future." His answer leaves me unsatisfied; I enjoyed our banter from the reception.

I rush to the bathroom and set down my clothes, then take out the remaining pins from my hair. Realizing I've forgotten my skincare items, I step back into the bedroom to retrieve them, only to find Alex wearing black boxer briefs and taking off his white form-fitting undershirt. I manage to catch a glimpse of his toned abs as he lifts it, the muscle definition trailing from the top of his hip, dipping lower beneath his—

"Like what you see, princess?" Alex pulls his shirt back down.

I avert my eyes and yelp, "Sorry! I was getting my makeup case. I didn't know you were changing."

I peek through my fingers, as he takes out a tee from the suitcase. "It's too warm for the joggers he packed. So, if I'm only wearing underwear, we're *not* sleeping in the same bed."

"It's one night. It'll be fine," I scoff, pulling my hand down and turning my body away from him. "I'll put a pillow between us."

I sense him approaching, making a shiver run down my limbs in anticipation. "Do you really think that's the best idea?" The timbre of his voice is low and sultry.

Probably not...

For years, Chris has been unfaithful, but that doesn't mean I have a green light to do the same; two wrongs don't make a right. Confidence sets in as I remind myself that Alex is a gentleman and he'd never try anything.

I shut my eyes tight. "No, I just don't want us to get caught in this lie. We need it to look like we're happy newlyweds."

"And if you wake up in my arms tomorrow morning?" I turn to face him, and he tilts my chin up. When I open my eyes, there's no trace of humor on his face. My cheeks are hot, and a blush creeps from my neck and chest.

"I won't."

Leaning in, his cheek grazes mine, his admission coming out as a purr, "What if I want you to?"

So much for him being a gentleman...

CHAPTER 9
CHRIS

"He's awake," a woman calls as my eyes flutter open.

As my vision adjusts, a man's face comes into view. The noise is overwhelming—people talking over one another, the same beeping sound from before, and the shuffling of who the fuck knows what. The man flashes a light into my eyes, adding to my overstimulation.

"What happened?" I manage. My throat is on fire. I grip the front of my neck, and a nurse approaches with a cup of water with a straw, placing the tip of it in my mouth like I'm a damn child.

"You had another cardiac episode, Mr. Blake," the man in a white coat replies. "It wasn't a full heart attack, but you lost consciousness. Can you tell me what year it is?"

"2023."

"Good, do you know what day it is?"

"Friday, I'm... *Fuck!* I'm supposed to be getting married." In an instant, I'm flooded with memories of the accident on the way to the venue.

My heart racing. Airbags deploying and everything going black.

"Where's my aide, Cara?"

"I think it's best if you discuss it with your father. He's right outside. I'll bring him in once the nurses check your vitals."

A woman in pink scrubs approaches, takes my temperature, and tests my oxygen levels and blood pressure. When it all checks out, my father enters the room with a member of his secret service, and everyone files out. The man in all black scans the room and nods to my father before leaving us alone.

"Christopher," he says flatly, a slight gruffness in his tone. "How are you feeling?"

"Where's Cara?"

"She should be the least of your worries."

"*Where is she?*"

"You fucking killed her!" my father roars, and my heart jumps into my throat. Composing himself, he calmly adds, "Her neck snapped when the airbag deployed."

"No," I breathe, choking back a sob. "You're lying."

"I'm sorry, Chris. She died on impact," he continues. "We took care of it. You should be more concerned about how your brother married your fiancée."

"She... *dead?*" He nods. "And the news about Alex, that was real?" I thought it was all a dream. How the hell did Alex end up marrying Jaclyn?

"Jerry and I cleaned up the mess with the accident *and* paid off far too many people who know that you're here. You're supposed to be getting ready to go on your honeymoon with his daughter."

"She actually married him?"

He nods again and sighs. "Yes... and no. Alex pretended to be you. It was that, or politically destroying both of our families. If word got out that you killed someone..." Rubbing his hand over his face, he blows out a long breath. "You're legally married to Jaclyn as soon as you file the paperwork."

"And he just did it out of the goodness of his heart?" I laugh, and it hurts my chest and stomach. "I don't buy it."

My father shrugs off his jacket and takes a seat. "Your brother and I may not see eye-to-eye when it comes to policy, but he would likely be harmed by your actions— just as much as Jaclyn. He's not exactly selfless here. You share the same last name; he'd be guilty by association."

"It was an accident."

"Don't lie to me," he growls. "I saw the evidence before it

was destroyed. We had to stage it so that she got in the accident by herself."

"And Jaclyn?" I swallow hard. "Does she know?"

"About how the accident happened? No, but it's only a matter of time before Alex tells her. Jaclyn's a smart woman; even if Alex does tell her, she'll remain your dutiful wife... unless it leaks. Then, she'll have to protect her family." He stands and puts his jacket back on. "I need to get back to your mother. It's been a long day. Alex texted me to say that he'll be here in the morning with Jaclyn. Get some rest and prepare to grovel, in case she already knows."

Without another word, he leaves, and several nurses and doctors enter. "All right, Mr. Blake. I've reviewed all of your tests, and we'll be discharging you in a couple of days. We'll need to monitor your heart and do an echo tomorrow to see how it's doing. You'll also need to meet with a cardiologist regularly to discuss what can be done proactively to prevent another heart attack. We noticed elevated levels of methylphenidate in your system, so we believe that to be the culprit."

I shake my head. "I only take my ADHD medication once in a while." *When I remember.* "There's no way it could be *elevated.*"

"I'll add a drug test to the mix to see what else comes up. With how it looks now, you seem to have taken significantly more than your prescription dosage of your ADHD medication." He checks something in his chart, but none of this adds up. Why would I need a drug test when all I do is drink occasionally?

"Maybe I took an extra dose by accident?"

"We'll make sure there's no trace of anything else in your system. You should be out of here by the end of the week; hopefully within a couple of days, if everything looks good. Then, we'll have someone monitor you at home."

"I'm supposed to leave for my honeymoon tomorrow night."

"I'm sorry, Mr. Blake. I can't recommend traveling this soon. You'll have to postpone, at least until we can get your blood pressure under control."

I need to get the fuck out of here, or my brother is going to sink his teeth into what's mine.

CHAPTER 10
ALEX

In our stand-off, Jaclyn's chest rises and falls, her shaky, deep breaths blowing on my neck and chest. With my hand resting on her hip, I don't dare pull back. If I do, I know damn well the moment I see the slightest glimmer in those sapphire eyes, I'll do something both of us will regret.

It's a dangerous game I'm playing. One where we all lose.

With a delicate touch, her hands slide up my chest, and I fully expect her to push me away. And I'd deserve it. Bracing myself for a shove that never comes, I'm caught off-guard when her palms remain planted on me as she whispers, "I spoke sacred vows in front of family, friends, and God."

Growing up in a very religious family, I'm faced with the same dilemma. I promised myself to her. Standing at the altar with her felt wrong; I wanted to be up there with her as Alex, not as Chris. I can only imagine how she's struggling with this, too. After years of stuffing down my feelings, the moment I saw her in all-white and how her eyes lit up as she saw me, all logic was thrown out the fucking window.

I never should've suggested this charade.

"I know. I'm sorry. You're my brother's wife," I concede with a sigh.

We can't do this, shouldn't do this. Even if they weren't married, it's wrong to want her.

But, *fuck*, do I crave her.

"Because you're still in love with her, and you swore you'd love and protect her for the rest of your life in front of God," a little voice inside me taunts. *"Stop fighting your feelings for her."*

Jaclyn turns her face enough that if I did the same, I could claim her soft lips as mine. "It's just one night, you can stay in the same bed as me," she commands, though her voice is unsteady.

I ball the fabric of her dress in my fist and pull her body flush with mine, my hard cock desperate to escape the confines of my boxer briefs. She moans a quiet whimper, forcing a growl to get stuck in my throat. "*That.* That is why I shouldn't sleep in the same bed as you." Taking a step back, I add, "You love another man," and busy myself moving items in the suitcase, keeping my gaze anywhere except on her.

"I never said I love him." There's an edge to her words, but they feel honest.

"That may be true, but you'll hate yourself if I touch you, even if Chris cheated on you."

Shit, I shouldn't have let that slip. I shut my eyes tight, hoping she'll pretend I didn't say it.

"Everyone fucks around in Washington, especially Chris," she blurts, hands flying to her mouth. Her admission does little to remedy the hypocrisy of what we're doing. "I'm sorry, I—"

"How do you know he cheated?" Anger dances in my veins.

"He's been cheating for years." Jaclyn crosses her arms over her torso, rubbing her tricep as pain seeps into her expression.

I consider my options, and there's no use in lying to her. I could claim I didn't know, but I refuse to be like my brother. I'm sure he loves her—in his own way.

No, he doesn't.

"Why did you want to marry him if you knew he was cheating?"

Jaclyn's shoulders sag as she takes a deep breath. "There aren't a lot of honest men or women here. Greed, corruption... It wouldn't matter who I married, eventually my husband would cheat."

"My brother is a fucking idiot. You don't deserve that. I would never... I mean, *your husband* shouldn't cheat on you."

Her eyes soften, and a small smile threatens to appear at my admission. "I know you wouldn't. We may no longer be friends, but I don't take you as the kind of man to carry on an affair for years," she chuckles softly. "Or agree to what is essentially an arranged marriage."

All I want to do is take her in my arms and beg her not to file the papers. It's selfish, and would likely destroy plans set in motion by people with significantly more political influence than I have, but I've never wanted anything or anyone as much as I want Jaclyn right now.

I need to reel this in, or both of us will get hurt.

"You and I are not so different. You take your wedding vows seriously. I do, too. It's why we can't do"—I gesture between us—"whatever this is."

Her eyes narrow. "Neither one of us has done anything wrong. Especially you." Pausing to mull over her thoughts, she surprises me, asking, "Why haven't you ever married? You've been seen with dozens of women over the years."

"Dozens?" I laugh. "Don't believe what you read, princess. I've yet to find anyone who challenges me." *Since you.* "Or anyone who makes me want to be the best version of myself. You know the Washington game of smoke and mirrors; it's easier to pretend to be something you're not. I let everyone see what they want to see.

Having a date on my arm doesn't make me a playboy, as your father insinuated. I never go home with them."

"You went home with me," she jests.

"Well, princess, no matter how much I love the idea of spending the night with my face between your legs, you'd hate me in the morning. I can handle you hating what I stand for, but in no world would I want you to hate *me*." I rub the back of my neck, regretting sharing that with her. There's something about Jaclyn that makes me spill all of my secrets.

"You want to..." She shakes her head. "Men don't enjoy that."

"*That's* what you're focused on?" I laugh. "Jaclyn, if a man isn't making you come all over his face before he sinks himself inside you, he's doing it wrong."

She bites her plump lip, and my resolve is teetering. "We shouldn't be talking about this." The hint of flirtation in her tone is almost my undoing. "Why won't you tell me about the accident?"

I huff a small laugh, grateful for the change in the subject, and take a seat at the edge of the bed. "It's not my secret to share. Tomorrow, tell Chris I've told you 'everything.' And then... you wait. If there's an indiscretion to be shared, he'll share it. Go take a shower. Let's pretend that I didn't offer to tongue fuck you while in my underwear? And in the morning, you'll begin your life as Mrs. Blake."

*Unfortunately, not **my** Mrs. Blake.*

She takes a deep breath. "This is a nightmare."

"That's putting it lightly, princess."

The morning sun shines through the blinds, waking me before my alarm goes off, and... Jaclyn's snuggled up next to me?

When I got out of the shower last night, she was already fast asleep. I didn't want to wake her, and I sure as hell wasn't going to share a bed with her, so I opted to sleep on top of the scratchy comforter on the other bed.

So, how did she end up in my bed, with her head on my chest and her arm draped over my body?

"What time is it?" she asks sleepily.

I brush her hair off her shoulder and tuck a few rogue strands behind her ear. My fingers linger a moment longer than they should, and I drop my hand, landing on the soft, silky skin of her arm. I shouldn't enjoy touching her as much as I do. Yet, here I am, loving every second of having her this close. "The alarm is set to go off in twenty minutes if you want to go back to bed. But why are you in mine?"

"Why am I...?" Her eyes fly open. "Oh, shit! Alex! I'm so sorry." She pulls away and scrambles to cover herself, despite her wearing a tank top. "Why are you in *my* bed?"

I point to the bed to our right. "*That* is your bed."

"The housekeepers," she squeaks.

"...won't care. If it eases your mind, we can make a mess in here before we leave, so it appears that I took you in every possible position and on every surface. No one will be any the wiser."

"Are you sure?" Her face visibility relaxes, and I can't help admiring that she's even more beautiful with no makeup on.

Fuck, I need to get out of here.

"Come on." Sliding off the bed, my feet hit the worn, rough carpet. "If we hurry, we'll have time for breakfast."

Opening Chris' suitcase, I didn't think much of it's contents while rummaging last night. It's mostly casual clothes—including cargo shorts. Never in my life have I seen him wear anything but slacks.

"There are a lot of clothes in here for an overnight bag," I mutter, taking out a polo and dark gray slacks. They'll be a bit tight, since I have thicker thighs and broader shoulders than he does, but it'll work in a pinch.

"It's not an overnight bag," she replies, opening her own suitcase. "It's for our honeymoon."

I glance over and frown. "Honeymoon?"

"Yes, you know, when two people get married and take a vacation..."

"Very funny, princess. Why do we have your honeymoon luggage?"

She briefly draws her lips into her mouth. "Our flight is tonight."

"Tonight?" I huff a laugh, shaking my head. "You need to talk to Chris and postpone it."

Jaclyn hums thoughtfully. "Chris... Right..."

"You didn't think I was going with you, did you?"

"The thought crossed my mind, yes," she muses.

This can't be happening. I look to the ceiling and groan, "I'm in hell."

"I get it." Jaclyn shuts her suitcase forcefully. "I'm sorry if you don't want to spend two weeks with me. But I'm not calling the shots here; I didn't ask for this, either."

"Is that what you think?" She's busying herself with the clothes she pulled to wear for the day. When she doesn't look at me, I quickly put on the too-tight slacks and close the distance between us. "Come here." I open my arms wide, and with slight hesitation, she steps into my embrace. "I enjoy spending time with you. That's not the issue... You're the kind of woman a man could easily fall for... and you're *married.* This isn't easy for me."

"I'm sorry you got dragged into this. Nothing is going to plan," she sighs, her voice is wavering and holding back tears. I instinctively rub my hand up and down her back to console her. "You want to know something embarrassing?"

"Is it more embarrassing than the fact that I can't fit in these pants?"

She laughs and rests her chin on my chest, looking up at me. "I had a crush on you in college."

"A crush? What are we, thirteen?" I tease.

"You know what I mean! I liked you."

"We were just friends," I deadpan, rolling my eyes, but my heart squeezes at the thought. As old emotions come bubbling to the surface, I tamp them down just as quickly. "Nice try, princess."

"I'm serious. When word got around that you were supporting causes that didn't align with the party, I was *ever so gently* told it would never work."

"So, you married my brother instead?" I deadpan, cocking my eyebrow.

Shutting her eyes tight, Jaclyn hides her face in my chest, her voice is muffled when she admits with a wince, "Yeah..."

"Why him? You said it yourself, you could've been with anyone in Washington." It's a risk asking, but curiosity gets the best of me. "Why Chris?"

"Would you like the real or the canned answer?" I don't respond, though I'm no longer sure I want either. "I had to settle for second best."

I huff a small laugh, kissing the top of her head, and that damn hum of hers is back as I whisper into her hair, "You're full of shit, but I'm flattered." We stand there for a moment, neither of us moving, while I selfishly pretend the world around us doesn't exist and she could be mine. It's only a matter of time before Jaclyn will be out of my life and back in *his* arms, and the thought twists my heart. I take a deep breath and will away the fantasy. "All right, let's get dressed, mess the room up a bit, and grab some breakfast."

CHAPTER 11

JACLYN

P ulling up to an unmarked office building, I do my best to keep my expression neutral. I was an idiot thinking Chris would be in a typical hospital or medical facility—both of our fathers have access to armies of medical staff. The building passes as corporate offices; the perfect cover. Having been in an accident, Chris could be requiring anything from stitches to needing a new heart. I selfishly hope whatever it is will keep him here long enough for Alex to join me in Hawaii. Unlike when I'm with Chris, I can be myself with Alex, and two weeks where I don't have to be picture-perfect sounds like a dream come true.

Alex opens my door and offers me his hand as I get out of the car. It's wrong to want to keep my hand in his, but I do it anyway for as long as he'll let me. I'm enjoying Alex's innocent touches more than I should. The tug to be near him is unbearable—even though it goes against my better judgment. Holding his hand feels natural and keeps me grounded.

As he closes the car door, he makes no move to walk toward the building. "Don't lie to him about me telling you everything."

"Why not?" My brows pinch.

Reaching up to tuck my hair behind my ear, he replies, "Ignorance is bliss, princess."

"What happened yesterday? Was Chris with another woman?" The words leave a sour taste in my mouth. I can turn a blind eye to his cheating—but on our wedding day? Surely, it's not that hard to keep it in your pants for *one* day.

"Did you wake up in another man's arms this morning?" Alex smirks, and my chest constricts, my pulse thumping in my ears. "Don't be a hypocrite. You're better than that."

He's right; I'm absolutely a hypocrite.

"Will you be there with me?" I ask softly.

"No." He shakes his head. "Chris won't want to see me. I'll wait outside the room for you."

"You're his brother. Of course he'll want to see you."

Alex places his hand on the car, pinning me in on one side. Leaning in, he whispers, "I slept with his wife. He won't want to see me."

Our faces only inches apart, my breath hitches at the thought of him closing the distance and kissing me. He probably tastes like coffee and cinnamon from the French toast he had for breakfast. My eyes search his, begging him to do it.

What the hell am I doing?

"We only *slept* together, Alex. I know you're teasing, don't make it sound like you wanted more than a glorified nap."

"I thought I was clear what I would've done last night, if you were mine." A devilish smirk dances on his lips, an adorable dimple appearing. My eyes fall to his mouth briefly, but when his small smile fades, I glance back up. He's looking at the entrance of the building behind me. "Time to go find your Prince Charming and begin your happily ever after." His gaze returns to me. "Come on, princess."

Pushing off the car, he walks toward the building, and I follow two steps behind him. He stops abruptly, and I nearly run into him. "What's wrong?"

"Don't walk behind me," he grumbles with a frown. "We're equals. You walk beside me."

I'm taken aback by the comment but nod in understanding. When we reach the front door side by side, I grab for it before he can, opening it for him. "Since we're equals and all."

He holds the door above my head. "Nice try. We may be equals, but I'm still a gentleman." I roll my eyes, laughing to myself, and walk in.

The entry appears to be like any other office building, with a directory posted next to the elevator. Alex presses the 'up' button while I peruse the list.

Laura Crest, M.D. — Children's Psychiatry — 203
Timothy Meadows, C.P.A — 206
Joshua Hamilton — Target Investments — 208
Fredrick Milton, M.D, D.O. — Neurology — 210
Laura Gallagher — Gallagher Whiskey — 211
Kristina Dawson, J.D. — Criminal Law — 215

Why are they only on the second floor?

I don't have a chance to continue reading the most obscure list of tenants I've ever seen when the elevator dings. Alex gestures for me to step inside first and follows behind me, pressing the button for the fifth floor.

The building and elevator are older than I am, and the light above us flickers a light gold. The silence is deafening. "Why are there medical offices on the same floor as a lawyer and an accountant? And why is there nothing listed for the rest of the building?"

"You've been in your ivory tower too long," he chuckles, continuing to face the elevator doors.

"What the hell is that supposed to mean?" He doesn't have a chance to answer when the elevator ascends with a jolt; I hold on to Alex to keep my balance. As we reach our floor, the doors open to a metal wall. "What's going on? Where are we?"

He opens the small call box and punches in a four-digit code, holding the receiver to his ear. A few seconds pass, and he replies to whoever is on the other line, "Alexander Blake. Code word 'snapped.'"

Snapped?

The large metal door opens, and Alex steps out; I hesitate for a moment. "Don't you trust me?" He offers his hand, but I don't take it. It doesn't matter if I trust him, there are no prying eyes to put on a show for. If either of our fathers were to see us holding hands, there would be questions.

I take a deep breath and follow him down a dimly lit hall with light gray walls. There are no doors or office windows anywhere to be found as we continue turning left twice and then right. Eventually, we reach one that has the same metal as the elevator. Alex opens the call box to the side and types in a code. Like before, he states his name and a code word again.

The door opens, and the beeps of medical equipment fill the space. "Is this where Chris is?" I whisper, now wishing more than anything that I was holding Alex's hand. We approach one of four doors, and Alex opens a call box for a third time, going through the motions.

A man in a black suit and earpiece appears, likely part of one of our fathers' service details. "Mr. Blake. Mrs. Blake." I begin to correct him, but he cuts me off, commanding, "Right this way."

"You're no longer Jaclyn Taylor," Alex reminds me. The man enters a room on the right, and as I'm about to walk in, Alex stops me. "Ignorance is bliss."

I chew on my lip, wringing my hands. "Come in with me?"

"No, princess. I promise I'll be here when you're done." He offers a small smile and takes a step back. I breathe deeply and walk in without the slightest idea of what I might find.

CHAPTER 12
CHRIS

"You have a visitor," a man who is part of my father's secret service detail announces. I sit up and attempt to make myself presentable, my father doing the same in the chair beside my hospital bed.

Jaclyn comes into view, wearing a blue, sleeveless dress with a high neckline and hem that reaches her knees. It's form-fitting enough to show off her incredible curves but still conservative. I expect her to rush to my side, maybe even worry about what happened to me. Instead, she remains rooted in place, emotionless.

Did he tell her?

Seeing Jaclyn like this reminds me of when we started dating and I was unable to pierce her frosty exterior. Years later, nothing has changed. Her frigid tone matches her expression and posture as she breaks her silence. "How are you?"

I look to my father for the proper response, but all I get is a dip of his chin. I sigh in defeat; Alex must've filled her in.

Asshole.

"I'm sorry, Jackie. For everything," I rush out and her nostrils flare once. "As soon as I'm out of here, we'll start our life together. Just like we planned. Nothing has to change."

I reach for her in hopes she'll accept my apology as an olive branch. Her lips part slightly, and she glances at my father, then back to me. "You didn't answer me. How are you?"

"I had a heart attack," I sigh, pulling my hand back when she doesn't take it.

"Heart attack?" Her eyes narrow, but she looks otherwise relieved. The response makes me even more curious about how much Alex has told her. "What about the cardiologist appointments? Sleep studies? You said everything was fine."

"I... I'm sorry."

"For what, exactly?"

I take a deep breath, blowing out slowly. "For all of it. Mostly, for missing our wedding."

"You never saw your doctor, did you?" There's no anger in her voice; her calm tone is messing with me. I would prefer her to yell at me at this point. *Fuck, does she knows I've been lying to her for months... years?*

"No." I cast my eyes down, and my father groans.

"Our parents and Alex talked about having to clean up your mess. An accident. Was anyone hurt?"

Relief settles in my gut. She doesn't know everything, but there's no use in lying. "My assistant was with me."

"Will she talk?"

The question gives me pause; maybe she's only upset that I missed the wedding and knows nothing about Cara? "No. The heart attack caused a car accident, and I was told my airbag killed her."

Jaclyn gasps, her hand flying to her mouth and eyes wide. "Chris!"

"Yeah, I know." I sit up straighter in bed as the blood drains from her face. "She was, um—"

"No. The less I know, the better," she huffs. I'm irked by her hardly showing a shred of emotion, even if she hates me for this. "If she's not going to be a problem, then as soon as you're healed and cleared by doctors, we'll go on our honeymoon and pretend this never happened."

"Chris can't travel, and you can't postpone the honeymoon," my father interjects. "It's actually the perfect cover to give Chris enough time to heal."

"I'm not going on a honeymoon by myself," she deadpans.

"We'll have Alex step in for him." Jaclyn's breath catches as my father says his name.

"Absolutely not," I growl. "He's not taking *my* wife on *my* honeymoon."

"She's only your wife because of your brother," he barks back. "He saved your reputation, your chance at the White House, and Jaclyn from what could've been one of the most embarrassing days of her life."

"You're right. It'll look suspicious," she agrees at the same time I shout, "You saw what happened in committee!"

"He's helping the ranchers," Jaclyn spits, before quickly adding, "However... he should have considered your concerns about beef prices." I've never seen this side of her; the fire seeping from her poised exterior. This has to be *his* doing.

So help me, if he takes her from me...

No. Over my dead body. She's mine, my ticket to the Oval.

"Where's my brother?" I seethe, and Jaclyn looks at the door. "Is he here?"

"Outside," she meekly replies, her shoulders tensing.

"Perfect." Dad claps his hands and stands, moving for the door. I keep my eyes on Jaclyn. She draws her lips into her mouth for a brief moment, her pupils dilated as my father opens the door. "Good, you're still here."

CHAPTER 13
ALEX

As I step into my brother's room, Jaclyn is outwardly trying her hardest to keep her emotions at bay, but her eyes betray her. I shouldn't want to reach for her...

I shouldn't want to keep her for myself.

None of this makes sense, and I'm no longer confident I'll be able to walk away from this unscathed. Sure, I'm attracted to her, but it doesn't excuse my inexplicable need to protect her from all of this. We cannot and will not ever be more than acquaintances.

"Alex, you'll be going on a short, two-week vacation with Jaclyn," my father says a bit too cheerfully, clapping me on the back.

I choke on my own air, sputtering, "I'm sorry... *What?*"

"He isn't taking *my wife* to Hawaii," Chris insists, wincing as he attempts to adjust his position.

"Are you sure this is the best idea?" Jaclyn says with a nervous laugh. There's an unmistakable glimmer of mischief in her eyes, and I can't help but wonder if she planned this. At the very least, she's amused by it.

"*Chris* married Jaclyn. *Chris* has to go on his honeymoon. *Chris* can't go. If you want to fuck this up for all of us, now is your chance," Dad warns.

"I can't stay with her for two weeks," I bite back, but the pain on Jaclyn's face has my heart at a standstill. As much as I'd love to spend a couple of weeks basking in the Hawaiian sun with her, all it would take is one too many Mai Tais for me to take things too far. It's quite possibly the worst idea I've ever heard. Though I am speaking to my father, I can't take my eyes off her when I correct, "Jaclyn is Chris' wife. I can't do that to them."

"It's a fucking vacation! What choice do we have?" my father groans. "You're going with her." I can feel his eyes narrowed on me without even looking at him. "Unless we are doing some sort of sharing hour, and it's your turn to tell us a secret of *yours*."

My gaze snaps to him. "There are no secrets to tell. As long as my constituents are taken care of, I can go. Will you ensure we'll have two rooms?"

"Two?" He barks a laugh. "You're supposed to be Chris on his honeymoon. The reservations will remain intact; no reason to raise suspicion. You'll sleep on the damn floor for all I care, but you'll be on that plane later today *and* sharing a room with her."

"Don't you think he's done enough?" Jaclyn asks, treading carefully.

"You're going to let the fox into the hen house? What the fuck is happening?" Chris exclaims, and for the first time in nearly a decade, I want to agree with him.

"Jaclyn deserves a real honeymoon," I offer, and her molten eyes soften. I only hope Chris or my father don't notice.

"And she'll have it," Chris promises. "As soon as I'm out of here, I'm taking my wife on a cruise for an extended vacation."

"You don't have time off until October," Jaclyn reminds Chris. She's right. We won't for at least another month or two. Chris' accident is costing us all weeks of lost time, and now I have to worry about my father possibly fucking over my chances of reelection.

"I'm supposed to be campaigning," I insist. My father is a mastermind when it comes to political strategy. He understands how crucial it is that I'm in Texas as much as possible before next year's election; there's no way I can take two weeks off.

"If I can assure that you keep your seat, will you consider it?" The desperation in my father's voice makes my heart lurch. Granted, he's more concerned about Chris than me, but he's willing to pull strings for me and keep the sharks at bay. At least a dozen men and women would jump at a chance to take my seat if this blows up in my face; I'm tempted to take the deal.

Why not ask for the moon? I have nothing to lose.

"Pass the Livestock Bill. If all of this falls apart, make sure that I'm replaced with a moderate in Texas... And take care of Florida. Fuck knows if I see another 'Florida man' post on social media." I shake my head. "They need all the help they can get. I know it might flip the Senate, but this is all risky." I refuse to let Texas end up with someone in office who believes that people are expendable. Or worse, strip their rights away and only be there to line their wallet.

"That's a tall order," Dad laughs. "You know that between Jaclyn's father and I, we can do our best. Ultimately... it's up to the people."

"I know," I concede. "*Fuck!*" Raking my hand through my hair, I snap at Chris, "Why the hell did you have to do it? On your wedding day, of all days?"

"You're the asshole who married my *fiancée!* What all did you tell her?"

"Why was your aide with you on our wedding day?" Jaclyn steps between us, her back to me. "Alex only told me that you were in an accident. It's because of him that you even have a wife. You should be thanking him." She's keeping her composure, even if it's eating at her. Out of the four of us, she's the only one who has remained collected through all of this.

With a small chuckle, Dad leans in to whisper, "He's out of his league with her." For a man who wears a scowl ninety percent of the time, I'm pleased to see he's almost smiling, even at the expense of my brother. I'm unsure how much was divulged when I wasn't in the room, but it was enough to set off the hibernating lioness. Guilt creeps in—I never should've suggested marrying her. She'll be tied to Chris forever.

"You're not going on my... *our* honeymoon with *him*," Chris grits out.

"She is," our father demands. "Or would you rather lose your shot at the executive branch?" Chris deflates against the bed. "That's what I thought. So, he's going to pretend to be you. We'll make sure Texas is in the *right hands* in Alex's absence. And when you're healed, you'll have your wife, two-point-five kids, a picket fence, and a damn puppy if you want." He sighs. "It's the only way this works."

His emphasis on Texas being in the right hands stings. I won by a slim margin, and I've fought like hell to represent my state to give the people what they want. In the blink of an eye, it could be taken from me—from the people who elected me. One false move and my career is over, and everything I've worked so hard for with it.

As much as I ache for Jaclyn, I can't risk this whole thing falling apart. Unfortunately, I also have to play by my father's rules. My only choice is to put on a show and avoid her as much as possible. Hopefully, everything will be as I left it when I return in two weeks.

"Fine," I agree, though my teeth are clenched so tightly that my dentist will be putting in molar caps.

"No," Jaclyn breathes, though I can't tell why she would be upset. In the end, she gets everything she's ever wanted. I can't figure out what her endgame is.

"You have a plane to catch," my father reminds us, leaving no room to argue.

Jaclyn's eyes fall to the floor. "Of course."

Fuck, I hate that she feels the need to be subservient to our fathers. A flash of a memory of waking up to her in my arms dances before me. That's the Jaclyn I want—the one who gives herself because she *wants* to, not because she *has* to.

My father ushers Jaclyn and me out of the room. The moment the door shuts, he glances in either direction, keeping an even tone. "Keep your hands to yourselves in private, but you have to sell this in public, just like at the wedding. I'll send a few friendly media contacts to stumble upon you two. If you see a camera, you need to pretend you're in love."

"Are you sure about this?" Jaclyn tries to contest, but she sees the same beast in front of us that I do. We're both fucked if this goes south.

"Make sure you're not followed from here. Enjoy your flight, Mr. and Mrs. Blake." He brushes past me toward the exit, leaving Jaclyn and me in the worst possible predicament.

Two weeks with Jaclyn Taylor... Screw driving the bus, I'm already in hell.

CHAPTER 14
JACLYN

The flight to Hawaii is terrible. A storm on the West Coast has created turbulence for an hour, and I keep my fingers interlaced with Alex's for most of it, easing my nerves. Thankfully, there hasn't been a single bump for almost two hours since, yet our hands remain joined. I need to use the restroom, but if I do, I'm worried I won't have an excuse to be close to him anymore. His simple, sweet gesture has kept me from spiraling.

I can't take it any longer and get up to shimmy past him. After using the bathroom, I sit back down, placing my hands in my lap and looking out the window. Seconds later, he waffles our fingers again, and my heart squeezes as his thumb swipes across mine. My hope is shattered when I glance over, and his eyes haven't moved from his ereader, expressionless. We're technically in public on this plane; it's all for show.

I should be grateful for the large divider between our seats—a literal reminder to keep my distance. Neither of us has spoken more than three words to each other since we left the office building. There are so many things I want to say.

Thank you.

I'm sorry.

I wish things were different.

Why couldn't it be you and me instead?

I can't bring myself to tell him any of it.

The flight attendant approaches. "Mr. Blake, may I get you something to drink?"

"Yes," Alex replies and turns to me. "What would you like?"

Since the wedding, Alex has imprinted himself on my heart with simple little touches—this is one of them. It's such a small, polite act, but my heart stops at his words, making me stumble over mine. "Um... an Old Fashioned, with an extra cherry."

A genuine smile appears that reaches his eyes. And, damn, I miss that smile; I haven't seen it since before we visited Chris. "Make that two," he tells her, not looking away from me. When she moves on to the next passenger, he whispers, "And what is the special occasion, princess?"

"I'm on my honeymoon with my husband. Isn't that a big enough reason to celebrate?" I tease, biting back my grin. Unfortunately, his falls. "What's wrong?"

"It's going to be a long two weeks," he sighs, squeezing my hand and releasing it. When he returns to reading, I let out a defeated huff and put my earbuds in to listen to a memoir I started earlier.

While I didn't allow Chris to go into detail about the accident, I've been suspicious about Cara for the past six months. No matter how unfaithful he's been in the years we've been together, it doesn't give me a free pass to flirt with Alex. I have no right to hold his hand, and I especially have no right to imagine his face between my legs like he suggested yesterday.

Why do I want it? Why do I want *him?*

The flight attendant drops off our drinks, and we both thank her—yet another reminder of how Alex is nothing like Chris. While Chris expects to be serviced, Alex is appreciative. My mind wanders, wondering if that's true in all facets of their lives. Attending prestigious schools and being elected to the Senate are likely the only things they have in common.

Entertaining the idea would only lead to trouble, but my thighs clench anyway. There's an ache in my core that's never been there with Chris. I've never had the desire to have Chris touch me or to touch him. The way Alex has treated me in a single day, I find myself *wanting* to be on my knees for him.

A small whimper escapes me, loud enough for Alex to hear. "Are you okay?" he asks knowingly. My eyes widen, and he smirks. "What are you listening to?"

He tucks my hair behind my ear, and I swallow thickly as he traces the shell of it, taking out my earbud and putting it in his own. After listening for a minute, a wide grin splits his face.

Alex's cheek brushing mine, he whispers darkly beside my ear, "Political autobiographies get you wet, Jaclyn?" His voice is silk, sending shivers down my limbs and lighting me up inside.

"I'm not," I insist, though the fib is heavy on my tongue.

"You know, you shouldn't lie to your husband," he taunts. Alex looks around to make sure no one is listening, then groans, "Why do I want to slide my hand under your dress to find out for myself?"

My breath catches, my voice shaky as inside thoughts slip past my lips. "You should."

Alex's eyes darken, and his jaw tightens. He presses a sweet kiss to my cheek and sighs, "Fuck, I'm sorry, shouldn't have joked about that. You have no idea how much I want to, but... you're not mine." He hands me the earbud and sits back as pain mars his features. When he brings the Old Fashioned to his lips, he doesn't drink. Instead, he sets it back down. "That's not something I want to celebrate."

The lines have blurred so much between us since we began the charade. It's gone beyond flirting into unfamiliar territory. Chris cheated for years, and I'm confident his accident was because he wasn't able to keep his cock in his pants. And he killed Cara. It isn't sitting right with me.

Snapped?

Someone's neck doesn't break from an airbag deploying.

Unless...

"Her head was in his lap," I mutter to myself. Unable to help myself, I ask Alex, "Did you know about her?" He gives a look of warning. Anyone could be listening in, but I still repeat, "Did you know?"

"Yes," he replies simply. The admission hurts more than Chris' indiscretions and omissions. Chris had another woman's mouth around his cock on our wedding day...

Am I really that unlovable? That undesirable?

"Sn—" Alex presses two fingers to my lips. *Why is my instinct to run my tongue along them, maybe pull them into my mouth to tease him?*

"My father and the person I hired definitely have a twisted sense of humor by making that the code word."

I quickly pull back before I do something to further embarrass myself. "Why would you let me go through with it? Why not insist we cancel, like you originally suggested?"

"You deserve a happily ever after."

I shake my head, chewing on my lip. Being married to Chris would boost his political career, setting him up for a presidential run. He doesn't love me, and after he killed a woman, I'm certain I'll never love him. After the past forty-eight hours, I have no right to be upset. I'm as guilty as Chris is, even if I haven't physically acted on my attraction to Alex. How is that a happily ever after? If Chris hadn't survived that crash, maybe I would have had a chance at a fairytale ending. Instead, I'm married to one man while I'm craving another.

"What about *your* happily ever after?" I take a sip of my drink, the whiskey burning my tongue.

"Not everyone gets one in this story, princess."

"Good evening, this is your captain speaking. We will be landing in Honolulu in thirty minutes. It'll be a warm few days, still in the high eighties when we land. There isn't a cloud in the sky, so we should have a smooth touchdown. Your flight attendants will be coming around to collect any trash or unfinished beverages shortly. Welcome to Hawaii."

"Shoot, I was supposed to approve the final seating chart for the gala." I reach for my laptop, but he places his hand on mine. "It was due yesterday."

"It's okay, you can send it when we get to the airport or the resort."

Alex finishes his drink in three gulps, setting it down carefully, without the clang I'm accustomed to when Chris finishes hard liquor. I do the same, tossing it back, and my throat stings, making me cough.

"Easy there. You didn't need to finish it," Alex chuckles.

"Yes, I did. Need the liquid courage."

He frowns. "For what?"

"Tonight."

CHAPTER 15
ALEX

Jaclyn and I check in at the resort and make our way to a small villa on a private beach where there's not another person in sight. I'm actually looking forward to the quiet and waking up to waves crashing instead of cars driving past my apartment.

The captain wasn't kidding when he said it would be warm. Even with the sun low in the sky, the humidity makes it sweltering—cargo shorts make a lot more sense now. Our only reprieve from the heat is the ocean breeze that's also warm. First thing in the morning, I'm buying clothes that fit properly and investing in a few fans.

With the time difference and the eventful past few days, we're both exhausted. As I set the luggage by the front door, I suggest, "Why don't you lay down for a bit, and I'll see about ordering a late dinner for us? Oh, don't forget, you have to approve the seating charts." Jaclyn doesn't reply, instead taking my hand and dragging me through the living space to the bedroom, making me wonder if *this* is what she needed the liquid courage for. Guiding me to the bed, she has me sit, and no matter how much I want her, I admit, "You know we can't do this."

Jaclyn falls to her knees, and the sight has my cock thickening in my shorts, which are already too tight. Untying my shoes, she responds matter-of-factly, "You're tired. I'm tired. So... we're *sleeping* together."

"I can take off my own shoes," I laugh softly as she removes one and unties the other.

"I know. You've been taking care of me this weekend. When was the last time you let someone take care of you?" She stands once they're both off and moves to the side of the bed to pull the duvet back. "Shorts off."

"Excuse me?"

"Shorts. Off." She cocks an eyebrow. "Or do I need to remove them for you?"

Unsure of where she's going with this, I follow her directions and set them on the small chair to the side of the bed. "Anything else, princess?"

"Yes." Jaclyn tilts her chin up. In the most adorable attempt, she commands, "Shirt, too. I don't want his clothes in my bed." I can't imagine the war waging within her. Despite it being a terrible idea, I do as she asks. "Get in." She pats the bed, and I climb in under the covers. It's too warm, so I leave the top sheet on, pushing the duvet to my feet.

As she pulls her dress over her head, I warn, "*Jaclyn.*" She sets the dress beside my shorts, leaving her in a matching dark blue bra and panty set. I can't take my eyes off her.

"What?" It's as if the dormant fire inside her is suddenly ablaze. *I'm absolutely going to get burned.* On the other side of the bed, she slides under the sheet, removes her bra, and tosses it to the ground.

"What do you think you're doing?" I growl, quickly losing my resolve.

"I normally sleep naked. Should I remove my panties, too?" Her tone is a blend of sweet and teasing—faux innocence.

Fucking brat.

"You woke up this morning wrapped in my arms, while fully clothed. Do you really think this is the best idea when you're practically naked?"

"No more naked than you are." She shrugs and turns away from me. "Goodnight."

I groan, staring at the ceiling. "You've got to be kidding me."

"Oh, did you want to cuddle?" she asks over her shoulder.

Yes.

"I'm going to sleep on the couch," I grumble, my palms itching to reach for her.

Pulling the sheet tightly under her armpits, she turns and slides up next to me, resting her head on my chest just below my shoulder. I instinctively wrap my arm around her, blowing out a long breath as I pull her closer. It's wrong to touch another man's wife, especially my brother's. Yet, here I am, unable to keep my hands to myself, loving the feel of Jaclyn's bare skin under my fingertips.

If she's his wife, why does it feel like she's mine?

"You're not sleeping on the couch or the floor," she sighs, slinging her leg over mine. "I need you here."

"I'm not my brother."

"Thank God for that," Jaclyn laughs softly, settling closer.

"When we're back home, you'll be in *his* bed."

Jaclyn adjusts to look up at me. "No, I won't. Not after what happened. He killed a woman he was sleeping with... *on our wedding day*. That's unforgivable."

"You're topless in bed with your husband's brother; you aren't exactly innocent."

"He isn't my husband." There isn't a hint of teasing in her tone.

"What are you talking about?" I huff, hating the reality I'm living. "It's his name on the marriage license."

"It isn't filed. It's still in my purse. So, I'm not married. Not yet, anyway."

"It doesn't matter. We shouldn't be doing this." My words are meaningless. Neither of us move, accepting our sins—and our fate. I don't dare tell her she's not mine, again. At this point, that would be a lie. "It's been a long day, get some sleep."

Jaclyn takes a deep breath and settles in. My eyes are already heavy, and I drift off quickly, never letting her go.

CHAPTER 16
ALEX

I wake in darkness to the faint smell of smoke, with Jaclyn no longer in my arms. I turn on a light and slide out of bed, finding a large, brown-handled paper bag on the chair where our clothes were earlier. Curiosity gets the best of me, and I open it, taking out a black tee, a pack of boxer briefs, and gray sweatshorts. Popping off the tags, I smile to myself and get dressed.

As I walk through the living room, a faint glow illuminates the space from a fire pit outside. I step outside, the sliding door alerting my presence and making Jaclyn turn toward the noise.

Seated in the chaise chair next to the fire pit, she turns back toward the ocean. "Sorry. Hope I didn't wake you. I needed to approve the seating chart for the gala."

"You didn't." I step onto the patio, taking a seat in the chaise next to her. She's wearing her dress from earlier, but her golden blonde hair is braided now over her shoulder. "How long have you been out here?"

"About an hour. I hope they fit."

I glance down and pull my shirt away from my body for a moment. "They do, thank you."

"I want to burn all of his clothes."

"What?" I ask, barking a laugh.

"But then I couldn't stop thinking how wasteful it is." She turns her head to face me. "So, in the morning, I'm going to bag everything up and donate them."

"Remind me to never piss you off," I chuckle, earning me a smile.

Jaclyn returns her attention to the water, and we sit in comfortable silence for several minutes. Staring out into the dark ocean, her voice startles me. "What made you decide to run as a moderate?"

"Honestly? It was never my party; it's my father's." I shrug. "I could've run with his endorsement, but I always want to vote with my conscience. It's why I've never accepted donations from large corporations." Though, I leave out that I accept other types of help from time to time. "Most of my donations are ten, maybe twenty dollars. No one wants to be beholden to billionaires. I also don't consider myself liberal or conservative. I don't vote along party lines, and I think that speaks to a lot of people. So, I hopped across the aisle to distance myself from my father, and I've always been transparent that I will do what's best for my state."

"I wish it was that simple for everyone," she sighs wistfully.

"It is. You just have to stay true to yourself. There's so much hypocrisy from both sides. Sometimes, one side is right; sometimes, it's the other. It's okay to agree with someone across the aisle. Politics is more of a murky gray than black and white."

"But you still have to pick a side," Jaclyn counters with a raised eyebrow.

"Not always. You can show them that collaboration isn't the devil." I turn to face her. "Okay, rapid fire." She mirrors me, trying to hide her smile, while her eyes glimmer with intrigue. We did this all the time in college, and I'm hoping it will lighten the energy between us. "School choice."

"Every parent should have the right to have their child attend whatever school they want," she replies without hesitation.

"Who should fund it?"

"We should. Education should be free."

"True," I concede, and she bites her lip, thinking she won this round. Swallowing hard, I remain on topic, ignoring the fact that I want to take her plump lip in between my teeth, and ask, "Should a private for-profit receive the same funding as a public non-profit?"

She pauses before carefully admitting, "Yes."

"Should there be regulations to ensure the for-profit school meets certain standards?"

Her eyes narrow. "Is this a trick question?"

"No," I laugh. "Some people—*my father*—think we shouldn't regulate private schools, even if they were to hypothetically receive state funding. I can't get behind that. I'm not putting tax dollars into a school that isn't teaching math. But with criteria in place, I agree, parents should have options. Education isn't one-size fits all, and schools should have the choice of what curriculum they want to use to meet a child's educational goals."

"We both went to private schools," she laughs, no longer able to conceal her smile.

"The public school system was hard for Chris and me." I can't help laying my heart on the table when I'm around her. "There wasn't a lot of support for kids with ADHD back then. It's a lot better now, but I don't take for granted that my parents had a choice for my education, whereas other parents don't. Don't get me started on how messed up the IEP process is for kids and their families."

"Wait a minute, you have ADHD, like Chris? I had no idea."

"It's not something I announce with a megaphone when I meet people. For me, it's more hyperfixation, while Chris struggles with impulsivity—or at least he used to when we were kids." Talking about it only shines a light on the fact that Jaclyn is my fixation-du-jour. "Okay, that's enough story time. Next one. Gun control."

Jaclyn shuts her eyes and sits back in her chair, shaking her head. "I don't like this game."

"You're rusty, Taylor," I tease, and she laughs, just like she did when we were younger. Fuck, I miss how carefree she was. "You know the answer that's expected of you, but when you're representing a district, an entire state, or the country, you have to listen to everyone's voices. There is never *one* answer that fits. It doesn't have to be all-or-nothing."

Her fire is back when she asks, "Where do *you* stand on gun control?"

As she lights up, I can't help mirroring her smile, loving that she's willing to play. With a little work, she'll be ready to take office; I just hope Chris will support her when she does. For a brief moment, my mind wanders, imagining an alternate universe where we are prepping for her presidential debate with my face between her legs, or buried deep inside her. My cock twitches at the thought, and I quickly brush away the fantasy.

"This isn't about me, *wife*." Fuck... I like how that sounds a bit too much.

"I miss this," she laughs.

I miss you.

"Me, too." Her lips tilt up in a smirk, and I continue, "All

139

right, last one. What's more important, animal safety or cost of goods?"

"I..." She fidgets with the hem of her dress. "I don't know. Both?"

I lean over and tilt her chin to look at me. "*That* was a trick question. But I agree, they're both important. In the bill I was working on with Chris, the ranchers want their animals to be safe, and the large corporations are worried about cost. They are both right, so we need to find a way to help the consumer so they can afford to put food on their table, while also ensuring the animals are cared for properly. Both sides have dug their heels in, refusing to budge. Some people, *who shall not be named*, want tax cuts for the large corporations; they believe it will offset everything. If we're being honest, we all know the additional cost will be passed along to the consumers anyway. It'll just make the corporations richer."

I sit back in the lounge chair, and she sighs in defeat. "I love that you have the courage to speak your mind, but I could never do what you did. If I wanted a chance of running—*and winning*—it would have to be in my father's party, and I'd need to bend to the will of everyone around me."

Taking her hand in mine, I swipe my thumb back and forth along hers. "Run for a House seat next year or in the midterms. Be honest in your campaign with what you believe in. It doesn't matter which party—you'll win."

"Maybe in a few cycles. I'm not ready. Are... are the rumors true that you're going to run for President? Your approval ratings are incredible. The country needs someone to bring everyone together."

Like you...

"My staff and fellow senators want me to. I'm happy where I'm at, politically, and I have no desire to leave Texas. I can do so much more for this country as a senator. So, no need to worry, I won't run against your husband," I chuckle, but she finds no humor in it.

Jaclyn takes her hand back and reaches behind her, rummaging in her purse and taking out an envelope. I watch her curiously as she stands and stares into the fire.

"He doesn't deserve to run," she says quietly, ripping the envelope in half, and tossing it into the fire.

"Was that...?"

"The marriage certificate I'm supposed to file when I get back home," she finishes. "I didn't marry him yesterday. Chris didn't recite his vows in front of God. You did. The document is a lie. He only wanted to marry me because of my last name, as a one-way ticket to the Oval." Her gaze shifts to me. "Fuck that. I'm not his wife."

I try my best not to laugh at her rare curse. Realization settling in, the blood drains from my face at her admission. "By that logic, you're..." I can't speak the words. No. She's not mine, can never be mine, even though I promised myself to her at the altar.

"We're stuck in a web of deceit. When we're back home, I'll find a way out of it."

"And until then? What do you want?"

Jaclyn steps over her chair and surprises me by straddling my lap. Her hands resting on my chest, she replies softly, "The one man I shouldn't."

I grip her thighs, and a quiet moment passes between us, heat dancing in her eyes from the flames that mirror everything I'm feeling. "You know this is a terrible idea."

In the end, she'll go back to Chris, and I'll be left to settle for someone who doesn't make me feel half what Jaclyn has in two days. I'll be stuck on the sidelines, watching my brother spend the rest of his life with her. I don't get to keep her, but *damn it*, I want to.

As I cup her cheek, she leans into my touch. "You deserve so much more than the web of deceit, princess."

"So do you." Jaclyn closes the distance, tilting her head to the left, and kisses me. It's gentle, cautious, and full of promises neither of us will be able to keep. Her sweet hum is a knife to my heart—that she's already stolen and will break in two. As reckless as it is kissing her, touching her, I'll risk it all if it means Jaclyn is mine while we're here. I nip at her bottom lip, teasing her for entry which she quickly grants me. As my tongue sweeps across hers, I selfishly slide my hands up her thighs and grip her smooth ass, pulling her closer.

"Where's your underwear, Miss Taylor?" I ask, smiling against her lips.

She grinds her bare pussy against me, dampening my shorts. "Should I go find them, Mr. Blake?"

If she keeps it up, I'll end up coming from a damn dry hump; I need to slow this down. Shifting one of my hands to cup her pussy, I slowly circle her clit, and swallow her gasps. "If we're doing this, *really doing this*, you're coming on my hand *and* my tongue before you get anywhere near my cock."

Jaclyn moans into my mouth, and it beats her whimpers and hums by a long shot. "Wh-what about you?"

"Do you have any idea how much I want this, want you? Making you come is just as much for me as it is for you, princess." I slip two fingers inside her tight pussy, and she writhes at my touch. Jealousy and possessiveness overcome me, and I break away from her lips, trailing kisses along her jaw to her neck, whispering against her skin, "You're right. I married you yesterday. You're *my* wife, not his. You'll ride my hand until you make a fucking mess all over my lap, and when I take you over the edge, you scream *my* name."

As I curl my fingers, Jaclyn pulls her dress over her head and tosses it to the ground. She's an absolute vision, and I'm terrified that any minute now, I'll wake up from this incredible dream. Savoring her silky skin under my fingertips, I take my time sliding my hand up her side, needing to memorize every inch of her.

She grips the chair and grinds her clit against my palm, her eyes never leaving mine as she chases her orgasm. My name tumbles from her lips as a moan, making my painfully hard cock strain against my shorts. "Just like that, beautiful. Keep going."

I lean forward and take one of her taut, pink nipples between my teeth, swirling my tongue around it, then do the same to the other side. Her breath is broken, and I can't get enough, desperate to devour every inch of her.

"*Fuck*, do that again," she manages.

Swiping my thumb against one and teasing the other with my mouth, it's enough to send her over the edge. Her pussy tightens around my fingers, flooding my hand with her release as she breathes my name. I slow my curling to a lazy pace, my shorts soaked. Pulling my fingers from her, I bring them to my mouth, sucking them clean, and I'm fucking ruined—she's heaven on Earth.

Collapsing on top of me, her words are ragged. "That... was..."

The ache to feel her naked body pressed against mine is too much. As I kiss her shoulder, I whisper, "Sit back for one second." She does, and I'm able to remove my shirt before she settles herself on top of me again. I wrap my arms around her, unable to imagine a world where I'll ever be able to let her go.

How the fuck am I going to hand her over to my brother in a couple of weeks?

CHAPTER 17
JACLYN

H ow the hell am I going to say goodbye to this incredible man in a couple of weeks?

And why are his shorts damp?

"Alex," I shriek, sitting up. "Why are you all wet?" Cupping the back of my neck, he keeps his thumb on my cheek and kisses me softly. "This is serious!"

"Fuck, you taste good," he mutters against my lips. I attempt to scramble off him as he holds me in place. "You came, and it was the sexiest thing I've ever witnessed."

"You're all wet... *from me?*" My cheeks heat as embarrassment washes over me.

"And you're not anymore." He sits up and, in a swift movement, flips us until I'm on my back. "We need to remedy that."

Alex takes off his shorts and throws them onto the chair beside us, then spreads my legs wide. While I'm self-conscious about being on display, I'm desperate for him to touch me again. Regardless of how wrong this is, it feels so damn right.

"What are you doing?" I breathe.

"Something I intend to do every fucking day until we leave." He dips his head and licks up my pussy, circling my clit three times, then sucks hard. I cry out, and as he presses his fingers inside me again, the sensation is almost too much.

"You don't have to do this. I know you said you wanted to, but you can't *actually* enjoy it."

He nips my inner thigh, making me yelp. "Do you want me to stop?"

"I don't know," I whisper, chewing on my lip.

In an instant, he pulls back, and the emptiness is unbearable. As the fire reflects in his darkened eyes, he draws his fingers into his mouth, sucking them clean again. A rumble comes from his chest, and I swallow hard as a quiet whimper escapes me. There's something sensual—erotic even—about it, and I can't bring myself to look away.

Despite my pussy still ready and waiting for him, Alex doesn't tear his heated gaze away from my face. With the fire crackling beside me, and my desperation to have him touch me again, I'm too hot, feeling as if I'm about to combust.

"Why did you stop?" I whine.

"'*I don't know*' is the same thing as telling me to stop, princess. When—" He blows out a long breath. "When was the last time someone...?"

My brows pinch. "Someone what?"

"Tasted you, fucked you with their mouth, made you come all over their face." I can't help laughing until his eyes bore into me, cutting my giggles short. "Jaclyn, I'm serious. I've only had an appetizer and am looking forward to the main course. I want to fucking devour you." I reply with a shake of my head, my cheeks flushing. "Fuck, when was the last time anyone made you come? Was it with...?" The pain in his voice is unbearable, a knife slicing my soul.

"No," I reply honestly, shaking my head.

"Are you serious? When was the last time, then? By yourself with a vibrating toy?" He wiggles his eyebrows, and I adore that he's back to his playful self.

"*Alex*," I squeak and unconsciously lick my lip. "A lady never discusses her toy collection."

His knuckle traces down my inner thigh, making my breath catch. Without a hint of teasing, he admits, "I hate that you've been with him, but I love that he can't do this to you." Grazing my clit with his knuckle, a soft whimper passes my lips as a groan comes from deep in his chest. "Already so wet for me. Let me taste you again. I want to feel your clit swell on my tongue." I draw my lips into my mouth, stifling a moan. "Please, Jaclyn."

I should say 'no,' he's giving me an out. "Yes," I breathe, barely above a whisper, with no regrets.

Without another word, he lowers his head between my legs and licks once up my seam with a devilish glint in his eyes. I wriggle under his touch. He spreads me wider, licking firm circles around my clit. It feels beyond amazing, and I relax into his touch.

As I close my eyes, I grip the top of the lounge chair with one hand to keep myself steady while my other tangles in his hair. Continuing to swirl his tongue, he presses two fingers inside me, then a third. I'm so deliciously full, and so... *his*. Since we were younger, I've always wanted this —wanted Alex. I shouldn't have given in, but there's no point in denying myself of this perfect man anymore. Even without having sex, he's ruined me. I'm never going to be able to sleep with anyone else, let alone his brother, after tonight.

Alex's moans vibrate against me, and when he sucks hard, it's my undoing. My entire body buzzes as wave after wave of my orgasm crashes over me, almost in sync with the water in the distance. For a brief moment, everything goes black, but I'm not unconscious—there's still the sound of the waves, my heavy breaths, the crackling of the fire pit, and a feral, satisfied growl coming from Alex.

"Alex... I..." I pant, struggling to form a coherent sentence.

My vision comes back into focus, zeroing in on him swiping his bottom lip with his thumb, a cocky grin tilting his lips. "Can you stand?" I shake my head, and he offers his hand. "Sit up." He settles behind me, guiding me by my hips to sit between his toned thighs, my back pressed against his hard chest. Kissing the top of my head, he whispers into my hair, "You're fucking incredible... And you're *mine*, Jaclyn."

As I turn my head to look at him, he grips the front of my throat, capturing my lips with his. Tasting myself on his tongue as he deepens the kiss, I hum while reaching between us to grip his thick cock through his underwear. He pulls my hand away the moment I touch him, and I whimper in disappointment.

"Not tonight." Alex grabs a blanket hanging on the back of the other chaise and drapes it over me.

"Afraid to consummate the marriage?" I jest, and it earns me a hearty laugh.

"Oh, there will be *plenty* of consummation, but we've had an eventful couple of days. You need to rest."

We lay together quietly, listening to the waves crash as he keeps his arms wrapped tightly around me. I've never felt as safe and adored as I do with him. And I hate to admit, I trust Alex more than any other person in my life right now. Tonight complicates everything—my engagement, my plans... my heart. He said I'm a woman he could fall for. Now I'm worried that I won't be able to walk away from him in a couple of weeks.

After several minutes, he breaks the comfortable silence. "Are you ready for bed?" I nod, and he helps me up, wrapping the blanket around me again. "No one sees you like this but me." Taking my face in his hands, he kisses me. It's tender, sweet, and breaks my heart in two.

I wait while he extinguishes the fire, then he leads us to the villa, stopping in front of the sliding doors. Lifting me bridal style, he carries me over the threshold.

"What are you doing?" I laugh at his ridiculous gesture.

"What does it look like I'm doing, *wife?*" he teases back, walking us inside, but none of this is funny. I'd give anything to be married to Alex instead of Chris.

CHAPTER 18
CHRIS

Waking me for what feels like the fiftieth time in the past twelve hours, the nurse checks my vitals. She's pretty, though a bit too old for me. Still, if I wasn't laid up in this hospital bed, I'd bend her over for a quick fuck.

My mother walks in wearing one of her classic black pencil skirts and a gray blazer, with a somber expression to match. Catching me staring at the nurse's ass, she purses her lips and groans, "Can you give us a moment alone?" The nurse scurries out of the room, muttering, "Yes, ma'am." Once the door is shut, Mom takes a seat next to my bed. "Christopher, you need to get your shit together, or your father will *not* support your presidential run."

"What do you mean 'get my shit together?' I'm married to Jaclyn now. That all but guarantees the party's nomination," I sneer.

"You two have no chemistry." She takes out her phone and scrolls, tapping a few times. "Ah, here we go." She hands it to me, and I click on the article. It highlights how I appeared indifferent in our staged photos leading up to the wedding, and now a man in love on the big day.

Alex.

"After your little *accident*, do you really think a woman like Jaclyn is going to remain your dutiful wife?" She takes her phone back and tucks it in her purse.

"Relax, it's fine. She doesn't know about me and Cara," I insist.

"You've forgotten that your wife is an educated woman. If Alex hasn't told her the truth, it's only a matter of time before she figures out that you were fucking your aide on your wedding day. And I give her a few weeks before she puts two and two together that you've been sleeping with any woman willing to spread her legs, since you were eighteen. Sure, she'll stand beside you for photo ops, but she won't enthusiastically support you." My mother groans, and as I'm about to reply, she continues her rant, "Things are different now than they were when your father ran. Yes, she's a Taylor, but Jaclyn is the perfect choice because you need a First Lady who does something other than stand there and look pretty. If you want the White House, you have to win her over; you need to look at her the way Alex does."

"Can't you see he wants to steal *my* wife?" I growl.

"He's quite the actor. If he does manage to steal her from you, you deserve it. What you did..." She tsks. "You're worse than your father. Fix this, or you've not only ruined her life but yours, too." As she stands, she brushes her skirt to smooth out any wrinkles. "The wedding was beautiful, by the way. I'm so happy she went with lavender and white."

My mother is right; I'm throwing away my shot at the presidency. Fuck, maybe even reelection in Florida.

Once she leaves, the nurse from before comes back in, and my eyes fall to her full breasts as she coyly asks, "Anything I can assist you with, Mr. Blake?"

What's one last bit of fun before I'm saddled with the ol' ball and chain?

"I seem to have an ache I could use your *assistance* with, Nurse"—I check her name tag—"Wendy."

Wendy checks the door and returns her gaze to me. "I'm here to help, sir." She pulls back the blanket covering my lap and lifts the medical gown. "You have swelling. May I assist... *manually?*"

"I think it needs something warmer," I suggest, and she wets her lips.

As Wendy leans in, the door flies open, and she quickly pulls back. "Oh, good, you're still here," my mother chides as I scramble to cover up. "You're fired. And *you*..." She glares at me. "You should be wooing your wife, not your nurse. I was going to give you the good news that you'll be discharged later today. Perhaps I should tell them you need to stay here indefinitely if you can't keep it in your pants, Christopher."

Mom turns on her heel before I can protest, and Wendy rushes after my mother. When the door shuts behind them, I'm left alone for a moment with my hard cock. Needing release, I fist it, but the vibe left the room with Wendy. I manage to make out a few shouts before the door opens again, and a man in a white coat walks in.

"Good news, you'll be released later today, Mr. Blake, pending your echo results and drug test. We should have both shortly. Are there any arrangements you'd like us to make?"

"No, any arrangements can be made by my family."

He nods and walks out. As soon as the door closes, I relieve the ache Wendy couldn't take care of, surprised by Jaclyn's name passing my lips as I come.

CHAPTER 19
ALEX

My usual weekday morning alarm blares, waking Jaclyn. After a few curses to myself, I quickly silence it; there's no way I'll be able to go back to sleep. I cancel all alarms set for the next two weeks and set it aside.

"Shh, go back to sleep, princess. I'm going for a quick run. I'll be right back." After our night, she needs her rest.

She murmurs an intelligible response, and I slip out of bed. Looking around for running shoes, I quickly discover they don't exist here. "Between the two of us, we can buy whatever you're looking for later today," I'm able to make out from her sleepy mumbles, and disappointment settles in my gut. I miss having the pavement beneath my feet and the rush of beating my personal best. I need it— almost as much as I need her—and I haven't gone for a run in the past few days.

Fuck the shoes. A perfect, beautiful woman is in my bed all but begging me to claim her as mine.

"I was going to go for a run, but I need to pick up new shoes. Though, I can think of a few things we could do to burn calories."

"Alex," she giggles, "you're such a flirt." I strip off my clothes, and she sits up. "Wait—" I can't. I won't. I don't and climb back into bed with her. "I'm serious. I want to. It's just that I'm going to start my... um, *time of the month.* Any day now." It's endearing that she thinks that will stop me from my desperation to finally have her.

My bare cock nudging at the entrance of her tight pussy, I admit, "I couldn't care less, but we don't have con—" She locks her heels behind me and draws me closer, slipping an inch inside her. "*Fuck.*"

"You probably shouldn't come inside me; I'm not on birth control. But I need you, Alex." Her words are my undoing. *I. Need. You. Alex.* The four little words wash over me as she pulls me in another inch. "You feel so good," she whispers through uneven breaths.

She's wrong—she feels more than good, she's fucking perfect. I resist pushing in the rest of the way and kiss the hell out of this beautiful goddess in front of me instead. A selfish part of me wishes that I could get her pregnant, seeing her belly swell month after month while she campaigns with my brother, knowing it's mine.

"Are you sure about this?" she whimpers as I slowly rock in and out of her.

"I am if you are. You said you're supposed to start any day now, right? You took biology, so we both know it's statistically unlikely you could get pregnant." The realization is disappointing. I thrust deep inside her and hold, needing to be sure she still wants this, wants *me*. "Do you want me to stop?"

"No," she replies without an ounce of hesitation, "don't stop."

"Are you sure?"

Her pussy clenches around me as she bites her lip. "Absolutely."

My lips melt into hers, needing to be impossibly closer as I resume claiming her. Right now, she's mine. I want to ruin her, to have her thinking of me any time another man touches her.

No.

Fuck that.

I'll be the last man to touch her.

She's mine.

Possessiveness courses through me. We need to find a way out of this mess; there's no way in hell I'll walk away from her after everything that's happened. I break our kiss, trailing my lips down to her neck, and mark her for the whole damn world to see. As I draw her soft skin into my mouth and suck hard, she cries out in pleasure, clamping tightly around my cock.

It's too much, and to my own detriment, my balls tighten, and I come hard, painting the walls of her pussy with my cum. Almost immediately, she moans, gripping my back, but there isn't the same warmth from last night when she pulsed around my fingers, drenching my lap.

"Jaclyn," I growl, "what was that?"

"I came."

"You didn't come."

"Yes, I did," she insists, but she's so full of shit.

"I've been hard since the moment I agreed to marry you. Two days of blue balls will make any man come too fast. You came for me yesterday, and *that?* That wasn't an orgasm, princess."

"Sorry, I'm just used to—" She hisses as I carefully pull out of her and slip two fingers into her pussy, keeping my cum inside her. "What are you doing?" she rushes out as I begin kissing down her body.

Drawing one of her nipples into my mouth, I keep it between my teeth as I reply, "What does it look like I'm doing?" I curl my fingers, and her delicious moans fill the room.

"Kiss me again," she whimpers, and I continue my torture. Keeping my fingers inside her, I slide down her body, and she laughs, tangling her fingers in my hair. "I asked you to kiss me."

Once my face is between her legs, I lick two firm, slow circles around her clit. "You never said where." I could spend my lifetime between her legs, and it wouldn't be enough. Her hips buck once, seeking more.

"You came inside me," she breathes but makes no move to stop me.

"You seriously think I fucking care? Now, be my good little wife and come all over my face. If you dare try to fake it with me again, you won't be able to sit properly for a week."

After a morning in bed, Jaclyn and I venture outside the villa to try a seafood restaurant on the water that the resort concierge recommended. It's intimate with a spectacular ocean view, the perfect quiet place to spend time together where we can be ourselves.

The host leads us to a square table on the patio. When he steps away, I push in the chair for Jaclyn, and she winces as settles into her seat.

"Perhaps six is your limit," I whisper, peppering soft kisses down her neck.

"*One*. One is my limit," she grumbles.

"I respectfully disagree, Mrs. Blake," I retort with a chuckle and take the seat next to her. She glares at me, but I ignore it. Attempting to hide my smile, I open the menu. "What sounds good?"

"I'm not Mrs. Blake and"—she lowers her voice—"how are you so chipper and not exhausted?"

Not looking up from the entree page, I slide my hand onto her thigh. "For the next two weeks, you're *my* Mrs. Blake, and I think you can give me one more." I slip my hand under her dress, pushing it up as I glide my fingers along the inside of her thigh.

"Alex!" she whisper-shouts, gripping my hand and holding it in place.

"Yes?" I lean in and press a gentle kiss on her bare shoulder. "Are you already wet for me again?"

Jaclyn's breath catches, a light pink blush dusting her chest and cheeks. "Why do I think you're going to find out for yourself?"

"I regret not doing it on the plane." Setting down the menu, I slide my free hand into her hair and bring her lips to mine. She releases my grip on her thigh and spreads her legs enough that I find her panties soaked. My pinky grazes the wet fabric, and it earns me my favorite hum. I groan against her lips, "Until we leave, I get to play with this perfect wet cunt of yours whenever I want. As soon as we're done with lunch, I'm having you for dessert."

A small flash of light pulls my attention from her. Keeping my gaze locked on her, I spot three photographers hiding outside the patio from the corner of my eye. I've been so swept up in Jaclyn that I'm being careless. Granted, I'm supposed to pretend to be in love with her, but what we are doing is far from fake—at least for me. From where the photographers are stationed, they won't catch my hand on her thigh. I still pull back, her desperate whimper making my cock twitch.

"Don't look up, but we're being watched," I whisper beside her ear and kiss her pulse point.

She pulls back, brows pinched. "Who would be watching?"

"Could be paparazzi, or either of our fathers keeping tabs on us. I'm sorry, I should be more caref—"

Jaclyn's mouth crashes into mine, her soft lips parting and letting me selfishly take from her. I slide my hand into her hair, deepening our kiss. None of this is appropriate for a restaurant, and I stop my foolish heart from reading more into this; it's all an act, a show for whoever is watching.

A throat clears to my left, and Jaclyn and I break apart. Our waiter smirks. "My apologies for the wait. May I get either of you something to drink."

Jaclyn's eyes don't leave mine as she replies with a wide grin, "Two Old Fashioneds—with an extra cherry," giving me a glimmer of hope that everything I'm feeling isn't one-sided. "We're celebrating."

CHAPTER 20
JACLYN

O ver the last few days, Alex has spent his time either buried inside me or with his face between my legs, leaving little time for recreation. Not that I mind. If all we have is two weeks, I want to soak up every second with him—in and out of bed.

Our clock is ticking.

After the photoshoot I set up prior to this whole charade, we enjoyed a late lunch with some of the most delicious fish tacos I've ever had. We haven't seen much of the island, so at his suggestion, he drove us to one of the hiking trails, only for him to quickly discover that I am by no means a hiker. To appease me, he offered to take us on a scenic drive around the island to sightsee, and while it's not as relaxing as a day at the beach, I accepted.

Windows down and my ponytail whipping in the sea air, Alex keeps our hands joined. His eyes are trained on the road, which runs parallel with the ocean. He's so hard to read. So far, it's been the perfect, relaxing drive until he speaks the dreaded words, "Rapid fire."

Here we go.

"Gay marriage?"

Of all things to ask? "Which answer do you want?"

"Your opinion." His adorable dimple pops as he tries to hide his smirk. For a politician, he has the worst poker face. "What do you believe is the right answer?"

"This is a trap! Where are the hidden cameras?" I laugh, looking around.

"No trap." Alex squeezes my hand tighter and brings the back of it to his lips. "When you're on TV in a presidential debate, I want to know if I'm watching the real you."

"Wives of candidates don't debate," I deadpan.

"No, but after four to six years in the House, or maybe after the beginning of a second Senate term, you're going to run. I need to know who I'm voting for."

"*What?*" He's lost his mind.

"You've spent too long worrying about cherry blossoms; I want to know where you stand on important issues." There isn't a hint of teasing in his tone; he's genuinely curious.

I clear my throat dramatically. "It is my personal belief that marriage is between a man and a woman. A church should not be forced to perform marriages that go against

their beliefs. *However*"—he briefly glances at me—
"everyone in this world deserves to marry the person they
love. So, it's not up to me or any state to stop two
consenting adults from being legal spouses or to be wed
by a religious entity that supports them."

"Is that your official answer?" He cocks an eyebrow,
biting his lip and unable to hide his smile.

"No," I sigh and his face falls.

"Why not?"

I lower my head, eyes shut tight. Pulling my hand back
from him, my stomach plummets to the floor. "You and I
both know that in the end, I'll have to fall in line. If I can't
find a safe way out of the marriage, I'll have to support
whatever Chris supports." The car slows down, and I
open my eyes as Alex pulls over. "Why are we stopping?"

We park in front of a small coffee shop, and he turns the
ignition off. Hands gripping the steering wheel tight, he
grumbles, "He's not going to support you running."

"Once he's done with his four or eight years as President,
I'm sure I can convince him that a seat in the House, or
maybe a governor of a small state, is perfectly acceptable,"
I counter.

"Are you okay with that?" *Why does he think I can do
more?* "You're satisfied with not serving your country in a
position you were born for?"

"I'm a hypocrite. I have no place in a position of power!"
My hand flies to my mouth.

His nostrils flare. "Why?"

"*You. Because I want you,*" I want to scream, but I set my hands in my lap, with ankles crossed and posture straight —as I've always done. "To the country, I'm the loving wife of a senator. How can I say I support people marrying who they love when I'm in a loveless marriage myself?"

"You don't have to be." He turns his whole body to face me. "You don't have to stay married to him."

"No matter what angle I look at it, there's only one solution: I'll be Chris' wife when we return home." The thought of living with him has bile rising in my throat; Cara isn't the last woman he'll sleep with.

"I refuse to believe that's the only solution."

"Sometimes things *are* black and white."

"Fuck that." Alex cups the back of my neck and brings me in for a searing kiss that I feel all the way to my toes. I don't have an ounce of protest in me. Nothing about the two of us makes sense, and I'm just going to fall into an abyss of pain and heartbreak when these two weeks are over.

But I've never felt anything like this with anyone else.

I can't help giving in to Alex—he lets me set the pace, and tests me. I'm going to miss him so damn much. "You're unlike anyone I've ever sexperienced... *experienced.*"

He pulls back with a full laugh. "Oh, my sweet wife, you know *damn well* I'm both." I've stopped fighting it when he calls me that. As far as God is concerned, I'm Alex's. "I don't give a fuck if you go back to Chris in a few weeks. You're *mine,* Jaclyn." His growl and frankness give me pause. "I'll sneak around the White House if I have to, slide under the Resolute desk if I must, but you and I know this isn't over when we're back in Washington."

"The Resolute desk is in the Oval Office," I retort, hiding my smile.

"Where *you* will be sitting." He lets out a soft chuckle. "And I'll be feasting on you until you can't wait a moment longer for me to bend you over and fuck you. Hard and fast. Begging to come again. You know, as Queen Victoria intended when she gifted it to Hayes."

I can't help laughing at the ridiculous image he's painted, but the levity dies quickly in my chest. "If things were different, do you think you could handle being a First Gentleman? Not only has it never been done before, but I'm pretty sure your ego would get in the way."

It's a lie. All of it. If I was legally married to Alex, he would support me running for any seat or office I wanted. He would be the best First Gentleman that ever First Gentlemaned. Hell, he'd be the best husband that ever husbanded.

But that's not our reality. In no world should I entertain the idea of him being mine.

Except now.

These few weeks.

I yearn for it. *Ache* for it. I'm desperate for his love more than I've wanted anything in my life. I'm not naive, this isn't going to last. If we had more time, I would absolutely fall in love with him.

"I think I've proven otherwise, princess."

Shit, what were we talking about? His ego...

"That may be, but you weren't meant for the sidelines," I say carefully, knowing he'll fight me on this if I press further. Thankfully, he doesn't.

"I wish that we had more time, just the two of us." A cocky smirk tilts his lips. *Is he a mind reader now?* "I'm sure we'd fall madly in love with each other if we did."

"The wedding... The honeymoon... Do you know why I begged to come here?" He shakes his head and a small lie tumbles from my lips, "I chose a resort with private villas to get to know Chris better."

I never wanted to get to know him better, I wanted space after the wedding.

Continuing with the truth, I admit, "Instead, I'm falling for his brother. You have to see how wrong this is." A sigh pulls from my lungs, the next words coming out as a choked sob. "Even if you feel so right."

Alex brings me in for a sweet, gentle kiss, and I melt into him, not wanting to ever break apart. My heart begs to be closer to him, even with him sitting right in front of me.

I'll never be able to step into the role of Chris' wife without wishing I was with Alex instead.

"Are you falling for me, princess? Have you forgotten you're sleeping with the enemy?" he whispers between kisses. "You make your own destiny, *Madame President*."

If only he was right.

CHAPTER 21
CHRIS

"What the actual fuck?" I seethe, throwing the newspaper across the room. "Someone get me a phone. A laptop... *Anything* with internet."

I knew it, fucking knew Alex would do something like this if he went to Hawaii with Jaclyn. It's only been a few days, but with the way she's kissing him in the photo, there's no way he isn't sleeping with her.

A nurse rushes in. "Is everything all right?"

"No, far from it. When am I going to be discharged? I was supposed to be out a few days ago."

"Within the hour," a doctor behind her replies, looking over something in a manilla folder. "We're waiting on both former Presidents to sign off on it."

"I need to get out of here," I growl, sitting up and slinging my legs to the side of the bed. The nurse tries to help, but I snap, "I've got it."

I stand and do not, in fact, 'got it.' My knees buckle, and I fall to the ground, my ass hitting the hard vinyl flooring. The woman doesn't offer to help me a second time, both staring at me with pity. After struggling for a while, she leaves and returns a moment later with a wheelchair, and I'm able to pull myself up and sit in it. As I'm about to scold them for their terrible bedside manner, one of my father's secret service agents enters, glances around, and utters something into his headset.

My father walks in and addresses the doctor, "Are there any changes since we last spoke?"

"No, Christopher cleared all tests and will need to meet with a cardiologist in the next week or two to follow up. His primary or a psychiatrist will need to adjust his ADHD medication since it's what likely caused his heart attack." I hate that he talks about me as if I'm not in the room.

"Can we have a few minutes alone?" my father requests, nodding at the doctor.

"Of course." Everyone in the room files out, and my father pins me with an icy glare.

"You have to fix this," I plead, and his frown deepens. "You and Mom saw the headlines."

"Alex and Jaclyn are doing exactly what I asked of them; they're putting on a believable show while you heal. Why do you think your mother and I insisted you have a few extra days here?"

"She's fucking Alex! How are you okay with that?"

"I planted the photographers," he growls. "Jaclyn is a smart woman. She's supposed to be on her honeymoon, where most people fuck like damn rabbits after their wedding. It would be odd for her to turn her cheek or look like she was attending a damn tea party in public."

"I need to stop them. This is—"

"No. You're going to let them continue the charade until they return from their honeymoon. The media is eating it up; you are painted as a man in love. We put out a press release that Alex was hit by a drunk driver on his way to the wedding and is recovering from the accident. With the fake story, you'll need to be wheelchair-bound for another week, pretending to be him. From what I hear from the medical staff, that shouldn't be too difficult. One of my agents has your fake ID and credit cards in his name. You do not use *any* of your own until they are back. Is that clear?"

I swallow hard. "Crystal."

"Good. You'll lay low at his apartment in Fredrick. Under no circumstances are you to return to Florida until Jaclyn and Alex are home."

"Fredrick? You expect me to stay in *Fredrick?*"

A small smirk tugs at his lips. "He has a studio apartment there. Quaint." I roll my eyes, and he huffs a sigh. "Now that's all settled, I'm happy to hear your recovery is underway. Like your doctor said, you'll need to see specialists in the next month to ensure you're ready to hit the campaign trail. Your accident ruined more than your wedding; we've had to postpone your candidacy announcement. If you want to beat Berger and Thomas in the primaries, you'll have to make up for lost time as soon as she's back."

"Berger isn't a problem."

"No, *you* will be. You need to win Jaclyn over, or the country will assume you two are in the middle of a lovers' quarrel. She can fake it if she has to, but seeing as she doesn't know how the accident happened, she should have no problem slipping back into routine with you. You can't take the presidency without her. Get to know her. Fuck, at least pretend to like her."

"Woo my own wife? Shouldn't be too difficult."

"You've seen social media and the articles. You have your work cut out for you."

CHAPTER 22
ALEX

"Morning, beautiful," I whisper, kissing Jaclyn's shoulder. Waking up next to her has to be one of my top three favorite things I've experienced in my whole life. Her sweet hum as my lips touch her gets me every damn time.

"Morning." Her reply is groggy as she shifts to face me. "What time is it?"

"Nine."

She lets out a long yawn, slinging her leg over me but quickly retreats. "No!"

I rush to sit up. "What's wrong?"

"I'm so sorry!" Jaclyn grabs every stitch of fabric within arm's reach and wraps it around herself.

"What are you..." I follow her glance to my leg, which has a small smear of blood across it. "Get back here."

"No!" she shrieks. "I did that to you. I'm so sorry, Alex, I'm going to—" As she moves off the bed, I snatch her by the waist and pull her back to me. "Alex! We are not having sex. In fact, I'm going to move to the middle of nowhere, never to be heard from again."

I toss her onto her back, and she tries to hold back her laughter. "It's fine."

"It's *not* fine. Oh, shit! The housekeepers!"

What is her obsession with what hotel staff thinks?

"...will think you were a virgin bride. I know, super embarrassing. But I'm sure your approval rating will skyrocket if it gets out." I pull down the comforter and lick small circles around one of her nipples before grazing it with my teeth.

"This isn't funny," she giggles, wriggling under my touch as I blow cold air on her now-wet skin.

Ripping the comforter down, I kiss her stomach, sighing, "Sorry, little one. I really did try to make it happen. For fuck's sake, your mother is so full of my cum she should be knocked up with twins by now. Alas, this is where we part ways." She lets out a full laugh, and I look up at her while still talking to her belly. "So, we're going to hop in the shower, then strip the bed. And I'll make sure she's taken care of, no matter what."

"Alex," she breathes, her laughter ceasing, with a combination of relief and a hint of longing.

"Come on, my little wife, let me make good on my promises."

I slide off the bed and offer my hand. Jaclyn doesn't take it. Instead, she strips away the soiled comforter, keeping it wrapped tightly around her, and rushes to the bathroom. Thankfully, the villa doesn't have locks on any inside doors, and I'm able to follow her. As she turns the knob for the shower, I wrap my arm around her, splaying my hand across her belly and pulling her back flush with my chest.

"May I join you?" I ask playfully, the steam quickly filling the bathroom.

"Yes, but—"

I guide her into the shower, scalding hot water pouring down on me. I can't help hissing as it pelts my shoulders. "Do you always have it this hot?"

"You just told a non-existent child that you were going to take care of me. *This* is taking care of me. I need a hot shower, cozy pajamas, and probably at least two re-watches of *Pride and Prejudice*. Oh, and don't think you can get away with the short movie, either. We're doing the ridiculously long series, where he exits the lake in a wet tunic."

I laugh as I pull her closer, then press her against the shower wall. "Wet tunic?"

"Think you're up for it?" She winks, but I don't care if

she's joking. I'll happily watch a wet, swamp man on repeat if that's what she wants.

Gripping her chin with my thumb and forefinger, I bring her lips within a breath of mine. "Other than a Regency romance marathon, what else can I do to serve you?"

"I don't want to have someone serve me." Sinking down to her knees, she looks up with doe eyes, biting her lip. "I know you'll take care of me. So, let me take care of you."

Jaclyn slides her tongue along my shaft, making my cock impossibly hard. She's a damn siren, and in the span of less than a week, fucking owns me. As she takes all of me in her mouth, the only words I exhale are expletives. She licks and sucks until I hit the back of her throat, and she lightly gags. I grip her damp hair and pull back an inch, her eyes sparking with mischief. Reaching behind her head, her hand envelops mine, and she forces her mouth further onto me.

My cock hits the back of her throat again, and I groan, "Fuck, princess, you're so fucking beautiful on your knees taking all of me."

As she moans around my throbbing cock, it takes everything in me not to piston into her mouth. Sliding up and down my length, she massages my balls, and I have to brace myself on the wall behind her to keep my balance.

"I'm supposed to be taking care of *you*," I remind her, but she doesn't slow her pace. Her eyes are red with a mix of tears and the shower water, and I instinctively growl, "That's enough."

I'm not the man-slut the media paints me as; I rarely sleep with the women I go out with. The last woman I was with before Jaclyn was over six months ago, and I'm like a damn teenager about to come from a two minute blowjob. Since our first night, I've always made sure she's taken care of before me, and once I'm inside her, I almost always beat her to climax.

Not today.

Hollowing her cheeks and relaxing her throat, she massages her tongue along my length, refusing to relinquish control. With a fistful of her wet hair, I force her mouth off me. Worry flashes in her eyes. She stands, seemingly out of fear, and it pierces my heart. I don't think my brother has it in him to hurt her; I need her to know I never would. I brush the damp hair off her shoulder, kissing the sensitive spot between her neck and shoulder.

"You want me to come, princess? Earn it with that perfect pussy of yours. When you're on your knees for me, it's only because I've already taken care of you," I assure her, keeping my voice soft.

"You don't have to." A heavy breath leaves her lungs, and I take her face in my hands and tilt to the left, leaning in until the right of my nose is brushing hers.

She's branded on my soul, and I'll never escape it.

"I don't *have to* do anything. But, fuck, Jaclyn... You have to know how much I want you. And right now, I want *all* of you." Pulling back an inch, her enchanting blue eyes soften as the hot water pelts my back, shielding her from it.

We share a breath for a brief moment until her fingers tangle in my hair, pulling me closer until our lips are almost touching. I relish her soft curves as my hand slides up her leg, hiking it over my hip. Her eyes close, and a soft whimper escapes her as she whispers, "What happens after 'right now?'"

Fuck answering with words. I lick the seam of her lips, and her gasp allows me to taste her. She's no longer my brother's, and I want her to admit it, to show me that she's mine as much as I'm hers. Our moans mingle with the steam of the shower as it envelops us, and as I line myself up with her, no part of me gives a shit if we make a mess.

"We don't stop until you come," I growl against her lips.

"But I'm—"

I press an inch inside her. "I don't fucking care. You're going to come all over my cock, then I'm going to take care of your every need, every want... and every desire." I push in another inch, and her sweet whimpers spur me on. "You know I'm not going to be able to let you go when this is over." My cock throbs as I shove the rest of the way into her tight pussy. She gasps, and our shared breath makes me smile. "If anyone should be on their knees, it should be me. Let me take care of you the way you deserve."

A strangled sob passes her lips as they melt against mine. "I can't go back to him."

"Even if you do, you'll always be mine." I thrust hard and deep inside her. "Only. Mine."

I've never felt this kind of incessant need before. Obsession, if I'm being honest. We've talked it into the ground, and as much as I hate to admit it out loud, she'll inevitably have to play the perfect wife role for my brother. The thought sours my stomach each and every time I consider it.

There is no way out of this hell where my heart isn't shattered into a thousand pieces when we're back home.

He wins. I lose her.

But not now. In this perfect moment, I get to keep the woman I'm falling head-over-heels in love with.

As I continue to thrust in and out of her, Jaclyn's kisses are equally as desperate as mine. The devil on my shoulder is pushing me to claim every inch of her, despite knowing how wrong it is to ruin her. I selfishly want the ghost of my cock to haunt her when I can't touch her again. I don't believe in soulmates or love at first sight, but it's only fair that she feels the same ache I'll have in my chest. Jaclyn owns a piece of me, and when this is over, she'll leave a hole in my heart that I'll be forced to live with for the rest of my life.

Between kisses, she whispers, "I'm yours, Alex."

It pierces me in a way I never thought it could. I can't help myself, gripping the front of her throat and deepening our kiss, needing to brand every part of her as I promised. As she kisses me back harder, I chuckle against her lips, "Do you need more, princess?"

"Please," she breathes, her fingers sinking into my back.

"Please, what?"

Jaclyn pulls back, and there's a gentle understanding between us as she looks between my eyes. Every time I'm inside her, it becomes harder and harder to imagine life without her. She should be afraid of me, of whatever is happening between us, and run the other fucking direction. Instead, this impossibly brilliant woman is offering herself to me.

Me.

Her *real* husband.

I don't care what the fucking burned marriage certificate says. I stood up there, promising myself to her. She's my wife.

As her breath quickens, I press our bodies closer until we're fused together, pushing my cock deeper, and continue the same pace. She's almost there, but it's not enough. For a brief moment, she tenses, and I slow down, then build her back up.

Reaching between us, I circle her swollen clit, and I swallow her euphoric moans with my lips sealed on hers. As her pussy tightens around me again, her warmth coats my cock, and she cries out as she comes. Satisfaction fills me as *my* name passes her lips. The sound steals part of my soul every time. I thrust one final time and hold, never wanting to pull out of her.

Taking Jaclyn's face in my hands and kissing her deeply, I speak against her lips. "You did so fucking well, my little wife. We'll spend the rest of the day watching your swamp man. But, first, I need one more from you."

After breakfast and lunch in bed, and watching several hours of her favorite Regency romance, we fell asleep in each other's arms.

I wake to my phone vibrating on the bedside table and the bright orange glow of the summer sunset filling the room. Jaclyn snuggles closer as I kiss her forehead, whispering, "One second, I need to check my phone." Pulling my arm out from under her, I reach for it and find two missed calls from Ned.

Fuck.

I rush out of bed and slip on a pair of gym shorts, then leave the room to call him back. Once I'm on the patio, I take a seat on one of the lounge chairs facing the ocean, and I can't help but smile thinking about the first night with her. The way we both gave in, and she burrowed her way into my heart. My trip down memory lane is quickly derailed when I pull up his contact and press call.

"Took you long enough," he grumbles as he picks up.

"Any news?"

He huffs a laugh. "Your brother is out. He's staying at your place, and the media coverage is in your favor. I don't think it'll be for long—the Gallaghers don't trust Chris. The accident has been taken care of, but I'm more worried about how your brother will react seeing the photos that were leaked of you with Ms. Taylor in paradise."

"It's Mrs. Blake, and I'm supposed to *pretend* to like her," I defend. Glancing back at the villa to ensure Jaclyn isn't eavesdropping, I lie, "It's all for the cameras, or all of this will blow up in our faces."

"You were never supposed to marry her, but everything seems to be going according to the new plan. Between the clean-up and the story about *your* accident, you'll still have work to do when you're back. Also, the Gallaghers want to meet with you."

Mickey owns one of the biggest casinos on the East Coast; his brother, Finn, is the CEO of Gallagher Whiskey. Both are fronts for their less-than-savory business practices behind closed doors. The last thing I need is to be even more in debt to them, but I knew the risk when I ran for office. If I could, I'd wash my hands of all of it. "Of course. As soon as I'm back in D.C.."

"See you then, Mr. Blake."

He hangs up, and I stuff my phone into my pocket. As I wring my hands, I stare at the crashing waves for a moment, the solitude abruptly ending with the sliding glass door opening. Wrapped in a light blue silk robe,

Jaclyn sits next to me, taking one of my hands and interlacing our fingers. While I adore 'fun Jaclyn,' 'sweet, affectionate Jaclyn' takes my breath away. Coupled with how she instantly calms me with her presence, the trouble I'm in with the Gallaghers doesn't hold a candle to how much trouble I'm in falling for this angel of a woman.

"Everything okay?" she quietly asks, squeezing tighter and resting her head on my shoulder.

"It is now." I kiss the top of her head, breathing in her citrusy shampoo.

As she sighs into me, it's as if we've been each other's person for years, not days. "Do we have to go home? Can't we just stay here?"

"How are you going to change the world if you're here with me?" As much as I love the idea of staying, I have to protect her from the fallout, the consequences of my brother's actions, and possibly the Gallaghers.

"I'm sure we'd find a way."

"I'm sure *you* would." I offer her an earnest smile. "What do you say: In ten years, I steal you away, and we renew *our* vows right here on this beach?"

"You don't think it'd be suspicious, escaping D.C., just the two of us?"

I lay back on the lounge chair, and she sits between my legs, with the back of her head resting on my chest. Wrapping my arms around her, I breathe her in. "I'm sure you'd have a clever solution, being President and all."

"You're ridiculous. Why wouldn't you be the one in the Oval?"

"You know I don't want it. But you? You were born for it. So, what are we thinking? Lavender flowers again?" I quip.

"Absolutely not!" She shudders. "I hated the wedding."

"Hated it?"

"Well, I didn't *hate* it." Turning her head to look up at me, she adds, "I got to pretend to marry you."

"I wasn't pretending" I admit.

Jaclyn adjusts to get comfortable. "I don't think I was either."

"Then, why did you hate it?"

"I would've preferred blue but was warned that it would end up a political statement. Actually, *your* mother insisted on lavender as an alternative."

"Are you serious?" I laugh, pulling her tighter.

"So, if I get to choose, I want a blue rose bouquet, ranging from dark navy to pastel. Since we'll be the only ones seeing it, no one would be upset."

"Can we have live music? I was so confused why there was canned music for the ceremony when there was a small orchestral ensemble at the reception."

"Right?" Jaclyn playfully swats at my chest. "That was *my* mother. She insisted the acoustics were off, but I still would've preferred live musicians."

For the next hour, until she drifts off in my arms, we watch the purple and red fade from the sky as we plan our vow renewal that will never happen, but I allow myself to pretend all the same.

CHAPTER 23
JACLYN

Alex and I sleep in, missing his morning run before the sun comes up. His discipline for it still baffles me. As I drink my coffee and watch him jog down the beach away from the villa, it clicks why he does it—this time is just for him. It's quiet, except for the waves crashing or occasional bird. I soak in the serenity that's a stark contrast from Washington. The stress of the wedding and everything that followed melts away as I sit out here, enjoying the cool ocean breeze whipping around me.

With the gala rapidly approaching, I open my laptop, checking and double checking the details. Everything seems to be in order, except for the bachelor auction—we need two more. The gala is still a few weeks away; plenty of time to find a couple of eligible men of the right caliber. Chris typically participated, even when we were engaged. "It's for charity," I'd remind myself each year, only for him to come back from his 'date' liquored up, with lipstick on his collar. Thankfully, my dry cleaner assumed it was mine, despite my never wearing those shades of lip color in my life. Then again, he didn't need a gala auction to come home with the excuse that his mother hugged him earlier.

After spending an hour agonizing over the event and texting Ileah as mid-work procrastination, I head inside to make myself a third cup of coffee. It's been ages since I've had to prepare my own that didn't include pods, and I take pleasure in filling the pot with water, pouring it into the machine, scooping the grounds into the filter, screwing up the brew time, trying again and resetting it...

I'll need to make a point of insisting that I make my own coffee when I get home. Though, the thought of returning to Washington, and spending half the year in Florida, fills me with dread.

The smell of freshly brewed goodness fills the small kitchen, and as I'm pouring the coffee into my mug, the sliding door opens. "That was fast. Would you like a cup?" Topping my coffee with vanilla creamer, I hum as Alex kisses my shoulder and snakes his arm around me, pulling me against his soft chest.

Soft chest?

No.

"I'd love one, *wife*." The dark voice sends a chill down my limbs, and all the air leaves my lungs. My heart is stuck in my damn throat.

"Well, *husband*, would you like cream and sugar?" I manage with a shaky breath.

With a feather-light touch, Chris traces a pattern along the side of my neck and chuckles, "Someone's been busy."

"Oh, yeah, curling iron burns. From the wedding," I lie, though he has no room to judge me after what he did. He doesn't get to waltz in here and accuse me of anything. *He* was the one who broke us. "I was doing a touch up before the ceremony and should've had a professional do it. Ha-have you seen Alex?"

"No, but it's just as well," he replies knowingly. "We have *so much* to catch up on."

I'm able to step out of his hold to grab a second mug from the overhead cabinet. "Oh, my dearest husband, we definitely do." I finally turn and face the man who ruined my life with a fucking blowjob. If I'm being honest, perhaps he saved me. I married the one man I've wanted for years. A blessing, not a curse. I keep my posture straight and an emotionless expression, even while I'm screaming inside. "I'm happy to see you've recovered quickly."

As I set the cup next to mine, I pour coffee into his, but don't bother with adding sugar or cream. Instead, I take a seat at the small dining table—if he wants to doctor his coffee, he can do it himself.

Following my lead, Chris joins me with the coffee he wouldn't drink in a million years. His steps are slow; the pain is likely getting the best of him. I bring the mug to

199

my lips for a small sip, keeping my eyes on him, and as he's about to take a drink of his, he thinks better of it and sets it down.

His sinister tone from earlier is gone as he says the one thing I expect, "I'm sorry, Jaclyn."

"For?" I ask flatly. This is just like the hospital; it isn't as if I'll get an iota of truth from him.

"I told you, our wedding."

"And what about *before* the wedding?"

His jaw tics. "Alex told you, didn't he?"

"I'd like to know what happened, from you."

"An accident," he doubles down on his omissions.

I take another sip of my coffee, contemplating my next move. While I've never loved him, it still hurts that he cheated on me for years... including our wedding day, nonetheless. He's been doing it for as long as I can remember, but it's the blatant lack of respect that has scorching heat creeping up my neck. I'd love nothing more than to toss my coffee into his lap.

It's only a matter of time before we'll get a replacement marriage certificate, and I'll be tied to Chris for the rest of our lives. The pressure from my family was the only reason I entertained the idea of being married to Chris in the first place. I never should've allowed Alex to stand in for him.

If I could walk away, I would've years ago.

With a sigh, I groan, "Since you won't give me an honest answer, what now?"

Chris reaches across the table, offering me his hand. I reluctantly take it, curious about what will happen if I play along with whatever he thinks is happening. "You want honesty? I need you, Jackie. We're going to make me the next President Blake."

I inwardly cringe at the nickname, keeping my expression neutral. "And if you lose? What will happen then?"

"I won't lose." A cocky grin appears, and I want to slap it off his smug face. If he went up against Alex, there is no way he would win, but I doubt I could convince him to run against Chris.

The sliding glass door opens, and we both turn to find Alex carrying a bouquet of cornflower blue roses. I suck in a breath—they aren't a generic bouquet of a dozen red roses you'd find at a supermarket. There's also beautiful, lush green filler... *and not a hint of lavender in sight.* Stunning, in comparison to my wedding flowers. My heart swells as tears threaten to fall, and I quickly blink them away.

Alex closes the door behind him, only taking a single step before he spots Chris. Stopping in his tracks, he glances between Chris and me, his surprised expression quickly shifting to a glower directed at his brother. "Christopher. When did you get here?"

With Chris' attention focused on Alex, I give Alex a quick shake of my head, afraid of what might happen if he shows me the slightest bit of affection. Heeding my warning, he sets the flowers on the kitchen counter and casually leans against it, stuffing his hands into his pockets.

How can he remain so calm when I'm a damn ball of emotion?

Chris doesn't answer Alex's question, not that I would expect the King of Deflection to. "Thank you again for standing in for me on my big day, but I've got it from here," he sneers, squeezing my hand tightly. I hiss, and Alex pushes off the counter.

"He's right," I rush out, and Alex freezes. Keeping my tone even, my heart breaks into a million pieces as I add, "You've been so helpful in ensuring everything went smoothly. I appreciate all that you've done for us." A stray tear escapes my eye, and I refuse to let a second fall —I don't want to give Alex a reason to worry, or Chris the satisfaction.

Chris releases my hand and tosses his wallet on the table with a sly smirk. "Here. You can have your identity back. There's a ticket at the airline counter in your name for a flight that leaves in a few hours. You should be able to make it if you pack quickly."

"Don't you think it would be a bit suspicious to fly to and from Hawaii in twenty-four hours?" Alex grits out.

"I landed yesterday," Chris finally answers Alex's initial question and sits back in his seat, entirely too proud of himself. *Has he been spying on us?* My eyes widen briefly, but I quickly school my expression. "You can tell them you came to visit your brother—since you missed our wedding—and there's urgent business back home."

"The story is *I* was in an accident!" Alex's arms fly wide. "How am I supposed to explain traveling so soon?"

"There's a wheelchair in the back of the rental." Chris throws his car keys at Alex, who catches them with ease.

Alex pins Chris with an icy glare. "Are you fucking kidding me? And what about Jaclyn?"

"You mean *my wife?*" Chris chuckles darkly, and bile rises in my throat at the label. "I'm sure you've done quite enough." He gestures with a nod toward the flowers. "I suppose I don't have to worry much about you two getting close. Her favorite color is red, not blue."

Alex contains his smile, but the twinkle in his eyes betrays him. "Is that so? Well, it's a good thing her husband is here to set things straight. Here I was, trying to be a good friend." Calling me his friend stings more than Chris insisting I'm his wife. Alex shrugs and walks toward the bedroom, calling over his shoulder, "Give me ten minutes, and I'll be out of your hair."

CHAPTER 24

ALEX

Closing the bedroom door behind me, I lean against it and blow out a long breath. I suppose I should be grateful he's here; I'm falling for her harder by the minute. If I stay for the rest of the trip, I'll never give her up. Just seeing him here has me wanting to steal her away, never looking back.

What am I saying? I'll never give up Jaclyn.

She may remain legally married to him, but she's my wife.

Fuck. This.

As I'm about to storm into the room and tell my brother to give up the woman I love, a slew of vibrations in my pocket stop me. Taking out my phone, I find several messages from Finn Gallagher.

FINN GALLAGHER

> As you have discovered, your brother decided to pay you a visit.

> Get back to Washington so we can hash
> out the details.

> Mickey is fucking pissed.

I reluctantly shoot off a quick reply, letting him know I'm on my way. As much as I loathe being tied to the Gallaghers more than I already am, I need to ensure Jaclyn's safety.

Chris' clothes are long gone, and while I love the idea of leaving him with nothing to wear, I'll enjoy him not fitting in my clothes more. I take out a fresh pair of shorts, boxer briefs, and a tee, then strip out of my clothes I went running in to take the fastest shower of my life.

Once I'm showered and dressed, I grab my phone and scroll through my contacts. *How do I not have her number?* Taking a quick glance around, I spot a small pad of paper and a pen with the resort logo. I rush across the room and pull the cap off with my teeth.

I MEANT WHAT I SAID, PRINCESS. YOU'RE MINE.
IF YOU NEED ANYTHING, I'LL TAKE CARE OF IT.
346-555-1234

I bring the pen to the cap that's still between my teeth, then toss it onto the table. Ripping the paper from the pad, I begin to fold it, but I do a double take of the logo. At second glance, there's a small snake wrapped around the palm trees.

Snake?

It's odd for Hawaii. Shaking away the thought, I fold the paper and tuck it in my pocket. With a final survey of the room, I walk out, finding Jaclyn sitting rigidly at the table, her ankles crossed, and it's as if all the warmth I've come to love about her has left. She looks ready for a job interview, not like a wife enjoying coffee with her husband. I shake my head with a small chuckle as I move closer.

Chris' voice is low, and I'm unable to make out what he's saying by lip reading, but his eyes are pained. Hope fills my chest that she's not forgiving him for what he did, as if I could be so lucky.

"Hey, pri— *Jaclyn*, I seem to have misplaced my ereader. Have you seen it?" I pull the paper out of my pocket, keeping it hidden in my palm.

"Is it in the car?" Jaclyn asks curiously. "I think you took it on the waterfall tour."

We didn't see the waterfalls; that was on today's agenda. Perhaps my little wife has more fight in her than I give her credit for. Without waiting for a reply, she stands and rushes into the kitchen. I'm able to discreetly slide the paper into her hand as she passes me. Jaclyn squeezes mine for a fraction of a second before releasing me, taking the note and pocketing it as she grabs the car keys.

"I'll be right back," she announces.

As soon as the door closes, I growl at Chris, "If you dare cheat on her again, you'll find yourself in another *accident*."

207

"Is that a threat?" he laughs, making his way into the kitchen to dump his coffee in the sink. While he's generally getting around okay, there's a bit of a limp.

"A fucking promise. She's too good for you." My voice booms enough to echo through the villa. "She's Mozart and you're... Well, you're a four-year-old with a keyboard. You'll ruin her."

"Aw, do you have a crush on my wife? I can't say I blame you; she's beautiful."

"She's *my wife* more than she's yours," I spit. "I stood at the altar with her, swearing to love, protect, and cherish that perfect woman until my last breath. I'm a man of my word. If you hurt her, I'll fucking end you. I don't give a fuck that we're family."

"And how do you intend to do that?"

I cock an eyebrow and reply, "Who do you think cleaned up your accident? Mickey will be all too happy to take care of a second one." His eyes widen. I may have hopped across the aisle, but the Gallagher brothers have no issue with politicians on both sides in their pocket. I'll do whatever it takes to keep Jaclyn safe from him. No matter the cost.

My phone vibrates, and I check it, keeping one eye on Chris.

UNKNOWN

If I'm Wolfgang, you're my Constanze.

I try my hardest not to laugh at Jaclyn's eavesdropping as I stuff it in my pocket.

"You're right about one thing," I tell Chris loudly enough that she'll hear, "I care about Jaclyn. Get your shit together and make her happy." I bite my lip as a smirk tugs at the corner of my mouth. "Or I will."

The front door opens, and both of us turn to the sound. My brother's behavior has my blood boiling, but the mere sight of her grounds me. "Sorry, Alex. No sign of the ereader. Maybe we left it somewhere here, or on a hiking trail somewhere? If we find it, I'll mail it to you."

"Thanks for checking. Don't worry about replacing it; I'm sure I can buy a new one somewhere before my flight. I was in the middle of a memoir that I was enjoying a bit too much." Jaclyn draws her lips into her mouth for a moment, stifling a laugh. "Well, I best be off."

This is it. This is where I lose her.

At least for now...

I take the wallet with the fake ID and credit cards in my name, even though I still have my own, and swallow thickly. My heart is already aching for her, and I haven't even left. I was always supposed to walk away, but was foolish to think it would be easy.

Making my way to the door, quickened footsteps follow, and I turn to Jaclyn barreling into me, wrapping her arms around my middle. I hold her close, not giving a shit what Chris might think, and kiss the top of her head as I whisper, "Make him watch the whole series. It's the wet tunic, or nothing."

She sobs a laugh into my chest. "Damn it, Alex. I'm falling in lo—"

"No, princess, don't you dare fucking say it." With Chris approaching, I release her. "I'll always be here for you. Enjoy your honeymoon."

I can't get out of the villa fast enough, and, *fuck*, leaving her with him doesn't just hurt; I can't seem to unclench my fist long enough to open the car door. With my jaw tight, I take a deep breath through my nose, unlocking the door on my exhale.

As I take a final glance at the front entry, a stupid part of me begs for her to chase after me. I finally fling open the car door and slide in. It takes several minutes before I'm calm enough to start it.

Checking the rearview mirror, sure enough, there's a damn wheelchair. There is no way in hell I'm going to use it. Chris was in an accident, and he's not experiencing any mobility issues; there's no reason why my fake accident wouldn't have me walking around.

If it ever got out that I pretended I needed a wheelchair, I'd never live it down. Ben, one of the guys in my virtual running group, has a prosthetic leg. I'm sure he would fly his billionaire British ass all the way here just to lecture me... and maybe also a well-deserved punch to the face.

I roll the windows down and drive to the airport, wanting the sweet Hawaiian air in my lungs as long as possible. When I'm almost there, I roll them up to call Ned wanting to see what he knows about all of this, but there's an incoming call from Ileah. Curiosity gets the best of me, and I answer, "Hello?"

"Alex! You're okay! We heard about your accident. Tim and I were so worried when you missed the wedding."

"Oh, right, yes. The accident." *Fuck, I hate lying to my friends.* "I'm all right. Thank you."

"Sorry we haven't called sooner. We figured you were still recovering. That's not why I'm calling, though."

"Is everything okay with Tim?"

She chuckles nervously. "Yes, he's great. But I'm wondering if you could tell me what you know about Mickey Gallagher. I know he endorsed you... and you didn't accept his campaign contribution. He offered to donate to Tim's campaign. Between you and me, the Gallaghers seem sort of... *shady.*" It comes out almost as a question.

I bark a laugh, but my friends wouldn't be getting involved with the Gallaghers unless... "Ileah, are you in trouble?"

"Oh my gosh, no! I just thought it was strange that he approached me and not Tim, that's all. Forget I said anything... So, are you back in Houston? Or still in D.C.?"

Taking the exit for the airport, I don't have time to probe further about Mickey. "Sorry to do this, but I'm almost at my destination. Can I call you or Tim later?"

"Of course. So glad you're doing okay. I'll tell Tim you said hello."

"Okay." I huff a small laugh. "Talk to you soon."

We hang up, and I call Ned, who picks up on the first ring, "Hello, Mr. Blake. To what do I owe the pleasure?"

"You failed to mention Chris was on his way to Hawaii, *Ned*," I growl.

"It seems your brother doesn't listen to Daddy Blake." He lets out a long sigh. "Meet with Mickey and Finn. They'll decide what to do about the face-fucker." Ned pauses again. "I don't think the accident is all you have to worry about."

I pull into the lot for the rental cars, one of the attendants waving me down. "I'll see them tomorrow."

This charade ends right fucking now.

CHAPTER 25

JACLYN

Chris is here in Hawaii.

MOTHER DEAREST

No, he's here, staying at Alex's apartment.

No, he's in Hawaii! Alex just left. What is going on?

FATHER OF THE YEAR

Where is Alex?

I don't know.

He left when Chris showed up. What should I do?

FATHER OF THE YEAR

What you were always supposed to do, be his wife.

MOTHER DEAREST

Be safe, sweetheart. I don't trust him.

Show him that everything is fine.

M y own parents don't know what's happening, but they're still right. While my heart left Hawaii with Alex, I'm a Taylor—I can play house with Chris until I'm back home.

Slipping on my mask, I offer Chris my trademark, sweet smile, and stow my phone. "So, dearest husband, why are you here?"

And ruining everything that Alex and our parents set into motion?

"I'm here for my wife," he affirms but doesn't meet my eyes.

"Where were you when you said you were at the cardiologist?"

Chris finally looks up. "I... I lied to you. I was with friends."

"*Friends?*" I shouldn't be upset, considering I slept with his brother. Worse, I fell for Alex. I don't know if I can say the same for Chris and the woman he killed. But I'm better than this, or at least Alex thinks I am. Time to play the part and see how much damage was done. "I'm sorry," I sigh, "I didn't mean to imply—"

"No, you're right. I shouldn't have..." He shakes his head. "I shouldn't have lied to you about something like that."

I know in my soul he's hiding more than fucking his aide... but this is a game of chess, not checkers. "Your health is more important than a night with the boys."

Closing the distance between us, I imagine he's Alex as I tell him, "You're my husband, now. We don't keep secrets." There's a small clench of his teeth, a simple tell —we'll be continuing the game. There is no love here, not that there ever was. He wraps his arms around me, and I do my best not to stiffen.

"You're right. No more secrets." Chris' hand slides down to my ass, and he pulls me flush against him. "I've missed you. Maybe it's time I show you how much."

"I've missed you, too." I step out of his hold, feeling as if I'm cheating on Alex by allowing Chris to touch me. "I'm sorry, you can't show me *that way*. I'm on my period, we shouldn't..." He flinches, and it's another reminder of how these brothers are so different; Alex didn't blink twice when I told him.

"I didn't know. When, uh, when would be a good time to..."

"Fuck me?" My hands fly to my mouth, and his eyes widen. "What I meant to say was for us to be intimate."

Chris lightly licks his lips and lets out a small, unamused laugh. "How was my brother? Was he as good as me?"

Don't say it. He's testing me...

"Your brother has been nothing but a gentleman since he stepped in for you for *our* wedding. We've become good friends. Sure, it was unexpected, and he has some misguided political opinions, but Alex is a good man. He loves you and your family." The lies roll off my tongue a little too easily. *Is it my father's influence or Alex's?* "If you don't want to be married to me, I under—"

"No, I absolutely want to be married to you." He steps forward, and I bottle up my disgust. "You and me? We're going to take the White House."

It's all I'm good for.

A trophy.

A prop.

"You were born for it," I echo Alex's words to me. My palm itches to snatch my phone and call him. I should bide my time to be safe; Chris is already suspicious of me. "You've had quite the adventure. Why don't you take a shower, rest, and we'll work on strategy when you've adjusted to the time difference?"

"You're amazing, you know that?" Chris cups my cheek, and I begrudgingly cover his hand with my own and lean into his touch. He's nothing like Alex, who can command my body with a damn stroke of his thumb. Chris expects me to serve, and to be two steps behind, instead of alongside him.

Every moment since the wedding has opened my eyes wider to what's going on around me. While I don't agree with everyone on the other side of the aisle politically, they aren't the enemy I thought they were. The decades I've lost, fighting for causes I didn't fully believe in, supporting candidates that didn't represent me and my values... It's not Chris' fault, or my father's; it's mine. I allowed myself to be swallowed up by one side of the political spectrum when Alex is right—it's not black and white.

Chris' indiscretions aren't black and white, either. I've faked orgasms, played the perfect part in public... but we are otherwise strangers. I've never let him in, never let him get to know the real me. While it doesn't excuse it, I can understand why he might need someone else, if only to feel something... *anything*. I'm not innocent in this, none of us are, and I have no room to judge his motives.

"I'm sorry," I breathe.

His brows furrow. "Why?"

He's still probing, trying to confirm that I slept with Alex, and I need to listen to my mother; she doesn't trust him. So, I opt for a safe answer that would appease Chris and my family. "For not being the fiancée you deserved when we were back home. We can do better than an arranged marriage. Your brother helped me see that you and I need to work together if you still want to run. Can we start over?"

Chris offers a genuine smile that meets his eyes. "I love you... There isn't anything to start over."

If you loved me, you wouldn't have missed our wedding because of a damn blowjob...

As much as it pains me, I have to make this work—at least for the time being. "I booked our honeymoon here so we could get to know each other better. It's so easy to get swept up in everything when we're in Washington—or even when we're in Miami. Here, it's just you and me. We can let our shields down and be ourselves." Chris leans in to kiss me, and I stop him with my hands braced on his chest. "But I think we need this time to figure it all out, especially since you missed one of the most monumental moments of my life. I'm still hurt that you weren't there and that you've been lying about your doctor appointments."

His eyes are earnest as he sighs a laugh. "You're absolutely right. I'll get cleaned up, and maybe we can take a walk on the beach together?"

I nod, grateful that he's not pushing for more. "I'd love that." *I'm in hell.*

Chris presses a kiss to my forehead, and I rein in all of my negative emotions as he pulls back. "Give me twenty minutes."

CHAPTER 26
CHRIS

I'm going about this all wrong. There isn't a doubt in my mind that my brother fucked my wife, but it wasn't just sex with them. I can tell Jaclyn has feelings for him, and based on how he acted while he was here, Alex is head-over-heels in love with her. In the end, it doesn't matter. I don't need Jaclyn to *love* me; I need her to *help* me with my campaign. She needs to respect me, and that's a hell of a lot harder to earn than love. With our nuptials public, my candidacy announcement should come sooner than later.

I'm so fucked.

A long hot shower and fresh clothes have reset me. Though, I must've lost weight because they fit a bit larger —that, or Jaclyn ordered the wrong sizes for me for the trip. I pull out another shirt and check the size tag. A size too big. Jaclyn knows my measurements, so it doesn't make sense...

Alex.

With a groan, I suck it up, and wear the ill-fitting clothes. Once I'm changed, I join Jaclyn out on the patio. As I nervously open the sliding glass door, I find her on one of the lounge chairs with her laptop, talking to someone with a tinge of anger in her voice. I overhear the last of her conversation, "Take care of it." Her growling ends as she turns at the sound of the door. "We'll talk soon... Thank you." Hanging up, she offers me a sweet smile, void of love. "Hi."

"Mind if I join you?"

"Go ahead."

Her tone is clipped, so I tread carefully. "Everything okay?"

"No, nothing is going to plan for the gala. Story of my life," she huffs, defeated. With the event fast approaching, my best guess is that she's arguing with a vendor. Jaclyn is meticulous when it comes to the small details of an event. I'm sure it will be beautiful with her in charge, and no one will know if things are amiss.

I take the seat next to her to enjoy the cool ocean breeze and the sun glistening off the water. It's just the two of us, not another person in sight. One might even call it romantic. We've been together for years, and it's always been nothing more than a business transaction, with our marriage sealing the deal by signing on the dotted line. Sure, she's stunning, but we have virtually nothing in common; I've never met a more boring woman in my life.

Stepford wife in the flesh.

Jaclyn continues working while I marinate in the mildly uncomfortable silence. She doesn't reach for my hand, and I don't seek out hers. Despite our differences, she knows me better than I know myself most days, and I appreciate that she's not pretending with me. Though for the first time, guilt seeps in—she's always been at my side. She deserves a spouse who loves and supports her.

Am I able to give her that?

As I look out to the crashing waves, I'm lost as to what I should say. We're supposed to spend the rest of our lives together, and the thought gives me a deep sense of dread like I've never experienced. Being married to someone who doesn't love you is a special kind of torture. She'll play the perfect part publicly, but I can't wrap my mind around how I'm supposed to make her believe I love her, let alone have her fall in love with me.

We sit in silence for several minutes until I finally break it. "How was the wedding?" She groans. "That bad, huh?"

Finally looking at me, Jaclyn's reply is cold. "The wedding was the best day of my life."

"The best?" I laugh.

"What do you want me to say, Chris? That I hated it? I didn't. Even with the shitty coordinator, the boring color palette, our mothers overstepping, Alex taking the schedule off the rails..." She sighs deeply. "You want the truth? I don't regret speaking my vows to Alex in front of God, our friends, and family."

My jaw tics at the mention of him. "You're not his wife. You're *mine*."

"I would divorce you, but we're not even married."

I can't help rolling my eyes and scoff, "What are you talking about? My name is on the marriage certificate, *princess*. You're stuck with me."

"Don't call me that," she spits, her gaze molten. "And I'm not stuck with you. Our certificate isn't filed." Glancing over at the fire pit, she chuckles darkly, "Good luck salvaging it."

Perhaps Jackie isn't as boring as I made her out to be. "Well, that can be remedied."

"I know," she sighs in annoyance, and damn it, I'm fucking this up further.

"What would it take to make this right?"

"Depends. What's on the table?" Her question takes me by surprise.

"We have to make this work. So, I'll do *whatever* it takes."

"Whatever it takes?" Her eyebrow lifts, disappointment oozing from her. "Stop fucking your aides."

"I've never fucked my aides." The lie slips off my tongue with ease. "What else?"

"Does it matter? It isn't as if I get to make real demands; I'm not in control here."

She's fucking right, but I'm not in control, either... and I'm so damn screwed if I can't get her to fall in love with me. Or at least tolerate me.

As Jaclyn looks away, I keep my eyes fixed on her; it's been too long since I *really* looked at her. While she's devastatingly gorgeous, taking my breath away, she's got a backbone that I've never noticed before today. I want more of this sparring between us.

No wonder Alex is drawn to her.

"I want to fix this," I plead softly.

"There's nothing to fix." Jaclyn gets up abruptly. "I'm going to take a walk."

The last thing I need is her alone with her thoughts; it'll all but secure losing her. "Can I join you?"

Jaclyn doesn't protest, giving in to my small gesture, and we make our way to the water. Keeping my hands in my pockets, we walk along the shore in silence as I catalog the last few years, unable to remember the last time I took a walk with her.

*Have we **ever** taken a walk together?*

Alex has absolutely dug his claws into Jaclyn. Mere weeks ago, she was the perfect woman to have by my side —delicate and demure. My family is right; I need to woo my wife. If I fall in love with her in the process, even better.

Another apology won't do it. I need something big. Bold.

A grand gesture.

The gala for her mother's charity is in a few weeks. Too far away; I need something now. We're on our honeymoon, and as much as I feel like my cock could remedy this, the idea of fucking her after my brother repulses me.

Jaclyn wasn't inexperienced when we began dating, but sex was a chore. Even so, I loved that she was my dutiful girlfriend—mine when I needed her. Once I secure the presidency, I couldn't care less if she wants to take a lover... *so long as it isn't Alex.* I've worked too hard to get where I am to let it slip through my fingers because he wants to get his dick wet. For me, sex is just sex. It's more for him, and probably for her, too. If they spend any more time together, I'll lose her for good.

Walking beside Jaclyn is actually... *nice.* It's relaxing, only the sound of the crashing waves dancing around our feet as they meet the sand. I love that neither of us is trying to fill the silence with idle small talk. I'm comfortable with her, always have been, enough to admit aloud, "We're going to be all right."

Jaclyn keeps her focus ahead of us. "When are you going to tell me what really happened with the accident?"

"I had a heart attack," I answer carefully.

"And how did you have a heart attack, exactly? Were you doing any *strenuous activities* while driving?"

Fuck. She knows…

Denial is still the best course of action. "No, the doctors think I took too much of my ADHD meds."

"You always forget to take it." She huffs a laugh, though her tone is still flat. "How the hell did you take *too much?*"

"Honestly, I don't even remember taking it that morning."

Stopping in her tracks, Jaclyn finally looks at me. "Why don't you take your health seriously?"

"I don't *need* to take them; they help me focus sometimes." I shrug.

"You didn't need to focus on the day you were supposed to get married?" Jaclyn scoffs, and once again, I'm going about this all wrong. I feel like an even bigger asshole.

I take her hand and weave our fingers together, surprising myself with how much I enjoy it. Her gaze drops to our joined hands, then returns to me as I tell her softly, "You're right. I should take my health—and mental health—more seriously. I've just been under a lot of stress and pressure, between the wedding and preparing for our next big step…"

"*Our* next big step?"

"Yes," I chuckle. "*Our*. You and I are going to take on the world together. Why do you sound surprised? It was always our plan. If it got out to the media that I had a heart attack, it would ruin everything."

"Heart attack? You *killed* a woman." Pain is chiseled into her features. "How can you be worried about a campaign when a woman is *dead?*"

This isn't about Cara's mouth wrapped around my cock, and I can't help the relieved breath that passes my lips. Thankfully, I'm able to pass it off as pain. "I know. I'll make sure her family is taken care of."

Jaclyn nods in understanding, but her eyes say otherwise. "You want to make it right? Stop fighting with Alex. If it wasn't for him, your face would be plastered on every media site for the next four months."

"My brother and I have always fought." I reach to tuck wind-swept strands behind her ear. She doesn't flinch or pull away; she doesn't melt for me, either. "But this isn't about him. It's about you and me."

"You don't have to worry about me." I'm met with wall after wall with her, and I intend to tear them all down. As she tries to pull her hand away, I keep it firmly in mine. When she tugs a second time, a soft grunt escapes her. "I'm fine."

"You don't sound fine," I laugh.

"You don't love me, so why are you worried about me?" she huffs, and it stings far more than care to admit. It doesn't make sense, I shouldn't crave her attention or adoration. We've never had a romantic relationship. It's no different than my parents—an arrangement.

"I do love you," I counter, though it comes out as a growl. Taking a glance around to ensure we're still alone, I still whisper as I ask, "Do you love *me?*"

Her expression softens. "I love you as much as red roses."

"Well, if I'm your favorite..." I snake my free hand to her lower back and pull her flush with me. She catches herself with her palm on my chest. "You'll forgive me for missing our big day? Can I make it up to you with a night out, just the two of us? Maybe hide from the paps and enjoy an evening where we don't have to pretend everything is okay?" *But, mark my words, by the end of our trip, it will be.* "I think we could both use a night of fun."

Jaclyn blows out a long breath, and my eyes fall to her lips—lips my brother likely claimed for himself. Where minutes ago, the idea of being with her after him disgusted me, I now selfishly want her for myself. If I'm lucky, by the end of our honeymoon, she'll crave *my* touch, not his. We'll live in amicable bliss, and maybe in time, she'll love me more than red roses. I'm not sure if I'm capable of loving someone, but I need to try with Jaclyn. Warmth fills my chest, imagining her by my side, the picture-perfect family with our children, as I run for reelection.

I win.

"You know, I don't remember the last time we had fun." Letting her guard down, she offers a soft smile, and chuckles.

I lean in and kiss her cheek, not wanting to press my luck. "Then, let's go have a bit of fun."

CHAPTER 27
JACLYN

"This has to be the worst margarita I've ever consumed."

As I'm sitting to his left at the four-top table, I can't help laughing at Chris' expense. "You ordered a house margarita! What did you expect? But, honestly, we're in Hawaii. Why not drink a Mai Tai, or something with pineapple? The pineapples here are the sweetest you'll ever taste."

"I've tasted something sweeter," he flirts, briefly glancing at my lap. I'm genuinely confused—he hasn't had his face between my legs in years. Chris steals my shot of top-shelf añejo and finishes it in a single gulp, then sighs, "That's better." To my surprise, he flags down our waitress. "Could we get another shot for my wife? And I'll have... water. Water is the best option at this point."

"Water?" I cock an eyebrow. "I thought we were supposed to be having fun."

There go my plans; three or four more shots would have him loosening his lips about the accident.

Once the waitress is out of earshot, he sidles up next to me, close enough that I notice the blue in his hazel eyes— a reminder that he's not Alex. This afternoon, I've been falling into easy banter like I have with Alex; I need to keep my wits about me.

"Lest you forget, my dear wife, I was in an accident? I'm on pain medication and shouldn't be drinking at all." A moment later, the waitress appears, sliding the lime-garnished shot in front of me. Before she can get away, I order two more. When she leaves to retrieve them, Chris smiles brightly, shaking his head. "Didn't Alex let you drink? You were supposed to be celebrating."

I look out at the dining patrons, whispering to myself, "With an Old Fashioned, extra cherry."

"What was that?"

Blinking away the thought, I quickly correct, "Sorry, I was just thinking about something someone told me once —they only drink when they're celebrating. We have a lot to celebrate, so we should absolutely have a drink. You're going to be announcing soon."

"True." He chuckles to himself, then peers up through his lashes. "Does that mean we'll be drunk for the next couple of months?"

"I certainly hope not. Your campaign manager would

hate us." I can't help my smile; his campaign manager is a... *delight.*

"Remember the first year your mother insisted I do the bachelor auction for the gala? Fuck, we were so wasted." He lets out a full laugh, sipping his water.

"I spent so much money bidding on you!" I down my shot in one gulp, and suck on the lime to ease the burn. "Mrs. Bradley wanted you so badly."

"She's eighty! What could she possibly want with me?" My eyes fall to his lap, and his laughter ceases. "You can't be serious."

"We should have you do it again this year. You know, for charity." He doesn't bat an eye at me throwing his words back at him. Did he forget that he left with a celebrity and didn't come home until the middle of the night?

Chris leans in, his five-o'clock shadow lightly scraping my jaw. "I'm no longer a bachelor, Jaclyn." He kisses my cheek, and, *fuck*, it makes me miss Alex all over again.

I want a man I can't have, and I hate that my heart aches for him. There's no way Chris will let me go. He got what he wanted—the perfect wife and wedding to kick off his presidential run. Ever since I discovered Chris' indiscretions from a housekeeper at the hotel he frequents, I've been less and less confident that I'll have any sort of political future of my own. The past few days have solidified that there is no way out of this. I was foolish to entertain the idea that Alex and I could work. Even if Chris hadn't survived the heart attack or the accident, how could I ever sell that to the media?

Since I'm married to Chris for the foreseeable future, I need to make the best of this ridiculous arrangement. The accident has been swept under the rug. To drag it back out, I'd have to go up against not only my father but his.

I can be friends with a murderer and adulterer, right?

What am I saying? I'm not innocent, either.

Two morally corrupt people married to each other... Great.

Our waitress returns with more tequila, and I pass one to Chris. "One drink, a toast."

"What are we toasting to?" He lifts his glass, eyebrow slightly raised in question.

"Your swift recovery."

Chris rests his hand on the back of my chair, his genuine smile meeting his eyes. "No. To you. An incredible woman I don't deserve."

"I'm not incredible," I humbly stress, keeping the whole facade firmly in place. He only believes I am because he sees what I let him. Same with Alex, though I let my mask slip with him more times than I would like to admit. I've worked too hard to get to this point. Chris' accident put a wrench in things, but it should be salvageable when we return to Washington.

I can make this work.

"You put up with the dog and pony show, and you do it with grace, Jackie." He clinks his glass with mine and takes the shot with no chaser or lime. "I struggle most days. I don't know how you do it."

"What choice do I have?" *It isn't as if my father would approve of me doing anything that would make me happy.*

"You're the only reason I can do this." Chris reaches for my hand, and I turn mine over, interlacing our fingers. He feels just like Alex right now, and my breath is stolen from me. "I'm going to make everything up to you, and we'll go on a proper honeymoon."

"Honeymoon, right. Can't wait." I take my shot, no lime, wanting to savor the burn. My lie is surprisingly believable, a wide smile slicing Chris' face. Only a few dozen years of this, and maybe I'll no longer have to lie to him.

His gaze catches on my wedding ring, and the handsome grin is quickly replaced by a scowl. "Where's my wedding band?"

"Oh..." I look down at my ring. "I guess Alex still has it."

"Well, since you can't wait for our honeymoon, let's kick it off right." He lifts his free hand for the check. I don't have a moment to protest when he adds, "We'll start by finding a restaurant that's a bit more Hawaiian, then pick up a new wedding band. And maybe even pick up a pineapple along the way, too."

CHAPTER 28
ALEX

Landing in Washington, I expect to find my assistant, Abigail, waiting for me. Instead, there are no less than six men in black suits by the ground transportation sign, all with earpieces. At first glance, my gut instinct is that it's my father's service detail, but as I approach, there's a small green snake pin on their lapels that gives them away.

Fucking Gallaghers.

"Where to, boys?" I ask two of them standing stoically side by side. In an instant, I'm ushered into an unmarked black sedan. As I slip into the back seat, I'm relieved to see Finn, not Mickey. "Didn't know Gallagher Whiskey was so hard up that you had to resort to an airport pick-up service."

He doesn't answer until the car is in motion. "Why did you send Ileah to me?"

"I didn't send—" *The call...* "I didn't send her. Is she in trouble? Is Tim?"

Finn practically growls at the mention of 'Tim,' and glances out the window mumbling something that doesn't sound English. I can almost make out 'mo roon-hark.' I wasn't aware he spoke another language, he hardly has an accent.

"Ileah isn't in trouble. I'll make sure of it. No more referrals, Alexander," he replies, sighing deeply.

"It wasn't a referral. She asked about Mickey, not you. I didn't—"

"No. More."

"If this is about Jaclyn's wedding, I—"

"No," Finn snaps, and I don't bother explaining myself for fear of being cut off again. "You asked for my help to protect Jaclyn Taylor, not your brother. It was quite the clean-up to ensure it was staged properly." He pauses, and I don't argue or defend myself. "We can make him disappear."

"Make who disappear?"

"Christopher." His frigid tone sends shivers down my spine.

"No. He and I may not see eye-to-eye, but there's no reason for him to *disappear*."

The driver merges onto the highway, and we ride in silence for at least half an hour. We hit a patch of traffic, the eerie quiet making me take note of my surroundings in case Finn intends for *me* to disappear. There's nothing out of the ordinary, passing the botanical gardens and Wolf Trap until the driver exits where several hotels, restaurants, and retail stores are located.

Finn finally slices through the deafening silence as we pull up to a hotel that nearly every one of my constituents would balk at—only billionaires could afford it. "You'll be staying here tonight."

"I can't stay here. If word got out—"

"You either stay here, or your family will be very interested to know that you've tasted more than the delectable pineapples of Hawaii while vacationing with your brother's supposed wife."

"Finn," I growl, "you have to know how bad this looks."

"I do." He pulls out a hotel keycard, holding it between his middle and forefingers. "It'll ensure you do as we ask." My eyes fly wide. "Don't worry. It's only *mild* blackmail," he chuckles. "Room is in my name, not yours. Next time, be a bit more careful while feasting on a woman's cunt where anyone could see."

He tosses three photographs onto my lap, and my stomach tightens, my breath caught in my throat. The first two I could spin, the third... My face is buried in her naked pussy. No way in hell that I'll be able to explain that one. I could claim it's Chris, but even with media buy in, our families will know it was me.

My career—obliterated. Hers will be in flames before she has a chance to run.

I'm not ashamed of what we did, I'm pissed at myself for being so careless. "This is on me, not her."

"Are you sure about that?" he chuckles darkly, twirling the card in his hand.

"What do you want?"

"A small favor. Ensure Taylor takes the White House, and your secrets follow me to the grave."

"Taylor?" My brows pinch. "It's impossible. He already served two terms. You know as well as I that he can't legally do a third."

Finn forces the keycard into my palm. "She's smarter than you. Perhaps I should go straight to your wife." The mention of her has my heart stopping.

"Jaclyn? She's not mine." *Fuck, that hurts to say out loud.* "She's married to—"

The door to the sedan opens. "Your brother. Or at least she will be if you don't stop it. You don't have much time to make sure your little *princess* isn't stuck with Christopher."

There's no path that leads to me keeping Jaclyn safe, much less for keeping her for myself. I'll never be able to convince her to leave Chris, and if his surprise visit in Hawaii was any indication, he has every intention of announcing his presidential run soon. By the end of the month, everything will be up in flames—my career and Jaclyn's aspirations with it.

Would the Gallaghers really leak it?

As I slide out of the car, a defeated groan leaves my lips. "How long will you give me?"

"Four weeks. I have a few things to take care of before then. If you decide to help me with this little side project, neither you nor your wife will need to worry about me or Mickey."

"What about—"

"Enjoy your stay, Mr. Blake."

The car door slams shut, and they drive away without any indication of how long I'm supposed to stay here. How the fuck does he expect me to do this?

Turning to face the hotel I'd never be caught dead in, a man in a dark navy suit approaches. His disingenuous grin has me on edge. "Welcome, Mr. Gallagher. If there's anything you need, please don't hesitate to ask."

CHAPTER 29

JACLYN

"*You missed this cock, didn't you?*"

"*Yes,*" *I whimper as Alex slowly thrusts deeper. I missed a hell of a lot more than his cock. I fell hard and fast for the enemy. In the span of a few days, he somehow knows exactly what I need, giving it to me over and over. I don't just want his cock—I want all of him.*

"*Not as much as I missed your tight pussy, Jackie.*"

Jackie?

I gasp as my eyes flash open. There's an arm wrapped around my waist, pulling my back against a warm chest. It takes me a moment to work out where I am, but disappointment settles in my gut realizing it was only a dream. Alex is gone. I went to bed last night by myself; Chris took the couch. Why is he in bed with me, with his cock pressed against my ass?

"Chris?" I wince.

"Yeah, baby. You didn't think I was...?"

Yes.

I quickly turn in his embrace. "I was asleep and thought you were on the couch. It was disorienting. That's all."

"Fuck," he mutters, tucking stubborn strands of hair behind my ear that are determined to keep falling into my face. "You're so beautiful." *What?* "How did I get so lucky to wake up next to you every morning for the rest of my life?"

"We agreed you'd sleep on the couch." While it's mildly endearing that he's trying, I can't help my skepticism, still hurt by his actions. Even if I have no right to be after what I've done.

"I couldn't stay away."

As much as I want to roll my eyes, I stifle my groan. "How long have you been in bed?"

"You caught me," he chuckles and looks over his shoulder. "There wasn't an outlet by the couch for my CPAP, so when you fell asleep, I climbed into bed with you."

"Chris!" I squeak.

"You're my wife now. I know you're still upset about me not being there, but—"

"Still upset?" I laugh. "I said my vows to another man in front of God. Doesn't that bother you?"

With a firm hold on my hip, he pulls me close. "Of course it bothers me! I had to see pictures of you, fucking gorgeous in your white gown, promising yourself to *Alex*." He shudders. Playing my part, I cup his cheek, and he covers my hand with his. "I don't expect you to forgive me, but will you let me try to earn it?"

He can't be serious...

I close my eyes and press my lips to his, pretending he's Alex. As much as I hate myself for it, Chris has to believe I'm in love with him. After years of fucking other women, you'd think he would know the difference between love and lust, or at least detect when a woman isn't into it. Unfortunately for me, I know he'll attempt to take things further.

Being with Alex felt *right*. Our connection was magnetic and I rarely thought about Chris when Alex was here. He managed to imprint himself on my soul with that wicked mouth of his, promising himself to me with more than words. I miss him so much, it hurts.

Each sweep of Chris' tongue across mine chips away at the small part of me that thought I could salvage this—all of it is fake. He doesn't want me, never has.

Except for as a trophy that puts out occasionally.

I'm supposed to be his wife. Do I really have another choice?

Chris reaches between us, his fingers dipping into the waistband of my panties, and I plant my hands on his chest, pulling back. "I'm on my period," I remind him. My excuse will only buy me so much time, I only have a few days before I will have to sleep with Chris to keep up appearances. The broken heart card can be played a few times before it's no longer believable.

"Are you feeling okay? Do you need anything?" His concern is suspicious. The last time he made a move and discovered I was on my period, he ran off to Miami with Cara the next morning on an 'unexpected work trip.'

"No, I'm all right. Nothing a hot shower can't fix."

He slides out of bed, rounds it, and offers his hand. As I hesitantly take it, he smiles wide. "Quick shower and breakfast, then let's spend the day with our toes in the sand. No plans."

Chris *always* has a plan. He's driven and meticulous—none of this makes sense. It has to be calculated.

With a raised eyebrow, my curiosity gets the best of me. "Since when are you able to handle a day with no plans?"

"True. I'll probably only last an hour." Helping me out of bed, he pulls my body flush with his. "But it's a start."

CHAPTER 30
ALEX

Despite being in one of the most comfortable beds I've ever slept in, last night had to be the worst night of sleep I've had in a long time. Waking up without Jaclyn didn't help. I'm obsessed with her, and now I have to find a way to make her the leader of the free world?

How did I get saddled with this?

I rub the sleep from my eyes and grab my phone from the nightstand. Three missed texts. The first is from Finn.

FINN GALLAGHER

Your wardrobe will be delivered at 7:30.

I check the time, and I have an hour before they'll be delivered. After typing out a reply thanking him for arranging it, I check the next message from Ned.

NED COLLINS

Finn and Mickey expect you ready by 9.
A car will be downstairs.

Of course Finn wouldn't send me clothes out of the good-ness of his heart. The third missed text has my heart stuck in my throat.

JACLYN BLAKE

I miss you.

It was sent twenty minutes ago. With the time difference, it's 12:30 a.m. there. Throwing caution to the wind, I risk replying, even though it may wake her.

Have you been a good little wife for me?

Dancing bubbles appear at the bottom of the screen. They disappear, and I can't take the anticipation, hitting the call button just to hear her voice. It rings once but she sends me to voicemail.

Is he next to you?

Yes.

You better be wearing more than when you're in bed with me.

So naked right now.

Don't make me call him.

I dare you.

I switch over to the phone icon and call my brother's phone. It rings a few times when a text notification appears at the top of my screen. He's likely asleep and hooked up to his CPAP, so I hang up the call and click the notification.

Are you serious?

What are you actually wearing?

One of your shirts and a black thong.

You're so full of shit.

A picture comes through with the covers pulled back, her hand lifting her shirt enough to reveal black lace and toned bare legs. A growl settles in my chest, my cock jumping at the sight. What I wouldn't give to rip those off and taste her right now.

You're sleeping next to him wearing that?

He hasn't touched me, if that's what you're wondering.

Have you touched yourself?

No. That's your job.

Do you have your earbuds handy?

Yes.

Put them in.

I give her a moment and click the microphone in the message to send her a voice note, keeping my voice low and sultry. "You've been a naughty wife, Jaclyn, wearing that to bed with a man who isn't your husband."

> Should I take it off?

"The next time I see you, I'll strip them off with my teeth. I don't care if we're in the middle of the National Mall; I'll claim what's mine."

> I'll be sure not to wear panties from now on, just in case I run into you.

Jaclyn sends me a photo similar to the last, except her fingers are an inch into her waistband.

"Did I say you could touch yourself?"

> You didn't say I couldn't.

A moment later, she sends another photo without her lacy thong, her thighs splayed wide, bare pussy on display. It's a ridiculously dangerous game we're playing with Chris next to her, but I fucking love the idea of her touching herself, my name quietly passing her lips as she comes.

"Delete that photo. No one sees that beautiful cunt but me."

> Deleted.

"That's my girl. When was the last time you came?"

With you.

I love and hate that answer. "Fuck, I miss your legs wrapped around my head while you come all over my face; your tight pussy squeezing my fingers... Are you wet for me, princess?"

Yes.

Gripping my cock, I slowly stroke up and down my shaft, imagining it's her warm, wet cunt instead. "Slip those fingers between your legs, circle that slippery clit like I would. You have to be quiet for me. He doesn't deserve to hear you. Who gets to hear you come?"

Only you.

"That's right, my little wife, you're *mine*. Your orgasms belong to me now." I selfishly tug harder on my cock, swiping my thumb over the head to wipe away the leaking precum, wishing it was her tongue. "I know you miss wrapping that perfect pussy around my cock, riding me until I let you come... Should I let you come tonight? Or make you wait until I can fuck you myself?"

Don't make me wait, Alex. I'm so close.

Show me.

Jaclyn sends me a picture of her glistening pussy, illuminated with flash, her fingers spreading her wide for me... and there's a small, braided cotton string. I'm such an asshole for forgetting she's in her period, but the fact that she's willing to send it to me anyway has me so fucking hard. The ache to have her again is unbearable. I don't just want to sink myself inside her, I want *her*.

"If you've been my good little wife, come for me. I want you to soak the bed, wishing I was there to lap up every last drop."

> Will you come with me?

"I'm going to come deep inside you, filling you so full you'll feel me dripping down your legs the rest of the day, desperate for me to fill you again."

My sexy little minx sends me a voice note, and I have to turn the volume all the way up to hear it properly. There's heavy breathing and delicious moans until she whimpers my name as she comes. It fucking does me in. My balls tighten, and in four long strokes, I come all over my stomach, struggling to catch my breath.

"You're mine, Jaclyn," I pant. "My hand will never in a million years compare to you. The next time you come will be around my cock, with me buried deep in your tight, wet pussy. Understood?"

> I'll be touching myself every night, wishing it was you. And there's nothing you can do to stop me.

I can't help my smile at her adorable defiance and type out my reply.

> Good night, my beautiful wife. I'll be
> seeing you very soon.

I change her name in my phone from 'Jaclyn Blake' to 'Wife,' and toss my phone onto the bed. Grabbing a tissue from the nightstand, I wipe the cum off my stomach, then get up to take a shower.

As I let the hot water beat down on me, I'm acutely aware that I'm in over my head, realization after realization crippling me. "*Fuck.*" I pound my fist against the shower wall, though it gives me no relief from my shitty situation. We both know she'll never be free of my brother. Why am I torturing myself by letting this go on? No matter how much I want her, it's going to hurt too damn much to see her standing next to Chris if I fail.

Finn wants me to work some sort of political magic, but there's no way in hell Chris will step aside for Jaclyn. She could unite the country, actually listen to both sides like a good, selfless leader should. I have to find a way—not for the Gallaghers and whatever twisted plan they have for her. Because it's the right thing to do for the country.

And for me. I want Jaclyn for myself, and I'd give just about anything to have her.

CHAPTER 31
CHRIS

Listening to Jaclyn touch herself last night was torture. A torture I deserve after what I've done. Her moaning my brother's name hurt; it's worse than I thought. In a few short days, he's stolen her from me, and I'm determined now more than ever to get her back. For years, I've taken her for granted.

That ends today.

With her still sound asleep, I slide out of bed, feeling more sore than usual. My body is also fighting a strange dichotomy—my mind is calm, but my heart is racing. I check the medication on the bedside table, and there's a small chance I took two of my ADHD medication today, instead of the painkillers.

No wonder I had a heart attack on our wedding day...

When I get back home, I'm buying one of those pill dispensers that divide by day.

As I attempt to stand, I groan, not just from the pain. It wakes Jaclyn, and she stirs behind me. "What time is it?"

"Go back to sleep." It comes out gruffer than I intended. "Sorry, I just need to grab a glass of water and take my pain meds."

"Stay put, I'll get it for you," she offers, rustling behind me.

When Jaclyn comes into view, she's wearing the over-sized black shirt she went to bed in and... no pants? I distinctly remember her going to bed wearing shorts, but I'm used to her sleeping naked; any clothes are too many. She saunters to the bathroom and returns with a glass of water, handing it to me. I set it on the table and grip the front of her shirt to pull her closer. Stumbling two steps, Jaclyn braces herself with her hands on my shoulders.

"What are you up to, Mr. Blake?" she flirts, stepping between my legs.

"What do you say we catch the next flight back home?" I slide my hands up her thighs, lifting the shirt until I'm able to hook my fingers into her lacy thong. Her breath catches as I tug them down half an inch.

"You just got here."

I drag the lace down her legs, and she hesitantly steps out of them. Gripping her ass, I pull her back to me, and she willingly climbs onto my lap, my cock straining against my boxers. "Fuck, I've missed you."

"We shouldn't do this; you were just in an accident."

"I'll be fine." I want to erase every trace of Alex, make her forget the past week happened, and have her scream *my* name.

"You should take your medication." She nods to the bedside table, and I disgruntledly grab my pain medication. I wash down the two pills with the water she brought me, then take her ass in my hands again and grind her bare pussy against me.

"See, I'm fine," I hiss through my pain, though the friction feels amazing against my cock. I reach between us and pull myself out of my boxers, needing to be inside her.

"You're anything but fine. What did the doctors tell you about sex?"

"They didn't say anything."

"Such a liar," she chuckles. Her giggles cease as I grip her hips and rub the length of my cock across her clit. "What did they say about exercise? You've had some sort of cardiac episode. What if you have another?"

"You can tell the coroner that I died happy, buried in my wife's pussy."

"I'll need to go to the bathroom first to, um..." Disappointment must be written all over my face. She adds, "Unless you want to make a mess?"

"Sorry, I forgot... *again*." I sigh and kiss her neck, goosebumps erupting down her arms.

There's still a small bruise just above her collarbone that I'm sure my brother left behind, not a damn curling iron. I claim my own place on her porcelain skin, sucking hard on a spot between his mark and her ear.

She's mine, not his. And I want the whole fucking world to see... especially Alex.

Jaclyn sighs a moan, and even through both of our shirts, her nipples pebble against me. I can't help myself and pull her top over her head, tossing it to the ground. In a quick movement, I throw her onto the bed, towering over her as I kiss down her chest and draw one of her peaked nipples into my mouth.

"Fuck it, let's make a mess." As I swirl my tongue, I drag my teeth against it, loving the soft moans passing her lips. "I don't need to fuck you to make you feel good, Jackie."

"You don't need to do this," she pants, and I move to the other side. With her fingers tangling in my hair, I can't help smiling against her.

Yes, I do...

I swipe my thumb around her clit, and her back arches away from the bed. With her nipple still between my teeth, I ask, "How many times did he make you come?"

"What?" she rasps, gripping the sheets.

"Did he make you come?" I bite down harder, making her squeak. "Did he?"

"No," she breathes, but there's no way in hell she's telling the truth.

Pressing harder against her clit, I kiss down her body, my lips landing right above my thumb. I've never fucked Jaclyn on her period, and I sure as hell haven't gone down on her during it. I honestly don't remember the last time I did when it wasn't her time of the month, either. It has to be years.

No better time than the present.

I slide lower and replace my thumb with my tongue. Surprisingly, the slight metallic taste doesn't put me off, especially with her gasps filling the room, egging me on. I pay attention to how she whimpers softly, and how her body shakes as I suck.

"Chris, I'm going to—" Unable to finish her thought, she screams out as her release quickly coats my tongue and floods the duvet beneath us.

It's been far too long since I've tasted her, but I don't remember her drenching my chin like this. Even with her being on her period, the tang doesn't discourage me, since she's never this wet when she comes... *ever*. And, fuck, it's hot. I need her to do it again for me.

I slow my pace and kiss up her body, admiring the rise and fall of her chest as she catches her breath. I pinch the small cotton thread coming from her pussy between my fingers, and as I'm about to tug, my phone vibrates on the bedside table.

Whoever it is can fucking wait...

"It could be important," she whispers, still breathless.

As much as I hate to admit it, she's right. Between impersonating my brother to travel here and the fake wedding, the last thing either of us needs is to have a slip-up. I pull back to answer it, and when I check the caller ID, the number is unknown. After another ring, I pick up. "Hello."

"Good morning, Mr. Blake. Good to see you're doing well after your accident." He has a slight Irish accent, but other than the small detail, I can't place the man on the other end.

"Who is this?"

"Mickey Gallagher." My stomach drops. "Your father and I have discussed an arrangement. One you've already —*how do I put this*—royally fucked all the way up by traveling to Hawaii."

"I don't know about any *arrangement*. You have the wrong—"

"Mis-ter Blake," he enunciates. "Stop tongue fucking Ms. Taylor and come back to Washington. You have two days."

How do they know what I'm doing with her?

The line cuts out, and I glance down at the fucking perfect woman in front of me, sprawled out with her hair mussed. I don't fucking care if they're watching. As I'm about to resume where we left off, the phone rings again from another unknown number.

"Yes?" I answer it with a growl.

"Two days, Mr. Blake."

CHAPTER 32
ALEX

"It's done," Mickey insists, the small tilt of his lips almost resembling a smile. It fades as he glances at his CCTV feed and his jaw tics. "One moment."

He dials a number on his landline, growls, "Two days, Mr. Blake," then hangs up.

Fuck. Is Chris actually touching her?

"What happened?"

Despite my matching his gruff tone, he finds humor in my inquiry and chuckles darkly, "Don't worry. Your little princess is safe. She may have enjoyed herself a bit more than expected, but—" I'm halfway out of my seat when he gestures with his hand for me to sit. "*Ah, ah, ah.* That's not how this works. We need Ms. Taylor. Whether she has orgasms or not doesn't concern me. Now... How attached are you to your brother? He seems to be getting in the way of my plans recently."

"Please don't kill him," I sigh, pleading. "I told Finn not to. Chris may be an asshole, but we're family. Just... please?"

"Understood," he concedes. "Finn is chasing after a woman he'll never have. He's my brother. Even if it risks everything we've built, I'd never kill him over it. So, how do we make each other whole here? Your father—and hers—want Chris to run for President, with Jaclyn by his side. Finn and I, well, we *respectfully* disagree."

"I see. And how the hell do you expect me to convince everyone that Jaclyn should run instead? Chris isn't going to just roll out the red carpet for her. You have to see how ludicrous that is?"

As he's about to reply, Finn strides in with confidence I couldn't muster if I tried. "Sorry, I'm late. Traffic."

"Traffic?" Mickey balks. "There isn't another car for miles."

"Tractor?"

I stifle a laugh, but Mickey offers a cold glare. "Leave the poor woman alone. She's married, for fuck's sake."

"She won't be for long." Finn rolls his eyes, then addresses me, "Ned has taken care of everything for the accident and your little switch-up. Unfortunately, when your brother went rogue and fucked everything up by traveling to Hawaii..." He lets out a deep sigh, rubbing the back of his neck before continuing, "Christopher is a loose cannon and could ruin *everything*. As I'm sure my brother reiterated, get Taylor to the White House, or both of your families will have *fun* secrets that make their way into the media."

"And, *again*, how do you expect me to do that?"

A sly smirk tugs at Finn's lips. "Just make sure that your pretty little wife's hands are clean after the gala."

"What happens at the gala?"

"So many questions." Finn rolls his eyes again, then asks Mickey, "Are you sure we can't just work with the Taylor girl directly?"

Mickey grinds his jaw. "Figure it out, Alexander. You know the stakes."

"I don't know why I'm even here," Finn huffs. "I need to get home and let my dogs out before the gala."

I try not to laugh at the idea of a man like him owning a dog, much less *plural* dogs. Even if he does have pets, why isn't an assistant or one of his men working for him doing it? Instead of probing, I take it as my cue to leave, standing and buttoning my blazer. "Gentlemen, it's been an experience, but I should get back to Tex—"

"Sit. Down," Mickey snaps. "No one is going anywhere until I know with absolute certainty that Christopher is out of the picture."

Finn adjusts his cufflinks. "I can have someone take care of it."

"No," I confirm. "There's nothing to take care of."

"You weren't supposed to marry the Washington darling, Alex," Finn tuts. "Everything was in place. Ms. Taylor would be brokenhearted, and we'd be there to pick up the pieces. You ruined everything with your theatrics. So, from now on, you leave the rest to us."

"That was before you told me you want her to be President! I'm in agreement that she is a better fit, but... promise me you won't hurt Chris." I don't care how weak my voice sounds, I can't have my brother's death on my conscience.

"Your brother isn't moldable," Mickey says carefully. "He's unpredictable. We'll spare"—his nose scrunches for a moment—"his life, if you ensure his wife is running."

"She's not his wife," I blurt, then quickly correct with a lie, "I mean... their paperwork is filed. You're correct."

"That bonfire was lovely, wasn't it?" Finn adds, lightly licking his upper lip.

"Fuck! Was there anything you two weren't watching?"

Perverts.

"You tell me." Mickey turns his monitor to show Jaclyn in bed, wrapped in Chris' arms, and I can't help the anger bubbling inside me. He's touching what's mine. "As I was saying, take care of it. Or we will."

I let out a long breath, trying to calm my rage. "As you wish."

CHAPTER 33
JACLYN

E verything is a disaster. Chris claims he has an emergency in Washington, but if I want this to work with him, I need to stay as far away from D.C.—*and Alex*—as possible.

No one is perfect. I'm certainly no saint, especially after these past few weeks. Having done my own deplorable acts, I doubt Chris would forgive me if he knew everything.

After his first time ever making me come, he slid into bed with me, wrapping his arms around me like Alex did when he was here. It makes my feelings for them murkier by the hour. My heart and my head are at war with one another, and the more time I spend with Chris, the messier this all becomes. I don't love him, and likely never will.

There are worse things than letting your husband go down on you. Maybe I can make this work, after all.

Except I can't get Alex out of my head.

Why can't I let him go?

And why am I okay with Chris and I sleeping together?

Am I really going to throw everything I've worked for away... because of... men?

For all I know, both of them are lying, wanting a piece of me that I have too willingly given them.

I'm a fucking mess and have no one to talk to about it. "He's an asshole!" would be great to hear from someone right now. I would call Ileah or Evelyn, but I would have to give them the most watered-down version of everything. It isn't that I don't trust them; I don't want to burden them with it.

Chris slides out of bed at the sound of his phone buzzing. He begins a string of curses, and since his primary aide died in the accident, my mind immediately goes to who could be his next blowjob victim—maybe his campaign manager?

Fuck, why does it hurt to imagine him with yet another woman?

No.

You're Jaclyn Fucking Taylor. You deserve better than this bullshit.

How is it fair that he gets to fuck anything that moves, and if it ever got out that I slept with Alex, I'd be crucified by the media? I take a deep breath and collect myself as Chris has a meltdown of epic proportions.

"Is everything okay?"

"No," he sighs, shoving Alex's clothes into his suitcase.

I should probably donate those when we get home.

I rush over to help him, but as I try, he tugs too hard, and his elbow hits me square in the eye. I push back, both hands flying to my face. "Fuck! Jackie, are you okay?" He pulls them away, no matter how hard I try to hold my hands in place. "Shit, let me call a doctor."

Chris moves for his phone, but I stop him. "No! I'm fine. The last thing we need is rumors that I'm a battered wife." While I mean it as a joke, I'm also serious. This clusterfuck of a situation doesn't need someone saying I've been abused on my honeymoon added to the mix.

I rush off to the bathroom to assess the damage in the mirror, and Chris comes up behind me, genuine worry etched in his eyes in the reflection. "Please, let me take a look."

"It'll be okay. I just need some ice." Everything is too heavy; I can't do this anymore, pretending to love a man that I don't. Tears track my cheeks as I brace myself on the counter and stifle my sobs.

"If you need ice, I'll call for someone to bring us a fucking gallon of it. But you're *not* okay."

"I'm... not okay," I concede, though it has little to do with my eye swelling.

"Please let me take a look?" he repeats, moving my hands away, and I reluctantly turn, keeping my eyes shut tight. He kisses my tears away, pulling me to him; it only makes me sob harder. "I'm so fucking sorry, Jaclyn. For everything." Wrapping me tighter in his embrace, he sighs deeply. "I love you more than I ever thought I could. I hope you know I didn't mean to hurt you."

The confession is lost on me—he didn't once think about me as he fucked other women. While he's promising oaths I never asked for, I'm stuck in a world of fiction. None of this means anything.

No longer fighting him, he wipes away my tears with the pads of his thumbs and whispers, "I'm going to find some ice and over-the-counter pain medication. I'll be back in ten minutes. If I'm a minute later, you can castrate me, but I doubt that will serve either of us."

I let out a soft chuckle as he rushes out the door, and I'm back to wondering if I can make this work with him.

Not likely, but I may as well let him attempt to grovel.

As promised, Chris returns seconds after what would be ten minutes, panting, "Acetaminophen, ibuprofen, and naproxen. Pick your poison." He dumps a small bag of medication onto the counter and holds up a bag of ice.

Maybe his pain from the accident will spike and he'll take both ibuprofen and naproxen.

What is wrong with me? I shouldn't be wishing an ulcer on someone!

"Thank you." I take the bag from him and pull out a couple of ice cubes, placing them in a washcloth to press against my eye. With a deep sigh, I throw him a bone. "You're a lifesaver."

"I did this to you, the least I could do is get ice." He places his hand over mine, pressing the cool washcloth against my eye. "I'm so sorry. Truly, for everything. I love you, Jaclyn... We're going to be okay."

My head is screaming, *"You're so full of shit,"* while my heart promises, *"We can make this work."* Luckily, my heart and head agree to keep him at arm's length.

"Thank you for bringing me ice and a plethora of pain medication. I think I've got it from here."

"Oh. Right. I understand," Chris pulls his hand back, slinking away in defeat. I shouldn't care what he thinks after years of infidelity and our wedding day, but if we stand a chance of salvaging this, I need to try.

"No, stop," I whisper, the cold, wet cloth still pressed to my eye. "Thank you. It was just an accident." He perks up at my admission. "I know you didn't mean to hurt me."

This time.

I pull the ice away and he kisses my eyelid. "I promise I'll never hurt you again. You have my word."

While his promises are empty, I can almost get behind the idea that I might get the happily ever after Alex promised me. Granted, it's not how I imagined it, but maybe Alex is right that things aren't as black and white as I thought before I became involved with him—or even Chris. If I can make my husband fall in love with me, he's more likely to support my dreams.

Congresswoman Blake... No. Congresswoman Taylor.

He resumes packing and demands I wait on the couch with the makeshift ice pack. As I'm posting a photo on social media that I took of the sunset last night, a text alert from an unknown number appears at the top of the screen. I click on it, and my breath catches as I read.

> UNKNOWN
> Secrets always have a way of coming out, Ms. Taylor.

CHAPTER 34
JACLYN
ONE WEEK LATER

"There's... *another one*," my assistant, Rose, announces almost singing, placing a single sapphire rose on my desk.

"Are you sure they aren't for you? A rose for Rose?" I chuckle.

"This one has a note." She clears her throat. *"For my beautiful wife. Miss you, princess."* Rolling my eyes, she gives me a knowing look, handing it to me. "Last time I checked, I'm single. This one's all yours, *Mrs.* Blake."

I've successfully avoided Alex since being back in D.C., and with Chris preparing for his big announcement, I've hardly seen him. I've been busying myself, focusing my attention on the upcoming gala. Deep down, I've known these daily roses were from Alex, and this note is the nail in the coffin.

The longer I'm away from him, the more the brain fog diminishes. My desperation for him—*my heart ripping from my chest at hearing his name mentioned*—has subsided significantly. Since all of my plans have been derailed, I need to make the best of everything, and that includes forgetting about Alex. Even though he's making it incredibly difficult with the flower deliveries.

I offer a sweet smile. "Chris is such a romantic."

Rose clips the stem at an angle and places it in the vase on my desk, joining the other five. "If this is going to be a daily ritual, perhaps we should invest in a few more vases?"

"I'm sure he'll give up after a dozen." If it were Chris, he absolutely would. Alex? No. Alex will ensure I consistently have a dozen fresh cornflower roses in a vase.

I have to end this. Now.

The moment Rose leaves my office, I snatch my phone from my desk and type out a text to him.

> Thank you for the roses.

> But you need to stop.

ALEX

> Make me.

I choke on my own breath, stifling my laugh. Serves me right for trying to negotiate with a politician—he's a man-child.

> I'm serious.

So am I.

As I take a moment to contemplate my next move, another message comes through.

I won't apologize for doting on my wife, Jaclyn.

I'm not yours.

The lie hurts to type, but it has to be this way.

Are you sure?

You're certainly not married to Chris.

I checked, and a replacement marriage license isn't filed. The embers are still burning in that fire pit from the original.

Why are you making this harder for me?

You think it's been a damn cakewalk seeing you with him?

Admit it, Jaclyn, you're mine.

I can't give in to the fantasy. It'll end with my heart shattered on the floor. Tears prick behind my eyes as I type, wishing with all of my being that I didn't have to do this.

I'm married to Chris.

And I'm married to you.

I fall into my office chair, and my heart sinks with me. He's never going to give up.

In no world would Alex and I work. If we did, I'd take the leap and be with the one man who made me feel more in a single glance than any other man has made me feel... ever.

But staying with Chris is the only option, or I'll lose everything. Other than the cheating and the lies, there's no reason I can't be content staying married to him.

We'll get him through eight years, and then it'll be my turn to shine.

The office door opens, and I sit upright, throwing water on my emotions as if they were hot coals. Rose brings in a dozen red roses and sets them on my desk. "It appears Mr. Blake has upped the ante."

No. He hasn't. The Blake brothers are at war, and I'm stuck in the damn middle. "Is there a note with these, too?"

"Yes." She pulls it from the arrangement. "I love you more than red roses." It takes everything in me not to laugh. With a frown, she asks, "What's with the red and blue roses? Are you finally planning on running for office?"

Rose has been with me for three years, and not once has a single flower been delivered to me. She's also one of the only people in the world privy to my political dreams. I can't blame her for wishing along with me.

"No, not me. Chris is planning to announce his presidential candidacy soon. I'm sure it's just a sweet patriotic gesture to get me excited."

"He is?" She purses her lips, deflated, then quickly corrects her tone. "Congratulations! Don't forget us little folk when you're First Lady."

"How could I? You'll be right there with me. I'd be lost without you."

Her smile is wide as she fluffs the flowers. "You're really living the dream, *First Lady Jaclyn Blake*."

You mean a nightmare?

"Let's not get ahead of ourselves," I reply with a light chuckle. My phone vibrates, and I turn it face-down before she can see the text preview. "Would you mind arranging lunch with my husband for tomorrow? He's been working so hard lately. I miss him."

"Of course."

She rushes out of my office, and as the oak door shuts, I quickly check my phone to find the one message I can never reply to.

I love you, Jaclyn.

CHAPTER 35
ALEX
TWO WEEKS LATER

"Almost done. You should make it with plenty of time for the bachelor auction."

I groan as Laura helps me into my tux jacket. It may not be legal, but I'm also no longer a bachelor—I'm Jaclyn's husband. I'm not sure how I got roped into this misandry as fuck auction, but I want out.

The only positive about any of this is the gala downstairs will bring me closer to my wife, if only for the evening. Unfortunately, I'll have to see her flirting with my brother. Watch him openly touch her. It doesn't help that she hasn't responded to my texts... or the blue roses I've sent daily since she returned to D.C..

"Are you almost done?" It comes out as more of a growl than I intended.

"I'm sorry, sir," Laura says carefully.

"No, *I'm* sorry. I'm just on edge," I sigh and ask about my aide, "Where is Abigail? She was supposed to make sure I wasn't attending, let alone being sold off like prime real estate in a buyers' market." I huff a laugh at the ridiculous fundraiser.

"She'll be here shortly. But, I assure you, you look amazing, sir." Calling me 'sir' a second time, I pause; there's an Irish lilt in her voice. It's then that I notice a small snake tattoo behind her right ear. If the Gallaghers wanted to spy on me, they should've picked someone a little less obvious.

"Great. And what time will Finn be here?"

"Should be any minute now," she slips up. The brothers are getting sloppy.

"Grand," I reply with a faux-Irish accent, making her suck in a breath. "Yeah, tell your boss that if he wants to meet with me, I'm ready for the evening." She busies herself with hair and makeup products as if I didn't just out her, my patience wearing thin. "Any time now, Laura." She scurries off, presumably to find Abigail or the Irish brothers.

Approximately ten minutes later, the door opens, and I bark, "It's about time you showed your face," assuming it's Finn or Mickey. I didn't look to see who was entering, but I sure as fuck should've.

"Hello to you, too." Hearing her velvety voice makes the hair on the back of my neck stand up, and a lightness settles in my chest for the first time in weeks.

"Well, hello, Mrs. Blake." I've never swiveled in my seat so fast in my life, finding Jaclyn standing before me in a crimson lace-adorned gown that trumpets at the floor. She's a fucking vision, leaving me utterly speechless. The majority of it is skintight, showing off her incredible curves, dipping low enough between her perfect breasts that I could easily slip my hand inside to play. Fuck. The damn dress is begging me to strip it off her.

Jaclyn lightly licks her upper lip, drinking me in, but sucks in a breath and quickly schools her expression. "It's come to my attention that you'll be participating in the bachelor auction."

"Yes, I am, at your mother's request... Or was it *yours?* Were you planning on bidding on me?" I taunt, but an idea strikes me: I can find someone to ensure I don't go home with anyone but my wife.

"No. I think Chris put her up to it." Jaclyn glances behind her to make sure no one is listening in, and my eyes zero in on a small purple mark on her neck that isn't from me. It's poorly covered with makeup and my jaw tics. *My fucking brother...* As she returns her gaze to me, her eyes widen. "What?"

I stand and prowl toward her, closing the door and guiding her backward with my hand on her hip for a step until I'm pressing her against it. Bracing myself with a hand above her, my eyes never leave hers. There's no way I could ever look away. When it's the two of us, she's my fucking world. As if the sight of her wasn't enough, her citrusy shampoo is like damn catnip.

Fuck, I've missed her.

Taking my time, I slide my hand up her side from her hip, loving the feel of the intricate fabric beneath my fingertips. Her chest rises and falls with a deep breath—one I want to steal for myself. Cupping her neck, I cover the mark my brother left behind and trace my thumb along her jaw.

He touched what's mine...

Jaclyn wets her pouty lips, and my jaw clenches as I resist kissing her. Instead, my thumb caresses her bottom lip. "Open." She does as I ask, and her tongue swipes the pad of my thumb as she draws it into her mouth. The sight of her scarlet lips wrapped around it has my cock thickening in my tuxedo pants.

Pulling it from her, I use the warm wetness to swipe away the makeup covering the hickey on the side of her neck, and a growl gets stuck in my throat as it brightens. She swallows thickly as I lean in closer.

"You let him touch you."

"Yes," she whispers. "He's my husband, Alex. I have to make it work with Chris."

I pull back, and a single tear leaves the corner of her eye. As I brush it away, I notice faint bruising above her cheek, masked with makeup but still visible being this close to her. While I can forgive her for sleeping with him, I'll never in a million years forgive him for laying a hand on her.

A rumble comes from deep within me. "When did he hurt you?"

"It wasn't like that. It was an accident a few weeks ago," she rushes out. "I'm just glad the swelling went down before tonight."

"Accident?" I growl. "If he hit you—"

"He didn't, I promise." Jaclyn places her hand on my cheek, and I cover it with mine, relaxing into her touch.

Fuck, I more than missed her. I need her.

Dragging our joined hands to my lips, I press a single kiss to her palm, and a light pink blush creeps up her neck and cheeks. "I swear he didn't hurt me. It was just an accident." I lean in to kiss her, but she braces herself against my chest, my lips a breath away from hers. "We shouldn't do this. I should go."

"Not so fast, princess." I tuck a few stray locks behind her ear that have escaped her bun. "Why haven't you replied to my texts?"

Her lip quivers. "I... I didn't know what to say."

"That you love me, too."

"I..." She opens and closes her mouth a few times, as if to admit I'm wrong—*or right*—and thinking better of it. *Say it, Jaclyn.* With swirls of pain etched in her irises, she whispers, "You should get ready for the auction."

I take a step back and make a show of adjusting my bowtie. "If you haven't noticed, I'm ready... Though it's false advertising, seeing as I'm no longer single." I lift my left hand, showing off that I'm still wearing my wedding ring.

"Alex," she breathes, reminding me of how all of this started.

I take her chin between my thumb and forefinger, then, not giving a fuck about the consequences, I swipe my thumb along her full, cherry-stained bottom lip again. "The game has changed, my little wife; this isn't pretend anymore. I know you feel this between us. You're *mine* as much as I'm yours. I'm not going to stand by and be happy that you're on my brother's arm. Because in the end, you know it'll be you and me."

There's a knock on the door, and I quickly steal a chaste kiss from her. I'm desperate to taste the one woman I've been unable to get out of my head since I left Hawaii—since college, if I'm being honest. Licking along the seam of her lips, she eagerly opens for me, allowing my tongue to dance with hers briefly despite her initial hesitation. If time was on our side, I'd explore every inch of her, reminding her that this is all real between us. I can't stop. She tastes too fucking good.

Whiskey, cherry, a hint of bitters.

"What were you celebrating?" I ask against her lips. My chest aches to be closer to her; kissing her feels like home. "Why are you here, Jaclyn?"

"Don't do the auction." As she pulls back, she briefly tugs my bottom lip between her teeth. "I know it's selfish of me to ask, but it'll hurt too much to see you..." She doesn't need to finish her sentence—it'll hurt to see me with another woman. Hope settles in my chest; this isn't over between us.

The door knocks again, but I'm sure as hell not letting her slip through my fingers. "I'm busy," I growl at whoever is on the other side.

"Too busy for an old friend?" Finn asks, and I still.

"I'll be downstairs in a few minutes," I call to him, and as I hear his footsteps retreat, I whisper to Jaclyn, "You were worried about a web of lies and deceit? There are bigger things at play than my brother murdering a woman. We need to talk and figure out how to get you far away from all. Meet me after the gala?" Needing her more than I need to breathe, I capture her lips, roughly kissing her a second time. Her sweet hum is all the reassurance I need that she's still mine.

My mouth travels to the opposite side of her neck that my brother shamelessly branded. She sucks in a breath, likely knowing exactly what I'm doing.

"You deserve the Oval, Alex, not him."

"I don't want it. It's yours."

"Mine? No, we talked about this." She pulls back. "Alex, I—"

"Go, my beautiful wife. We'll talk about this later." I kiss her forehead, my lips lingering. "You have the gala and, in a couple of hours, men to auction off."

"Which is supposed to include you." Jaclyn playfully pokes my chest, making me chuckle. When the soft laughter fades, her deep blue eyes dart between mine in question.

"Don't worry, I'll make sure I'm going home with you, princess."

"You know that's not possible," she sighs in defeat.

I need another taste. Not giving a flying fuck who might knock next, my lips crash into hers yet again, and I steal her moans. With each swipe of my tongue against hers, she willingly gives me this small piece of her, and I intend to fucking keep it. There's no way in hell I'm giving her up.

Not now, not ever.

When we break apart, a soft whimper escapes her, and I rest my forehead on hers. "Trust me, princess, I love you."

CHAPTER 36
CHRIS

"You're not running," Mickey insists, dramatically sipping his whiskey, keeping his eyes pinned on me.

"The fuck I'm not. You had an agreement with my father," I growl. "The whole point of me marrying Jaclyn was to guarantee my place on the ticket."

"'Was' is the keyword there, Mr. Blake."

I fucking hate that he calls me that. We're practically the same age, it's condescending as fuck, and it makes him sound like a movie villain.

Setting his drink down and slowly tracing the rim of the glass with his middle finger, he continues, "That was before we had to bring in my *associate* to clean up your mess. Couldn't keep your cock in your pants on your wedding day? You got lucky Cara didn't bite off your dick when you crashed." I scoff, making him chuckle darkly.

"It's quite curious that you had a heart attack; you're only thirty-six and *appear* to be in the best shape of your life."

"It was an accident; I took too much of my ADHD meds." It's still strange to me. I don't remember taking it that morning, let alone too much.

"You're quite accident-prone. Good thing you won't be President. When the gala is over, you'll go back to Florida and encourage your wife to run for office in the upcoming election. She should start small, maybe a congressional seat or a state position. With her turning thirty-five next year, you'll support her run in 2028."

"Jaclyn?" I bark a laugh. "You want *Jaclyn* to run? She'll lose. She's too much like her father. The country won't vote for her when she leans *that* far to one side politically. My own father had to become more centrist when he ran, and I intend to do the same. Plus, she's a woman. You really think you'll convince over half of the nation to support her? You've lost your mind."

"You underestimate your wife, Mr. Blake." He takes another sip of whiskey with a light hum as the liquid passes his lips. "She's more than qualified, and the country *loves* her."

I cluck my tongue. "Will they still love her when they find out she married Alex?"

"That reminds me." Mickey pulls out his phone and types for a moment before setting it on his thigh screen side down. Seconds later, a woman walks in that I recognize but can't place. "Your new aide, Lisa Johnson."

Lisa approaches and I politely stand, buttoning my tux. It's only halfway through the little slit when Mickey gestures for me to take a seat.

"Hi, I'm not sure if you remember me, I was your wedding coordinator." She offers her hand, but I don't take it.

"Why is she here?" I snap at Mickey.

"Alex and Jaclyn were careless discussing their fake nuptials," she answers for him, sitting next to me. "So, for half a million a year and a position on your staff, I'll remain here in D.C. to manage your office in your absence... Perhaps start a charity. What is your passion? Books? Animals?"

"No, absolutely not. Go work for Alex."

Lisa is about to answer when Mickey interjects, "Lisa *will* work for you. End of discussion."

"This is bullshit," I grumble under my breath. "So, I have to clean up Alex's mess, now? All because he couldn't keep his fucking mouth shut in front of her?" I gesture to Lisa with a wide swipe of my arm.

"To be fair, it was your father who was a bit too loud when speaking with your brother," she retorts.

I pinch the bridge of my nose. "Can't you just take the money?"

"No, I enjoy working," she replies with pride. At the same time, Mickey growls, "Lest you forget, Mr. Blake, who took care of your indiscretions? You're not in charge here. You'll return to Florida as we discussed, and Lisa will remain in Washington to run your office here."

There's nothing worse than being in debt to a Gallagher...

"Fine," I mutter, but he can't stop me from announcing. I won't do it at the gala and upstage Jaclyn after the progress I've made with her. Fuck Mickey, and fuck his ridiculous plan to make my wife President. Tomorrow, I'll find a way to get rid of this Lisa woman and coordinate everything with my media team.

"Wonderful." Mickey finishes his whiskey and stands, fastening the middle button of his tux jacket. "Now that's all settled, I'll see both of you at the event. I hear there's a bachelor auction again this year. Perhaps I'll see if they need another victim; it'll make for an interesting night."

He walks out, leaving me with Lisa. I don't have the mental energy to deal with her, so I excuse myself and make my way up to my room. Jaclyn should be ready and preparing for the gala, and I need some time to figure out how the hell I'm going to pull off announcing my presidential run... and not piss off the damn mafia.

Mickey is a fucking idiot if he thinks I'm handing everything over to Jaclyn. While I love her, the country isn't ready to. At least not yet. One day, but not for at least a few more decades.

CHAPTER 37

JACLYN

"Trust me, princess. I love you."

Can I trust him?

Alex opens the door and checks both ways down the hall to make sure no one is lurking. He presses a chaste kiss to my cheek as I step out of his room, and I inwardly chastise myself. I shouldn't have kissed him, but the moment I saw those brown-hazel eyes, every single fiber of my being begged me to.

My plan was to ask him to not do the auction. When our eyes met, all the air left my lungs, and I lost complete control of the situation. But it's over; I need to cut myself off cold turkey. It worked when he left Hawaii. I'll do it again. There is too much at stake.

As I approach the elevator, there's a man waiting, rubbing his hand behind his neck as he checks his phone. I stand next to him, watching for the numbers to climb from three to our floor, but they don't move.

"It's been stuck for a while. I think it's broken," he grumbles. After waiting in uncomfortable silence for at least three minutes, he looks up from his phone, and does a double-take. He offers a wide smile, one that meets his sparkling, emerald eyes. Even with my heels, he still has several inches on me, and I'm woman enough to admit he's an incredibly attractive man.

Find me anyone—doesn't matter if they are a man, woman, or anything in between—who doesn't love a green-eyed man, impeccably dressed in a designer suit. He's built like he could rail you on any surface, without breaking a sweat...

I sense a ruggedness beneath his tuxedo—this man has seen things. There's also a familiarity about him, and I'm struggling to place where we might know each other.

"Ms. Taylor. What are the odds that I'd run into you here?"

"Oh, I... um..." I'm not sure why I'm so flustered and stammering. Quickly squashing the spell I'm under, I offer a version of the truth, and reply, "I needed to deliver something to one of the bachelors for the auction."

"Ah, Mr. Blake, I presume? It's always fun to watch that one each year."

"No. Well, yes, actually. His brother is participating this year. My husband is no longer able to, for obvious reasons." I huff a small laugh, lifting the back of my hand and wiggling my fingers to show off my wedding ring.

"True, it would be inappropriate; Alexander shouldn't do the auction this year."

My breath catches at the mention of Alex. *Who is this guy?* "I'm sorry, you're mistaken. I'm married to his brother, *Chris*. Historically, he's done it, but Alex is in the auction this year, instead."

"Is that so?" He sighs a hum, then lowers his voice. "It's curious that the heart attack didn't take Christopher out hours before the wedding. Maybe Cara got the dosage wrong?"

Cara? Dosage?

I glance around and lean in to whisper-shout, "What are you talking about?"

"Forgive me, I've never properly introduced myself. Finn Gallagher." My eyes go wide, my heart coming to a halt. "Ah, so you've heard of me? Pleasure to finally make your acquaintance." He offers his hand, and I hesitantly take it. "Though it's a pity I missed your wedding. I heard it was beautiful." I offer a faux bright smile, and as I'm about to agree, he keeps his voice low. "Secrets always have a way of coming out, Ms. Taylor."

That little sentence feels eerily familiar, and it takes me a moment to place it. Blood drains from my cheeks at the realization that he could be the author of the cryptic text I received. Finn Gallagher, *the* Finn Gallagher.

The elevator dings, and when the doors open, he gestures to the empty space. "After you."

Keeping my posture rigid and my expression emotionless, I clear my throat and ensure my voice is light and airy. "That's all right, I'll catch the next one. Have a great time at the gala!"

"I insist, Ms. Taylor," he purrs.

I square my shoulders. "As you're aware, it's Mrs. Blake, now."

"Is it? I wasn't sure since your marriage license never left Hawaii." I look back down the hall at his challenge. Alex's door is still shut. There's no way I could make a run for it in this dress; I can hardly breathe in it as it is. "I can assure you, your safety is my utmost priority. We have *much* to discuss."

"Perhaps I should still seek a chaperone?" I jest, and as the doors begin to close, he forces them to remain open. "If you intend for us to take a turn about the room, you should make your intentions known." While I know the reference is lost on him, I can't help giggling to myself.

"I don't have time for Regency advice." On their own volition, my eyes nearly escape their sockets. "You, Ms. Taylor, are the future of our country. And if that weren't enough, my heart belongs to someone else. I have no desire to upset *mo rúnsearc* by her finding out I touched her friend."

Mo rúnsearc? What the hell does that mean?

Reluctantly, I step inside the elevator, choosing to believe this man who knows entirely too much about literature...

and me. I'm unsure who was loose-lipped about everything. How could he possibly know?

The hotel staff?

Alex?

Finn presses the button for the mezzanine level, and the doors close. It was incredibly reckless to get in an elevator alone with this strange man, but despite his reputation, he's given me no reason to fear him hurting me.

Except for the fact that he knows about the license, believes Cara tried to give Chris a heart attack, and is hinting that he knows about my fake wedding...

He wants something.

Pivoting the conversation away from me, I inquire, "I'm not sure which friend of mine is your '*mo rúnsearc*' or who you are worried about upsetting. All of my friends are married."

"She's the love of my life, but I wouldn't expect you to be privy to that information. She isn't exactly forthcoming about me, even with friends." Finn smiles with a twinkle in his eyes, tiny lines forming at the corners. It's almost sweet the way this ruthless killer lights up at the mention of a woman.

I rack my brain, trying to figure out who he might be talking about. *Is a friend of mine being unfaithful to her husband? With him?* Curiosity gets the best of me. Keeping my eyes fixed on the numbers counting up to our floor, I dare to mildly accuse him. "I don't recall your name on the guest list. Did you receive a personal invitation to the gala? Or are you attending as someone's plus one?"

"I was invited by your mother."

"My mother?" I suck in a breath and my head whips in his direction. "How do you know my mother?"

Finn whispers, "I know both of your parents, as well as the Blakes. You need to speak with *your husband*. The one you promised yourself to." He gives a knowing look. "The three of us have much to discuss regarding your political future."

"You sound like Alex." My hand flies to my mouth as the words slip out.

He chuckles, more wrinkles forming around his eyes at his genuine smile. "Would you prefer to start at the state level? Or jump right into a congressional seat?" The elevator dings, making me jump. As he steps out, he suggests, "You may want to take a ride back up to his floor. He'll have the answers you're looking for. While his brother is apprised of the situation, I don't expect he'll enjoy being pushed aside. You'll need allies in your corner, Ms. Taylor."

Finn walks away as if he didn't just word-vomit an evil plan on me. I don't know what to make of it and head toward the gala side door.

As if my day couldn't get any more screwed up, an all too familiar woman sprints toward me.

What the hell is she doing here?

"Jackie! I'm so glad I ran into you. Chris is finishing up a meeting with a... *donor*. Is there anything I can help with?" I'm dumbfounded, and if Lisa's smirk is indication, she damn well knows it—may as well be written all over my face in marker. "I work for Christopher now."

The fuck you do...

And, donor, my ass.

After my run-in with one Gallagher brother, I'm inclined to assume the other is talking to Chris. I don't know their angle, and that scares the shit out of me. Things have gone sideways, and I'm not sure who I can trust—it sure as hell isn't *Lisa*.

I was supposed to be a trophy wife, guaranteeing I'd have a ticket to any political post that would have me.

First, Alex was hinting at me in the Oval.

Now, the Gallaghers are asking me to run?

The coincidence is too much.

Is it all connected? It has to be. What the hell am I going to do?

It's said you should play the hand you're dealt. Unfortunately, my hand is absolute trash—Alex knows more than he's letting on, this shitty event planner has somehow weaseled her way in, and now, I'm strangely tied to one of the biggest mob families in the United States.

Nothing is going to plan...

"Can I help with anything, Mrs. Blake?"

I snap back to reality. "Sorry, no. Thank you. It's so great to see you," I finally reply, attempting to brush past her, but she grabs me by my forearm. Anger boiling inside me, I grit my teeth and snap, "I had to deal with you at the wedding. This is *my* event. If you touch me again, I'll make sure you'll never work in this town again."

"Oh, Mrs. Blake." Her grip tightens, but I don't flinch. "If I didn't make myself clear, I'm now one of your husband's aides. We'll be seeing so much more of each other."

"Oh? Did you suck his cock, too, just like the others?" The words tumble from my lips, making her loosen her hold as she lets out an audible gasp. It's all for show. She's not the least bit offended. Though, neither am I, with her insinuations and accusations.

I wouldn't put it past Chris to sleep with her at some point, even with his attempts to win me over. She's pretty, he'll fuck her.

"Don't worry, *Leslie.* You won't dislocate your jaw. But he's thick, so you might gag a little."

"It's *Lisa*, and I've never—"

"Fucked my husband? No. I don't think you have. Not yet, anyway. If you *dare* to try and threaten me again, I can assure you, you'll have more than just that stick up your ass."

Her irises blown, she nods vigorously. "Understood, Mrs. Blake."

"It was *so great* seeing you again," I say sweetly, moving past her, spotting Finn within ear shot leaning against a post.

Fuck, I'm an idiot.

As I walk past him, my chin is held high until he whispers, "You're ready, Ms. Taylor."

For what? The Presidency? No, absolutely not.

CHAPTER 38
ALEX

Abigail and Laura still aren't here, and I'm growing impatient by the minute. There are far too many variables, and the longer I'm away from Jaclyn, there is more of a chance that Finn or Mickey could get to her. The only reason I'm attending this ridiculous gala is to keep tabs on everything and protect her from two of the most dangerous men I've ever met.

And to torture myself seeing my wife with my brother. The masochism is strong tonight.

I stow my phone in my breast pocket, button my jacket, and head for the door. After double checking I have both hotel keys, I step out and take the elevator down to the gala. It should be starting in about an hour, but I may be able to sneak in early and watch Jaclyn in action as she puts on the finishing touches for the event.

As I steal a glass of champagne from an unmanned tray, I find Jaclyn talking to a woman with a clipboard and headset. I can't tear my eyes away; my wife is a fucking vision. Sipping the cool bubbly, I smirk against the glass when our eyes meet. For years, I've admired her from afar, and I don't intend to stop now, especially now that she's mine.

Jaclyn excuses herself and makes her way over, hips swaying with each step. When she reaches me, she takes my glass and tosses back the crisp champagne in a single gulp. "Easy, princess. There's more where that came from." The faded marks on her neck are covered with additional makeup, but still visible. Part of me knows Chris attempted to claim part of her for himself, hoping I'd see it. He may have even thought it would be enough to keep me away, but Jaclyn's mine. I won't give her up over a damn hickey.

"Do you have a minute?" Her voice is void of her usual levity; I nod without hesitation. "Come with me."

She leads us into a small conference room next to the ballroom, and I take out my phone to check for mics. With no visible cameras, if it weren't for the floor-to-ceiling windows spanning the wall, I'd lay her down right here on this table and take back what's mine.

Arms folded, I rest against the oak table while she shuts the door and pushes a button that drops the blinds of the windows surrounding us. It's pitch black for a brief moment before she turns the lights on and turns to face me. "I'm only going to ask this once, and you need to be honest with me: Are you working with the Gallaghers?"

"Yes," I sigh, "but it's not what it looks like."

"I think it's *exactly* what it looks like." She crosses her arms to mirror me, lifting her pert breasts an inch higher. I force my gaze to meet hers, finding her eyes boring into me. "I can't believe you're involved with them! They are basically"—she lowers her voice—"*mafia.*"

"I believe the politically correct term is 'organized crime,'" I tease.

"This isn't funny, Alex! Why did Finn Gallagher imply that I should run for office?"

My breath catches, and my arms fall to my sides, itching to pull her to me. Gripping the edge of the table is a safe bet; the temptation to touch her is too much. I have to remind myself there are more pressing matters. "You talked to him? Why were you talking with a Gallagher? Did he threaten you?"

"No. No one threatened me. I ran into Finn when I was leaving your suite. Is he the reason you keep saying I'll be President one day? Was"—her voice shakes before she sucks in a breath—"any of it true? Or was all of it their idea?" I push off the table, reaching for her, but she shrugs away. "Don't touch me."

"Jaclyn," I plead. The simmering war she is fighting in her mind is visible in her deep ocean eyes. I would throw everything away if it meant she didn't have to feel an ounce of this. "I'm sorry I didn't tell you everything. But I've *never* lied to you. *Ever.*" As I cautiously take her hand, thankfully, she lets me, and I gently swipe my thumb over hers. "I believe in you with my whole heart; you're the best choice for our country. None of this was supposed to happen the way it has. From what I was privy to, Chris was supposed to get caught with his aide before the wedding, giving you the pity of the nation. When he got in the accident and killed her, that plan went out the window."

Her brows pinch. "I'm not following. Why do you and the Gallaghers want *me* in office?"

"You, *my extraordinary wife...*" I bring her knuckles to my lips, dusting them with a gentle kiss, my eyes never leaving hers. "You are the bridge. It has nothing to do with the Gallaghers. The country has been in the hands of old-as-fuck men for far too long. We need a familiar name that will appeal to one side of the aisle, but the other will also vote for you if you campaign as a moderate. We need to fix this country, Jaclyn." I chew on my lip for a brief moment. I hope with all my being that she knows this is real... It always has been. "I won't apologize for that."

Jaclyn blows out a long breath, and I allow her the time to work through everything without interrupting. "Why didn't you let Chris get caught for the accident? Wouldn't that have solved everything?"

"I should've." Cupping the back of her neck, I kiss her forehead. "I wish I had done a lot of things differently." With a deep sigh, she wraps her arms around my middle, and I envelop her with mine, loving the feel of her warm, bare skin of her back against my palms. I should thank the designer of her gown for the lack of fabric. "If he was caught, the attention would be on vehicular manslaughter, not on you. I went against the Gallaghers when I stood up with you at the altar. I'm selfish, Jaclyn. Marrying you meant I had a reason to be close to you."

"You're so full of it," she chuckles softly, but I still feel it everywhere. My heart aches for this, for her. I need the lightness we had for those few days more than the air in my lungs, void of this nightmare we're currently living. "I thought you said you wouldn't lie to me?"

"I promise, I've never lied. Falling in love with you wasn't part of the plan, either. It just happened. So, even if it rips my soul in half, if you want to stay with him, I'll respect your wishes..." I shake my head, pain and disgust washing over me. "No. I'm sorry. I can't do it. *Fuck,* please don't ask me to... What if I can figure out a way for us to be together, would you consider it?"

I have no plan, but I'll fucking come up with one if there's a chance I get to keep her.

Jaclyn rests her chin on my chest, looking up at me. "As long as it doesn't include that hot Irishman or his brother... Even then, how would that even be possible? I can't risk it. My hands are dirty enough. I don't want to make it worse."

"Wait... did you just call Finn 'hot?' I don't blame you, he's an attractive man, but you should've figured out by now that I don't share." She laughs, shaking her head, and I can't help asking, "In all seriousness, what do you mean your hands are dirty? You won't get caught for marrying me instead of Chris. If you do, you can feign ignorance. I'll take the fall if it gets out; tell them I tricked you." Stepping out of my arms, she starts and stops a few times, only getting out a syllable at a time. I cock an eyebrow. "What are you hiding, princess?"

After taking a long, deep breath, she finally admits, "I knew about Chris cheating because of one of the house-keepers at one of the hotels he stayed at. I paid them off so they wouldn't talk. If it leaks that I bribed them..."

"That's your biggest worry?" I laugh and open my arms wide. "Come here, my adorable, little wife."

"No." About to step into my arms, Jaclyn shakes her head, retreating as her words tumble out of her. "This was a mistake. We shouldn't be in here. If we get caught... This, you and me, it's impossible. There's no way out of my marriage to Chris without it getting out that you stepped in for him. It'll burn both of us."

"The marriage license, did you file it?" I remind her. She chews on her lip, lowering her head; the answer I've been hoping for. "Then, as far as I'm concerned, you're married to *me,* not him."

"As sweet as that sentiment is, what are we supposed to do?" As she lifts her gaze, any joy that was there previously is absent from her glassy eyes. "You're working with the Gallaghers, and from the sounds of it, so are both of our parents... And I'm supposed to be married to your brother."

"I love you, Jaclyn. I'm not giving up on this, on us. Stay with me, fight for this. I know you feel the same way."

"What do you want me to say? That I'm falling in love with you?" Her voice raises, arms wide. "It doesn't matter that I have feelings for you. We can't do this!"

"Shh. We have to keep our voices down. You never know who may be listening in." I take a step forward, but she moves back.

"You think?" she whisper-shouts, then returns to normal volume with a huff. "On top of everything else, my *favorite* wedding coordinator heard a little too much and blackmailed her way onto Chris' staff. Or at least that's what I took from my interaction with her earlier."

"What the hell?" I can't help my humorless laugh.

"We don't have time to get into it," she sighs. "I'm more worried about the Gallaghers. I think they wanted Chris dead, or at least wanted him to have a heart attack. I can't wrap my brain around why."

It's as if I've been slapped in the face, and I'm still reeling from it. I know there are more details to all of this than either of us is aware of, and the Gallaghers hold all the cards.

"They didn't want him dead," I admit. "They needed him to get caught with Cara."

Jaclyn's shoulders fall. "I don't think it's that simple. Finn said something about Cara getting a dosage wrong. Chris was always terrible about taking his medication, but I saw the toxicology report. He took so much more than what he was supposed to. That's not an accidental second dose. It could've killed him."

Did they try to kill him? Sure, they hinted that he was a problem, but to go through with it...

"You're right. That doesn't sound like an accident. If you want, we can go on a fact-finding mission after the gala."

Taking another step away from me, she swallows hard. "They're dangerous."

"I know. For now, the best course of action is to pretend everything is normal. You're going to go out there and ensure the gala goes as planned." I take a small, slow step closer. "You're going to auction me and a dozen other bachelors off for the damn cherry blossoms." Another short step. "As much as it'll kill me, when it's all over, you'll go home to Chris, not letting him know *anything* we discussed tonight." Closing the distance, her chest is nearly pressed to mine. "And tomorrow morning, you'll tell him you need to run an errand and come to my suite."

Jaclyn's breath hitches as I reach behind her. Unzipping her dress, I slide my hand inside until I'm gripping her bare ass, pulling her flush with me. She whimpers a soft moan and doesn't stop me as I continue, "And after I have you screaming my name with my cock buried deep inside you, we'll make a plan for how to walk away from the Gallaghers, keep my place in the Senate, and give you a seat at the table." Brushing the right of my nose with hers, I whisper a breath away from her lips, "But he does *not* touch you again. He may be your husband to the rest of the world, but you're *my wife*, Jaclyn. If you let him, there will be consequences."

"Wh-what kind of consequences?"

I squeeze her ass firmer, and I'm unable to hide my grin. "You'll be my good fucking girl and do as I asked, or I'll mark every last inch of you until you look like a damn cheetah. There will be no denying that you're mine. I don't give a fuck who sees the bright red and purple bruises I leave behind with my mouth."

There's a faint knocking at the door, and I pull my hand from her dress, quickly zipping it. "Mrs. Blake? Are you in there?"

"It's my assistant," Jaclyn whispers, then raises her voice. "Yes, I'll be there in a moment, Rose. I'm briefing someone on tonight's events."

"Okay, great. I'll just... wait here?"

Jaclyn's shoulders sag as she steps out of my hold, glancing down and swiping at her dress. "You're beautiful," I assure her.

With a small smile that meets her eyes, she calls to the woman, "No need, I'll be in the ballroom momentarily." There's the faint sound of retreating footsteps, and when it's silent again, she asks, "What is this?" She gestures between us.

"We both know you're mine, but what do you want, princess?" I counter with a smirk I can't contain.

She chews on her lip and lets out a long breath. All of it makes me feel uneasy as anguish overcomes her features. "I'm sorry. Even if it breaks my heart—or yours—I have to try to make things work with Chris."

"You can't have both of us." I resist the urge to unzip her dress again and show her with my face between her legs why it's supposed to be me, not my brother. "But no matter what, I'll always be *yours*, Jaclyn."

Pain continuing to etch her face, she whines, "Why are you making this so hard?"

"Because you're worth fighting for." There's no use hiding how I feel. It goes beyond pretending to be married to her, I want Jaclyn for myself. She's *my* wife.

Period.

No, scratch that.

Fucking exclamation point.

And I'll give up everything to keep her.

Jaclyn lets out another deep sigh, and the ache in my chest is too much; she's giving me no indication of what she's thinking. I fucking hate it. All I want to do is throw her over my shoulder, and run far away from my brother, Washington, and two very untrustworthy Irish brothers.

"I... I'll see you in a few," she whispers sheepishly.

Fuck. That.

After this, she may push me away, choose him, take the easy route, and further entangle herself with the Gallaghers. On the off chance she does, I need one more moment, one more *second* with her where it's just... *us*. Capturing her lips with mine in a bruising kiss, she moans into my mouth, confirming this isn't one-sided. I know in my soul she loves me, but her situation is significantly more fucked-up than mine is.

Jaclyn slides her hands up my chest until they're around my neck, pulling me impossibly close to her. The desperate need to have her is overwhelming.

Refusing to end our kiss, her words contradict her actions as she mutters against my lips, "We can't do this."

"Then, stop kissing me."

"I can't," she whimpers. "I'm falling in love with you." A possessive growl rumbles in my chest. With an insecure shakiness in her voice, she adds, "You have to know this is breaking my heart," and mine skips a beat at her admission.

"I'd rather die than hurt you, princess." She stills in my arms. "Too soon? With the accident?"

Jaclyn huffs a soft laugh. "Probably."

"Don't do this. Stay with me, choose *me*, and I'll find a way out of this mess." I finally break our kiss, needing her to see how serious I am when I confess, "I love you, Jaclyn. Fuck, I need you more than I need to breathe. Choose. Me."

"It's not a matter of choice." She places my hand over her heart. "You stole this and I don't want it back. I'm trying to do what's right for us and for the country."

"We'll do it together." I slide my hand into her hair and keep my thumb resting on her cheek, unable to tear my eyes away from hers. She melts into my touch and I'm a fucking goner. "And I'm trying to be a gentleman, but I swear if you don't get out of here, I'm going to bend you over that table until you're coming all over my face and cock... twice."

"Promise?" she taunts, a small light beaming from her that I haven't seen in a while.

"Later, my little wife. Go be magnificent, and I promise you won't regret waiting."

CHAPTER 39
JACLYN

What the hell am I doing?

Each and every time I see Alex, I'm swept up by his sweet words, my undeniable attraction to him, and the way he can command my body with a single touch. It's maddening how charming he is. The logical choice is to run far, far away, fake a happy marriage with Chris, and pray each night that I'll be forgiven for my sins.

What if he's right?

What if the Gallaghers can help me find a cozy spot in the House or maybe even something at the state level? Alex and Finn are irrational for thinking I could ever run for President, but maybe if I give in...

"You're rusty, Taylor," echoes in my head, and Alex is right. I am. I need to stay sharp. I've been complacent; there are too many enemies tonight.

Making my way to the ballroom, everything seems to be in order. With the staff bustling between tables to ensure every last detail is perfect, I take in the expertly decorated space, and pride swells in my chest. Perhaps I was an event planner in a past life; attention to detail is certainly my strong suit. Each table is covered with crimson tablecloths, set for dinner service. While I think gold and silver would've been gorgeous, my mother insisted we make a statement with red. Despite our short-lived disagreement, it's still beautiful.

There won't be much to celebrate if everything falls apart, so I cross the room to one of the bars and order an Old Fashioned with an extra cherry—there's nothing wrong with a little pat on the back for things running smoothly.

The bartender makes quick work of preparing my drink, giving me a third cherry and a wink as he pours the whiskey over the muddled sugar and bitters. Sliding the drink to me, I'm about to thank him when a strong arm wraps around my middle from behind. Immediately, I sense it's Chris and not Alex, and it's confirmed when he kisses my bare shoulder.

"You look delicious enough to eat, Mrs. Blake." It's for show—everything is with Chris. His goal is achieved as the bartender's shoulders slump in defeat.

I spin his embrace. "What do you say we auction you off one last time?"

"Only if you'll bid on me." He wiggles his eyebrows. "How much do you think I'll go for?"

Things have been easy with Chris since we got back from Hawaii, and I genuinely feel like he's trying to make this work. Granted, his motives are likely not entirely pure, but this—whatever it is—is tolerable. A few decades of light banter is *fine*. It'll help me avoid the Gallaghers, the media will never know what Alex did, and no one gets hurt.

Except Alex.

And me.

*We **both** lose.*

I rehearse my manifestation statement over and over: *Congresswoman Taylor*. If I say it enough, maybe I'll forget about Alex and how he stole a piece of my soul.

Offering a bright smile, I finally reply, "Oh, I don't know, maybe a quarter mil?"

"That's it?" he playfully scoffs, pulling me into him by my lower back. I steady myself with my hands placed on his chest, and the simple touch has his entire posture relaxing. "I would've thought at least a half."

"I'd stop bidding at three-fifty, wait until the very last second, then outbid some sweet old lady... Just to see you sweat up there. Then again, I'm the auctioneer this year, so I can't bid on you. You're on your own."

Kissing my forehead, he asks quietly, "Why wasn't it like this before?" while smiling against my skin.

"What do you mean?" I pull back and frown, even though I know *exactly* what he means.

"I don't remember us having fun. Everything was so rigid and scheduled." Chris grins at me and mocks, "*Dinner at seven-thirty with your parents tomorrow, charity event the next afternoon, media appearance that evening...*"

"That's not how I sound," I laugh, swatting his chest.

"I know, but that's how it felt. It doesn't excuse anything, but I'm realizing now more than ever that I was such a fucking idiot. I should've taken you out more, gone on more vacations, spent quality time together. Just... *more.* I've missed years with you."

Chris leans in to kiss me as a woman's throat clears behind him. "Hope I'm not interrupting."

I peer around him and find Ileah and her husband, Tim, both looking exceptionally nervous. Unable to hide my smile, and with no one else around, I step out of Chris' hold and hug her tightly.

"Not at all. I'm so happy you were able to make it." When I pull back, Chris' eyes are in narrow slits, pinned on Tim. "Chris," I say cheerfully, "You remember my friend Ileah? And, of course, you know Tim."

Chris' jaw is tight, as he musters, "Yes, of course, how could I forget?"

Inviting Ileah and Tim was a risk, but if Chris really wants this to work, I don't want to sneak away for secret coffees or book club chats. I don't expect Chris and Tim to be friends, I want to be able to invite her into our home and not have anyone feel uncomfortable.

"*You are the bridge,*" Alex's voice repeats in my head.

I take my Old Fashioned and shake it side to side. "So, am I the only one drinking tonight?"

Ileah looks at my drink for a moment longer than necessary. "Old Fashioned with extra cherry? You know, a friend of ours drinks those"—she gestures to my glass—"when he's celebrating. Tim, who was it?" *Seriously, Ileah?* He gives her a knowing look, and I am so utterly screwed. They're friends with Alex, of course they know what he drinks. My stomach twists into knots. "Are we celebrating? I hope so."

"Oh? Is it Alex?" I offer, grateful Chris didn't pick up on it first. "He told us the same thing when he came to visit us in Hawaii. Didn't he?"

Chris doesn't answer right away, so I lightly nudge his side with my elbow. "Oh, right. Yes. We were celebrating the wedding my brother missed. Drunk driver. So sad."

Fuck, how is this man in politics when he can't even tell a simple, believable fib about a drink?

Ileah shakes her head with a chuckle, likely able to see right through our lies. "Yes, your brother! That's who it was. Didn't you drink those at your wedding, Chris? I didn't realize you and Alex had so much in common." *Fuck, does she know it was Alex?* "So, what are we celebrating?" She turns to the bartender. "Excuse me, may I have a Gimlet when you have a moment?"

Directing her attention back to me, Ileah opens her mouth to say something when a silky voice behind her interrupts, "I'll have what she's having." With her eyes wide, she slowly turns until I'm able to see his side profile.

Finn.

Chris wraps his arm around my lower back, tightly gripping my hip. It's possessive and protective. "The attendees will be entering shortly, Jackie," he grits out, fear dripping from his voice.

I nod and excuse myself, "Ileah, it was so great to see you and Tim. I have to check on the silent auction. Catch up with you two later?"

Shit, she looks like she's seen a ghost. I'll have to ask her about it when there's more time. Maybe I should stay? "Yes. Later," are the only words she's able to manage.

Chris guides me away from the three of them, and once out of earshot, he quietly mutters, "The Gallaghers are dangerous men. Why did you invite him?"

"He wasn't on the guest list." *Not entirely the truth or a lie.*

"I need to find my father and see what's going on. I ran into his brother earlier, and we discussed... a few things."

I knew my intuition was correct. "Something's wrong. Are you going to be okay?"

I paint on my signature, sweet smile. "Of course. I'll be fine."

Chris pulls me into him, holding me close to his chest. As he kisses me on my forehead, I allow him to keep me against him until his heart rate slows. Once I step out of his embrace, he rushes off to find his father, and I glance behind me; Finn is no longer at the bar with Ileah and Tim. Chris is right. Something about this doesn't sit right with me, but with the gala about to begin, I don't have time to figure it out.

The auction is in full swing, and we've already raised three million dollars for my mother's foundation from the first four bachelors. If this keeps up, we won't need to do another one of these for half a decade.

I'm about to call up our next bachelor when my stomach drops, and my mouth goes dry, seeing who is still on my list to come on stage. With all eyes on me, I swallow hard and announce, "Next up, we have Mickey Gallagher." There are whispers and gasps in the crowd. "Mickey enjoys reading science fiction novels, whiskey tastings, and swimming laps in his Olympic-sized pool." I cover the mic and ask, "How much do you want me to start at?"

"How about three hundred thousand?"

That's all?

I blow out a sigh of relief. "We'll start the bidding at three hundred thousand dollars."

"Three hundred," a woman shouts, raising her paddle.

"Three hundred, do I have four hundred?"

"Four," another woman yells.

"Do I have five? Five hundred thousand for this beast of a man. Go ahead, give us a twirl, Mickey." He obliges with a smirk, raising his arms to put himself on full display and spinning slowly in place. The man truly is a beast. Easily six-five, and a wall of muscle, he's built differently than Finn, who is still tall but with a leaner physique than Mickey.

"Five-fifty," the first woman bids.

"Seven," another belts out.

It goes on for what feels like ages until a final bid of three million wins Mickey. Cheers fill the space, and I cover the mic again as he leans in, whispering, "Meet me at my office on Monday. Bring your husband with you."

"Which one?" It slips out, and I draw my lips into my mouth, stifling a laugh. If Finn knows what Alex did, surely Mickey does, too. I'm poking the bear, except the bear is a damn mafia don.

I may have had a couple of Old Fashioneds tonight, but that doesn't explain why I'm feeling so bold.

Mickey smiles wide. "I knew I liked you. Bring the one who can't keep his eyes off you tonight." I glance into the crowd and can't find Chris *or* Alex. "He's to our left, about to punch a wall because I'm talking to you." As I look over Mickey's shoulder, I spot Alex seething like a bull about to charge a matador. He pulls my hand from the microphone and says proudly into it, "Can we have a moment to applaud our beautiful auctioneer tonight? She's raised millions of dollars for our beloved cherry blossom trees."

The entire room must be drunk, with everyone erupting in excited applause. My cheeks heat at the attention, and Mickey exits the stage. I auction off the rest of the men, leaving the best—or worst—for the end.

"Last, but certainly not least, we have my brother-in-law, Alexander Blake. He loves evenings at the beach, rapid-fire debates, and long drives with intriguing company."

Really, Alex?

He takes the stage, and the moment the spotlight hits his face, his scowl is replaced with a million-dollar smile. Under his breath, he speaks through his gritted teeth, "Very funny, princess. I'm not your brother-in-law."

I knew calling him that would get under his skin, but it was worth it to see him so riled up. "We'll start the bidding at one million dollars."

There are murmurs in the crowd, just like when I announced Mickey—likely since I haven't started anyone else at a million. It only takes a few seconds before a woman raises her paddle. "One million."

"And so it begins," I chuckle. "Do I have one point five?"

"One point five," a woman with a thick Irish accent in the back bids. I don't recognize her, so she must be someone's date for the evening.

"Two," the first woman shouts forcefully.

Alex huffs a laugh beside me, drawing my attention to him. He's enjoying this far too much, and when our eyes meet, his face falls, and he quickly clears his throat. I'm distracted for far too long by his gorgeous hazel eyes that when I finally look away from him, the women are already deep into a bidding war.

"Five point five."

"Six and a quarter," the Irish woman growls.

"Seven and a quarter."

"Do I just let them duke it out?" I quietly ask Alex. He doesn't answer as the women keep going until the bidding reaches ten million dollars. There's a brief pause. "Ten million, going once... Going twice..." My heart breaks as I announce, "Sold to number four hundred fifty-six in the back." The crowd roars with excitement, while I stifle a groan.

As applause continues, Alex covers the microphone. "That's Mickey and Finn's cousin. She bought me... for you."

"For *me?* What are you talking about?"

"I was never going to go home with anyone but my wife. I'll see you in the morning, princess." He discretely slips me a hotel key card and walks off the stage.

It takes a moment for me to collect myself. This man, *this beautiful man*, had a woman buy him... for me? I inwardly swoon at the notion until reality sets in. He doesn't have ten million dollars.

The Gallaghers.

CHAPTER 40
CHRIS

The two women bidding on my brother was embarrassing, especially since I never raised more than three million... and the fact that the woman I planted in the crowd to bid on him lost. If it keeps him far away from Jaclyn, I don't care who won. The auction is for a single date, to anywhere the bachelor chooses. With the beautiful, eager redhead winning, I have no doubt that the tides are turning in my favor. It's only a matter of time before he forgets about my wife and moves on.

Jaclyn and I are exhausted after the busy few weeks we've had, so I suggested we make it an early night. As soon as everything wrapped up at the gala, we skipped the afterparties and headed to our room. I made sure to reserve the largest one available—a metaphorical honeymoon suite.

Despite my apprehension before the accident, I love being married to Jaclyn. The more time we spend together, the more confident I am that the two of us will survive this. She's the perfect woman, and the biggest regret of my life is not noticing it sooner.

I unlock the hotel door with my key card and drop it onto the front entryway table, flicking on the lights. I hold the door for Jaclyn, who looks as tired as I feel, as she carries her red strappy heels in one hand and a clutch in the other. Only a few feet inside, she places her clutch on the table and tosses her shoes haphazardly onto the floor.

"Can you unzip me?" She huffs out a breath. "I'm probably going straight to bed with my makeup on."

I guide her by the small of her back further into the suite, turning on lights as we go. On the dining table, I find the red roses that I had delivered next to a single blue rose. Jaclyn pauses for me to help her with the dress as a growl is stuck in my chest, unable to tear my eyes from the flower. There's no card, but I know damn well that rose is from my brother.

"Everything okay?" she asks sleepily.

I pick the rose off the table and toss it into the trash. She follows my movements but doesn't react. Either she's too tired or doesn't care.

Maybe she's already over him, and chose me?

"Yeah, everything's fine." I step behind her to unclasp the top of her dress and unzip it until it stops just above her ass.

Holding the crimson fabric with her arm over her chest, she turns. "Thank you."

Jaclyn's hate that she used to hide behind her eyes has diminished, and I breathe a sigh of relief that this woman may finally be mine. I close the distance and slide my hand into her hair, kissing her softly. She doesn't melt into me, but she doesn't fight me, either.

"Tonight was amazing; you did an incredible job. While you get ready for bed, I'll set up my CPAP, and we'll call it a night."

It earns me a small smile, and she makes her way through the bedroom to the ensuite, turning on the shower. Opening my suitcase, I take out a pair of boxers and set them aside. As much as I'd love to sleep naked with her, I don't want to push my luck.

While she showers, I pour distilled water into the plastic compartment of my CPAP machine and make sure everything is plugged in properly. The water shuts off in the bathroom after what has to be the quickest shower Jaclyn has ever taken. She emerges from the ensuite with a white towel wrapped under her arms and another on top of her head, twisted in her hair.

"My turn, already?"

"You could've joined me," she chuckles coyly.

I shrug as nonchalantly as I can as my heart leaps at the thought that things are starting to really look up between us. "I didn't think you wanted me to."

343

"I mean, you probably would've had to hold me up. I almost fell asleep in there." She gestures with her thumb to the bathroom.

"We should get you to bed before you fall asleep on your feet, Mrs. Auctioneer." Grabbing my boxers, I head toward the bathroom, kissing her cheek as I pass her.

After taking a shower, I climb into bed, finding her asleep. Her damp hair is braided, and she's naked for the first time since the accident. Looking back and forth between the CPAP and my wife, there's no way I could curl up behind her with that thing strapped to my face. At first, I wrap my arms around her, loving the feel of her naked back pressed against my chest, but as I begin to drift off to sleep, guilt seeps in. The last thing I want is to wake her with my snoring; she needs her sleep after the busy night we've had.

Jaclyn's right. I should take my health more seriously.

I kiss her shoulder and whisper against her soft skin, "I love you, Jackie."

Her sleepy, mildly robotic sigh of "I love you, too" is all the reassurance I need. *We're going to be okay.* I turn over and fit the mask over my nose and mouth, then turn on the machine. As I breathe deeply for several minutes, my mind begins to conjure 'what ifs.'

What if she's forgiven me, and we get to live in marital bliss, putting this all behind us?

What if when we get home, she suggests we try for a baby?

The thought of practicing has my cock tenting in my boxers as I drift off to sleep.

~

"Yes, baby, right there. I'm so close."

"Fuck, I missed this tight pussy, Jackie," I grit out between thrusts.

Meeting my rhythm, her hips piston against me, taking me deeper. Her nails digging into my triceps, I'm trying my best to keep from coming. Our breathing picks up, and she's right fucking there. I'm desperate to have her sweet cunt pulsing around my cock as she comes with me, but I can't seem to catch my breath.

With thrust after thrust, the air has completely left my lungs. I try to clutch at my chest as the vision of Jaclyn slowly fades away—first her hair, then her dark blue eyes, then the remaining features of her face... until I'm left with nothing but dark gray clouds surrounding me.

This delicious dream has turned into a fucking nightmare, and I need to wake up. I reach to pinch myself, but my limbs are heavy, and I'm no longer able to feel anything. I'm left only with an ache in my chest as I plummet into the darkness.

CHAPTER 41
ALEX

Another morning waking up alone without Jaclyn. I hoped that after I slipped her my hotel key card last night, I'd wake to her soft body tucked into my side. Fuck, I miss the feel of her in my arms, the sweet citrus scent that lingers on her skin, how fucking delicious she tastes... Mostly, I miss how my heart jumps out of my damn chest the moment she walks into a room. I blow out a long breath, unsure how much more of this torture I can take. Rubbing the sleep out of my eyes, I glance over at the alarm clock, worry coursing through me as I notice it's blinking 12:00.

Shit, what time is it? And where's Jaclyn?

A small shred of light slips through the curtains, but the room is otherwise dark. I slide out of bed and open them one at a time. They must be black-out, doing their job, because based on where the sun is in the sky blinding me, it's around eight or nine. I squint at the brightness, closing the curtains and turning on the lamp on the bedside table.

Checking my phone, there's a missed call and text from Jaclyn. I can't help my smile as I swipe to open the text.

> WIFE
>
> I need your help.

Fuck. Fuck, fuck, fuck.

It could be anything—the Gallaghers, Chris, the media...

My mind is reeling at the possibilities. The time stamp is from twenty minutes ago. I quickly text back to inquire about which room she's staying in. As soon as the room number appears on my screen, I'm scrambling to get dressed in dark gray slacks and a white button-down.

Dressed and ready to save my wife from whatever danger may present itself, I pause at the door.

I don't own a gun.

I don't even own a fucking knife.

What if she's in trouble and I can't help?

If Chris hurt her, my fist will do in a pinch. How am I supposed to protect someone I love against a bullet?

With my hand poised on the nob, I take a page out of Jaclyn's book—she always pays attention to the little details. I'll have an easier time getting to her, and potentially saving her from a shitty situation if I look like my brother. Rushing to the bathroom, I wet my travel comb and glide it through my locks until the reflection in the mirror is Chris, not me. *Close enough.* After a quick once over with my razor, I hurry to her room.

I rap my knuckles on the door incessantly until it opens. My stomach bottoms out at the sight of my gorgeous wife in a white terrycloth robe with bloodshot eyes and tear tracks down her cheeks. In an instant, I take her in my arms and hold her tight.

"What's wrong, princess?" She shakes her head, making my shirt damp as she cries against my chest. "Did he hurt you?" She shakes her head again, and I step inside, closing the door behind us. Cupping her face, my eyes search hers for an answer. "Jaclyn, you can tell me. I won't hurt him." It's a bold-faced lie. If he so much as looked at her the wrong way, I'll rearrange his face.

As I wipe away her tears with the pads of my thumbs, she sniffles with a choked sob. "Chris is..." She cries harder. "Alex, he's gone. I don't know what to do."

"He left you? *That bastard.* He couldn't have gone far. I'll call someone to track him down." I'll make sure they don't look very hard.

"No."

"No? Do you know where he went?"

Jaclyn takes a deep breath, then swallows hard. "Bedroom."

With a frown, I glance behind her to the open door leading to it. I kiss her forehead and march into the room, ready to rip into him for making her cry even a single tear. I reach the door, spotting my brother asleep in bed, his CPAP mask off and dangling from the machine by the thick tube.

"Wake up, asshole," I growl, but as I move closer, he's... gray? I'm afraid to touch him to check for a pulse. Using the back of my hand, I feel his forehead.

Ice cold.

No. This isn't happening.

His chest isn't moving.

"Wake up, asshole," I repeat, trying to shake him awake. When I finally check his pulse, there's nothing.

My mind is racing a million miles a minute as my own tears begin to fall and all the air leaves my lungs. I pivot in place, spotting Jaclyn where I left her. Except she's clutching her knees on the floor, shaking and crying. Did she kill him? Or maybe the Gallaghers? They mentioned on a few occasions they wanted him out of the way. But this? If they are responsible for taking my family from me, they will fucking pay.

Finally able to catch my breath, I will away my tears and return to Jaclyn. Legs tucked into her chest, I fall beside her and brush the hair away from her face. "Shh, I'm here. It's going to be okay." It's the first lie I've ever told her, but it's the best I've got, and I want it to be true.

I lift her onto my lap, and we weep together in silence for several minutes, though it could be several hours. Time doesn't exist. One thing's for certain, I know in my soul Jaclyn isn't to blame for this.

A swirl of grief and anger courses through me from discovering my brother dead in their bed, but even through my pain, I can't imagine what she's going through right now.

My beautiful, sweet, incredible wife had to wake up next to his lifeless body...

I'm still in shock as pain fills my chest. I lost a man who I've shared everything with since we were conceived—fuck, we even shared Jaclyn. As much as I love her, I'd give up what we have if it meant he was still alive. He wasn't a good man, but neither am I... He didn't deserve to die.

"I'll kill him. And his brother."

Pulling back, she studies me. "Wh-what?"

"The Gallaghers, they have to be behind this."

"I don't... I don't think so. There was some sort of power outage." She points to the time on the microwave, which is blinking 12:00. With her breath shaky, she cries, "This is all my fault! He was supposed to see the cardiologist and pulmonologist tomorrow. I should have insisted he bring the other machine. The CPAP at home has a backup battery; he brought the travel one. It was off when I woke up."

With the power out in my room, too, the whole hotel must have been down at some point last night. I breathe a little easier; it wasn't a targeted attack on my brother. Tears threaten again, but this time, I don't let them fall. I need to be strong for Jaclyn right now and keep a level head. I'll need to make sure that she talks to a vetted psychologist when this is all over. Fuck, we both should.

"It's not your fault. If the CPAP stopped working, any number of things could've happened. A medical examiner will confirm if it was an accident."

"What do we do? Do we call the police?"

"No." I shake my head. "I'll call Ned. He'll know what to do."

Jaclyn nods, wiping her eyes and nose with the sleeve of her robe. I help her up and settle her on the couch. After taking a couple of deep breaths, I take my phone out of my back pocket to call him.

"Mr. Blake. To what do I owe the pleasure?" he answers on the second ring, grunting as if he's lifting weights at a gym.

"We have a... *situation* in my brother's room at the hotel the gala was at last night."

"I can come by in an hour or two. I have another *situation* right now."

"This is a *'life or death'* one," I grumble. "If you catch my drift."

Ned chuckles, "Oh, yeah? Seems to be a lot of those

happening this morning. Are you and Ms. Taylor all right?"

"Depends on what your definition of 'all right' is, *Ned*."

"Down, tiger. What do you need? A doctor? Someone to handle PR? I can send whoever you need."

"Not sure yet." I shake my head, and begin pacing, raking my hand through my hair. "We need to keep this between us for now until we figure out what to do. What time can you be here?"

He grunts, and there is a loud thud through the phone. "I can call a guy to wrap up for me here and be up to your room in about fifteen minutes."

Fifteen minutes?

"Are you here? At the hotel?"

"You know, I cannot confirm or deny that," he laughs. "See you in fifteen, Mr. Blake."

I keep Jaclyn tucked into my side for the next twelve minutes, stroking her hair and praising how well she's doing with everything, all the while trying to keep my own emotions stuffed down. I don't know how I'll tell my parents or what we'll tell the world, but right now, my only priority is making sure my wife is all right. I can fall apart later.

CHAPTER 42
JACLYN

There's a knock at the door, and Alex kisses my temple, whispering, "I'll be right back, I promise."

He slides my legs off his lap and answers the door to a tall man, with dark hair wearing all black, who I can only assume is Ned. As he enters, Alex whispers something to him, and he blows out a long, exaggerated breath, shaking his head. Once Ned spots me on the couch, he crosses the room and takes a seat on the coffee table in front of me, elbows on his knees and hands steepled. I do my best to rein in my emotions, but the tears still track down my cheeks.

Ned's voice is quiet and reassuring when he speaks to me. "Ms. Taylor, I'm Ned Collins. All of this has to be incredibly scary for you. Rest assured, I'm here to help. I've worked with more than half of Washington, including your family, and when someone is in a bit of a pickle, they call me. I know it's a lot to take in, but consider me your personal genie; your wish is my command."

"He's dead," I croak.

With a sad smile, Ned nods in solidarity and reaches out his hand. I take it and he envelopes mine with both of his. "I heard. There are a few options for us at this point since resurrection isn't my specialty." My lip tilts at his attempt at humor. He releases my hand and sits back, ticking his pointer, middle, then ring finger as he rattles them off. "We can move Christopher and stage his death elsewhere; call the police and tell them the truth; or my personal favorite, have him go missing for a month until a random person finds him in the Alaskan tundra."

"What happens with each option?" Alex chimes in. His tone is void of all emotion and I'm not sure what to make of it.

Ned glances over his shoulder at Alex, then back to me. Bouncing his gaze between us gives me confidence that this is really a joint decision—I don't have to do this alone, and neither does Alex. "If we make his death an accident somewhere elsewhere, the country will mourn, but ultimately, everything will go back to normal. If he goes missing, his name will be in the news for weeks, maybe even months. So, as fun as that one is, you'll be on edge until the body is found. And if we call the police, well, you risk being a murder suspect. Though you're not guilty... You're not guilty, right?" I nod. "It won't matter. Even the idea that you could be will put off voters."

"We should move him. Give him a dignified death," Alex replies confidently, but I know him. He doesn't sound sure of himself, looking to me for strength.

"Yes, we should move him," I agree, and Alex gives me a small lopsided smile.

"I'll warn you; the country believes you're married to Christopher. So, there's a good chance you could be appointed as the new Senator of Florida until the next election. You and the other Mr. Blake will never be together."

Alex's jaw is tight, eyes full of pain. He's lost his brother, and now he's about to lose me. As he rubs the back of his neck, he lets out a short, humorless laugh. "Well, princess, welcome to the Senate."

"No." I shake my head vigorously. "I don't want it. I mean... I do, but not like this. If I'm serving our country, I want it to be because the voters wanted me."

Ned chuckles. "No wonder Finn and Mickey like you. There is one more option, but it's risky, and we would need President Blake and President Taylor's buy-in. Both of them need to support it for it to work, but it means you two could be together like a fucking romance novel."

"We're piling lies on top of lies here," I sigh and wave my hand dismissively. "So, sure, what is this risky option?"

I pull my robe tightly around me as Ned says the words I never expected. "Alex dies."

"What?" Alex and I bark in unison.

"Alex dies," he repeats. "We move Chris and put together an incident report that Alex died in some heroic effort. Pick whatever feels more on-brand. Saving a child from being hit by a bus? Falling to his death when climbing Mount Kilimanjaro? I don't care what story you go with, but we kill Alex. Then, we bury Chris as Alex."

"How does that solve anything?" My brows pinch, unable to follow his logic. He studies me for a minute until it hits me. My eyes widen with hope. "Alex runs for President."

"Not quite." Ned huffs a laugh. "There are people I work for that will never allow that to happen. So, if you want to do this, Alex continues the charade he began at your wedding. You remain the dutiful wife of the Floridian Senator. But Christopher Blake will *never* be President."

"Why not?" I inquire. "Alex would be an amazing president, even if he's pretending to be his brother."

"I wouldn't. And you've thought about this a bit too much, Ned," Alex grits out, arms folded over his chest.

"Nah, I came up with this one on the fly." Ned winks. "My mind is just sick and twisty from schlepping dead bodies today."

Dead bodies? Plural?

"What about Jaclyn? Out of all the options, when does she get a seat at the table?" Alex's eyes burn into me, not with the anger or sadness from earlier, but with love. "This should be her choice, she deserves"—he swallows thickly—"she deserves better than being a senator's wife."

"As adorable as that is, with Chris dead, the Gallaghers will probably back an extreme candidate to win the next presidential election. It's my understanding that you're both privy to their insistence that Jaclyn will take the White House in 2028 as a moderate?"

"Why does everyone want me to run?" I stand and move toward the window. It isn't a pretty view, mostly office buildings and traffic, but I need my space to think; if only for a minute.

Can I do this?

"I don't want it. I'll arrange Chris' vacancy," Alex announces. "Jaclyn can have Florida."

I spin in place. "This is your chance to make big changes there. You always talk about how you can do so much more good in the Senate than the White House. Florida needs you, just like Texas does."

A hint of smirk pulls at his lips. "They need *you*."

"Alex," I breathe, "I'm not ready."

"What about Texas?" Ned offers, looking at his phone. Alex and I keep our focus trained on him. "If we fake his death, Texas will be up for grabs. I'm no political scientist, but based on what I'm reading here, they'll call for a special election. Throw your name in the hat?"

"I don't want Florida," Alex seethes through gritted teeth. "I'll step down."

"Then do it. What you do or don't do with Christopher's seat doesn't concern me." Ned waves him off dismissively before addressing me, "Ms. Taylor, this is your call. I am beholden to no specific person, so if your parents, or even the Gallaghers, don't agree, they can eat glass. Figuratively, but also literally for the right price. Right now, I work for *you*... Within reason, of course."

Alex crosses the room and wraps me in his arms, kissing the top of my head and speaking into my hair, "I've had enough loss for one day. I can't lose you. I'll be Chris, if you want, but in the end, this is your choice." He keeps his voice low. "I'll happily retire from politics if it means I get to see you as Madame President."

"I won't let you throw away your career. I've told you, I'm not ready," I sigh and tilt my chin to look up at him. Alex's brown-hazel eyes don't leave mine, and part of me lets the world around us fade away until it's just us in this moment.

Ned stands and loudly brushes at his thighs. "Okay, lovebirds, if we're set on moving the body, I'll arrange another room for you to stay in and hash out what happens after."

Ignoring Ned, I tell Alex, "You can't do this. It's not worth it. We'll bury Chris, and I'll live my best widow life. I can't let you throw away everything you've worked for on top of this."

"I won't lose you, Jaclyn. I can't. Chris is gone. He's fucking gone. I'm not"—Alex chokes on a sob—"I refuse to lose the love of my life on the same day that I lost my brother. I won't survive it." Alex breaks his gaze from me to tell Ned, "I'll do it. Arrange my death, we bury Chris as me, and Jaclyn will run in the Texas special election, if she wants it."

"Ms. Taylor? Is that what you want?" Ned cautiously asks.

I shake my head, chewing on my lower lip. "What if I lose Texas? Then, what? All of these lies will be for nothing."

"You won't lose, you're ready, princess. You've always been ready. Let me do this for you?"

Alex's eyes are so earnest that I can't help believing him. "I'll need a lot more rapid-fires."

"Oh, fuck," Ned groans. "Don't tell me you're adding arson. You know that's an extra charge, right?"

"No," I chuckle softly, not letting Alex out of my sight. "If Alex thinks I'm ready, we'll do it."

Ned's face morphs into a wide, genuine smile. "Well, consider it done. How is it that I'm able to satisfy four clients before I've had lunch? The stars must be aligned. I should find some astrology chick to confirm tomorrow's plans are equally compatible... First, I'll reach out to both of your parents to iron out a few details and make sure everything is set to move Christopher."

"What about Chris?" Alex asks Ned. "We need to make sure he has a proper burial."

"And he will. I'll leave the story up to you and your parents, but I'll take care in moving his body, and once you agree on how you want him to die as Alex officially, I'll stage it. I still think you should go with the Alaskan tundra."

"You enjoy this far too much, you know," Alex rebuts.

Ned shrugs. "It's my job. But what are we going to do about you two?" He gestures between us. "Legally, you're not even married to Chris."

"Then, it's about time my wife and I made it official."

CHAPTER 43
ALEX
TWO WEEKS LATER

"My brother was an incredible man who did so much for Texas and our country. I can't think of a better way to honor Alexander's memory than to have another Blake represent the state he loved so much. Regardless of the outcome of the special election, I will not be seeking reelection in Florida, to support my wife in her political career."

Cheers erupt from the large crowd, and I tuck my wife under my arm, kissing her temple as they chant "Tay-lor" over and over. I insisted that Jaclyn keep her maiden name, and thankfully, both families agreed. I'm unsure if glass eating was threatened for everyone to fall in line, but when Ned is involved, no one can be sure.

It's no surprise that the people of Texas love Jaclyn, and though my heart is broken after my brother's death, I'm finding it easier with each day that passes. Having Jaclyn by my side helps; the nights are hard for both of us.

When no one is around, we let our masks fall, and I'm grateful neither of us has to do this alone.

A week ago, we buried my brother—technically me. The staged incident involved 'Alex' assisting with the building of a homeless shelter in El Paso, and falling off the roof in a tragic accident. We went out of our way to never say 'Alex' during the funeral, to properly pay our respects to Chris.

Attending your own funeral is an interesting experience. No one has a negative comment about you, and the general consensus is that you died 'too soon.' At one point, I had to keep from laughing at the celebration of life party my family planned when my grandmother insisted that the wrong brother died. Whiskey has always been her weakness. Ironically, Gallagher Whiskey is her favorite.

Jaclyn agreed to run, so long as the Gallaghers stayed far away from her campaign. Though, I have no doubt they are 'helping' in the background. The meddling isn't what you would expect from a crime family. Their most recent, quiet endeavor is funding additional polling locations in suburban and rural areas of swing states. Despite their noble efforts, I still don't trust them.

Watching my wife make the announcement she was born to in front of a sea of no less than three thousand people, I've never been so proud of someone in my life. Yet, the little voice in the back of my mind chastises, *"She deserves this more than you do."* It stings that I have to put my career on hold, but I have my whole life to serve my country, even if I have to do it as Chris. She would've waited for him; I can wait for her.

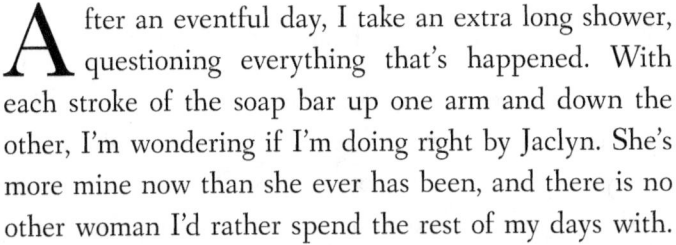

After an eventful day, I take an extra long shower, questioning everything that's happened. With each stroke of the soap bar up one arm and down the other, I'm wondering if I'm doing right by Jaclyn. She's more mine now than she ever has been, and there is no other woman I'd rather spend the rest of my days with. But... this isn't the life she signed up for. Scrubbing the shampoo in my hair, my guilt gets the best of me. The suds aren't washing away the overwhelming feeling of inadequacy—I don't deserve to enjoy or keep her.

The sliding door opens, and Jaclyn steps inside. She doesn't give me a moment to say anything when she wraps her arms around my middle, pressing her cheek to my chest as the water soaks her hair and back. I hold her close, and we stand there in silence for what feels like seconds and years simultaneously. Having her in my arms grounds me, banishing any doubts I ever had that we were made for each other.

Resting my chin on the top of her head, I whisper, "I love you, princess."

"You shouldn't. I was going to stay with Chris," Jaclyn quietly admits, hugging me tighter. "I was going to make it work with him and try to forget about us." It stings to hear her speak the words that I already felt were true. "You know that poem about the road less traveled?"

"Robert Frost?"

"That's the one. I wasn't ready to fight for this, for us."

Our hearts beat in sync as I dare to ask, "And now?"

I pull back enough to tilt her chin to look at me, and her eyes are so full of love and regret. "You were right. It was always supposed to be you and me. I still can't believe he's gone, but I need you to know I made the wrong choice. Alex, I'd throw everything away, any chance I have in politics, if it meant that I remained *your* wife. We can still make an announcement that you're seeking reelection, and I can—"

My lips crash into hers in a searing kiss. "No," I sigh as that cute little hum of hers makes me smile. "It's your turn to shine, princess."

"You shine enough for the both of us." Jaclyn melts into me as she continues speaking against my lips. "I couldn't do any of this without you." Her tongue tangles with mine and I let the world around me fall away. When we break apart, her words burrow deep into my soul. "The love I feel for you isn't like what I had with Chris or... *anyone.* I'm sorry he died too young, but I'm trying to see the good in the bad. *You* are my husband, even before he died. Through all of this, you've been my rock, my cheer-leader... You're the love of my fucking life." I can't help my chuckle at the rare curse. "I don't deserve you. I love you so damn much, and... I'm sorry. I'm sorry I didn't choose you."

"I don't blame you." Taking her face in my hands, I brush a soft kiss to her forehead. "There is nothing to apologize for."

"Are you really sure about all of this? You're giving up the state you love."

"I've never been so sure of anything in my life. Yes, I love Texas, but I love you and our country more. The moment we stood up in front of our families, I knew that this was never going to be fake for me. When I spoke my vows to you, I meant every word."

"You went off script," she chuckles.

"Are you sure?" I cock an eyebrow.

"We should have that vow renewal we talked about when we were in Hawaii." Lifting onto her toes, she presses her warm, wet lips to mine, and I can't help kissing her back harder. The soft hum every time my mouth touches her settles me in a way I never imagined possible. I nip at her bottom lip, and she repeats the vows I spoke to her when she married me, "I pledge to love, cherish, protect, and be devoted to you, now and forever... *Alex.*"

CHAPTER 44
JACLYN

A feral rumble comes from Alex's chest as I speak his vows back to him. Before I can properly tease him about sounding like a damn animal, he has my legs wrapped around his waist, roughly pressing my back against the shower wall.

We haven't touched each other since... *Hawaii?* Has it been that long? Why does it feel like it was just yesterday that we spent our days on the beach and nights with him buried inside me?

With the whirlwind of returning from paradise, the gala, Chris' death, and my political campaign, it's no wonder he hasn't touched me. I've missed it, missed *him*. This beautiful, selfless man did delicious things to my body that set my soul on fire. More than that, he always believed in me. To say I love him is the understatement of the century.

His fingers dimple my ass as he pulls me closer, his cock testing my entrance. "Say it again, Jaclyn." It comes out as a growl, and I'm selfishly pleased that Hawaii wasn't just a fluke. None of this was.

"Which part?"

He tilts his head to the left, our noses brushing, stopping short of kissing me. "Say it." His voice is almost pained; my fun, playful Alex is nowhere to be found.

"Hey, what's wrong?" As he sucks in a choked breath, I instinctively wrap my arms tighter around him and kiss my favorite spot on his neck. "Alex," I say softly, nipping at his earlobe as I pull back. I need him to look me in the eyes when I tell him my truths. "I love you. I married *you*. You're my husband. I chose a man who may have loved me in his own way, but he wasn't..." I take a deep breath, unable to help smiling. "He wasn't you. It was all a mistake. I. Love. You. And if I weren't a coward, I would've loved you the way you deserve years ago. I lo—"

Our lips collide in a swirl of lust and desperation. "You're perfect," he murmurs against my lips. Yes, I want him inside me, but I need him to really hear me. I'm not the perfect one, he is. Alex is handing over everything he's worked years to build, I don't take that lightly.

In the end, he's mine, and I'm his.

"Wait, wait, wait! One more thing... Rapid fire." His hearty chuckle fills the bathroom, and I think it's the first time I've heard him this light since...

I shake away the thought.

"Okay, princess, what'cha got for me?"

"Birth control."

His eyes are molten, just like I hoped they would be, and a cocky grin tilts his lip. As his cock glides against my clit, I stifle a moan when he answers, "Should be left up to the couple using it."

"Is that an answer on behalf of a senator or my husband?" I pant, unable to contain my desperation for this beautiful man.

"I'm going to claim every inch of you as mine, and if that results in a child... Well, it's a good thing I'm no longer seeking reelection."

My fun, mischievous Alex is back, and my heart does a damn summersault. Sadly, my glee comes to a screeching stop as my impostor syndrome seeps in. "What if I lose?"

"You won't."

"What if you're wrong?" I groan at the friction of his thick cock grinding against my clit, wishing he was already inside me. "I'm unprepared."

"You know I'm *never* unprepared. So, you won't be either." He finally slides me onto him until our hips connect. I don't care if this is stress, mourning, or Alex's breeding kink that he absolutely hinted at in Hawaii. I need him more than I need to fucking breathe. There's no other man I'd rather have a child with than him.

As he thrusts in and out of me, my gasps become louder and unavoidable. I reach for the shower lever to shut off the now-lukewarm water, and Alex carries me over to the bed, both of us still drenched.

"I haven't had you since..."

"Hawaii," I finish. "I know."

"It feels like it's been a hundred years."

"So dramatic." I playfully roll my eyes as his sear into me.

"Fuck, I love you," he laughs, his beaming smile I missed so dearly lighting up his face.

Alex tosses me onto to the bed, and with his hands braced on either side of me, I reach between us to guide him back inside me, but he swats my hand away. "No, my beautiful wife. What did I tell you about that?" I bite my lip and scoot up the bed until my head hits the pillows. Spreading my legs wide to taunt him, he growls, "*Fuck.*" It's drawn out and heady. Heat pools between my legs at the single word.

"You said you want to claim every inch of me. I can think of a few places you can start."

A delicious snarl erupts from him as he lowers his face to my pussy, slowly licking up my seam and groaning. How he can enjoy it is still beyond me, but when he sucks on my clit, I'm lost to my own bliss. Pressing two fingers inside me, he starts carefully, and I'm quickly full when he adds a third. I can't seem to catch my breath.

"You can take it, beautiful. You've branded yourself on every inch of my soul, it's my turn to return the favor. Tomorrow, you're going to wake up so fucking spent, there will be no doubt we belong to each other," Alex assures me.

My fingers tangle in his wet hair as he laps at me like a starved man. I feel initial shame as my legs shake and clamp around his ears, until he spreads me wider, and I have an out-of-body experience. The moment his fingers curl inside me, my back arches against the pillows, and I scream out, already so close to coming. Chuckling against my pussy, he thinks this is a damn game, and I can't take it a moment longer. Falling further into ecstasy, he thankfully doesn't make me wait, and in an instant, my vision blurs, and I'm lost to my orgasm.

Alex slows the pace of his tongue and carefully drags his slick fingers from me. I anticipate this being a mirror of Hawaii, but he doesn't suck his fingers clean. His hand wanders lower until he's teasing my...

"What are you doing?"

"I thought I was clear: I'm claiming every inch of you tonight. I need to be sure you're ready to take my cock." He is so sure, not an ounce of hesitation in his voice, as if this is no different than ordering a coffee or scheduling a business meeting.

Ass fucking at five? Let me consult my schedule... Why, of course I'll fit it in.

It will not in fact fit in. There's no way.

"Alex," I carefully warn, "I thought that was just a sexy thing to say." I keep my tone light, almost singing.

"When have I ever lied to you?" He cocks an eyebrow.

"No one has ever..." I can't even finish the damn sentence.

"Do you trust me?"

I reply with a nod, but confess, "I just assumed you'd suggest a game of 'how many times can I make Jaclyn come before the melatonin kicks in,' or something. But... *Wait*. No. I didn't mean *that* 'butt.' I—"

He barks a laugh. "You know that I'll never hurt you, princess, and if something doesn't feel right... Strike that, if something doesn't feel *amazing*, we stop." I'm so out of my league here, doubt creeping in—maybe this is why Chris was never faithful? "Jaclyn," he growls, bringing my attention back to him. "I'm not Chris."

"How did you... Did I say something? I thought I was a master at keeping my thoughts internal but—"

Alex lays down beside me, pulling me into his chest and intertwining our legs like a human pretzel. "Shh. Come here. You're the love of my life. My wife. Mine. As much as I love the idea of you choking on my cock, then fucking you until you're blinded by your orgasm, followed up by having you ride my face, and finish by taking that beautiful ass of yours... More than anything, I need *you*. It's never been only physical for me."

"Well, when you sell it like that..."

"I have a lifetime to fuck you in every position in the damn Kama Sutra if that's what we want to do. You're too tight for me to fuck your ass tonight, anyway." He huffs a small laugh, and I can't help joining in the levity. "For now, having you in my arms is more than I ever could've asked for."

I turn us until we're both on our sides, and my leg is slung over his hip, then reach between us until his cock is nudging at my soaked pussy. I expect him to fight me. Unwilling to risk another grandiose declaration, I desperately grind myself onto him until he's seated inside me, his balls hitting my ass. My adorable husband isn't having it and rolls me onto my back until he's able to thrust deep and hard into me.

His name comes out as a strangled whimper from my lips, making him chuckle darkly. "That's right, princess. I may be Chris to the rest of the world, but when I fuck you, you scream your *husband's* name."

"Harder, Alex," I manage through ragged breaths.

"Is my good little wife needing more?

"*Yes.*"

My pleas spur him on—driving into me harder, deeper, but because it's Alex, never faster. Our bodies collide feverishly, as if the other person might disappear. I don't realize my eyes are shut until my head falls back further onto the pillow, and Alex grips the front of my throat, pulling me to him, capturing my lips with his. Continuing his punishing thrusts, I'm moments away from coming, and I hook my legs behind him, forcing our bodies impossibly closer.

My orgasm rolls through me, wave after exquisite wave, unlike anything I've ever experienced. I can't speak, I'm not entirely sure I know how to breathe, my whole body is buzzing. Kissing me fiercely, Alex keeps the same pace and, in a few shallow thrusts, joins me in this oblivion.

Even several minutes after our heart rates have slowed, I refuse to let go of him, and he doesn't pull out. Rocking me onto my side and remaining inside me, he kisses my forehead with his sweet vow, "I promise to love, cherish, protect, and be devoted to you, now and forever," as both of us drift off to sleep.

EPILOGUE — JACLYN
FIVE YEARS LATER

Cheers explode in the large venue as my best friend is announced as the Vice President Elect. Winning the presidency with Ileah as my running mate has my heart swelling with pride. While a two-woman ticket was incredibly risky, even more of a gamble was having a two-party ticket. Over the past couple of years, we have worked hard to ensure our platforms are moderate enough to appeal to the majority of voters, giving us the highest approval ratings in the Senate. It all paid off.

I never wanted help from the Gallaghers, and thankfully, Alex and Ileah ensured they never interfered with the election. We ran a clean campaign, and won by a slim margin, with a last-minute endorsement from the Governor of Arizona. He helped us swing the state in our favor, to win exactly two hundred and seventy electoral votes to secure the White House.

Ileah takes to the podium, while her husband and their one-year-old daughter, Devon, remain backstage with Alex and me. We've tried for our own children, but even after several rounds of IVF, I wasn't able to conceive. The stress of the campaign trail didn't help. As soon as I'm out of the White House, we plan on trying one more time, and if it isn't meant to be, we'll be adopting.

For now, I make one hell of an auntie to Devon. She's adorable, with bright green eyes and a hint of red in her otherwise light brown hair, always moving and wanting to run before she can walk—so much like her father. He keeps her on his hip as Ileah gives her speech. If it were up to me, I'd let Devon crawl around the stage. Publicity be damned.

As I'm listening, I notice a small, black toy in Devon's hand. She's fiddling with it, and Alex's grip on my hip tightens, hissing my name. Devon continues playing with it, and my eyes fly wide.

"Hey, Devon, sweetie. Where did you find that? It's mine. May I have it back?"

Her dad looks down at the toy, which isn't a toy at all. It's a remote to a vibrating butt plug Alex bought for us. My poor husband's pupils are blown, and I immediately regret asking him to use it.

"I got you two presents for tonight. Thought we could have a little fun while you announce to the world that you'll be the first Madame President."

I open the box and burst out in laughter at the sight of a small clit vibrator, and an anal plug. "If you're going to make me wear it, you're using this." I hold up the plug.

"Well, if I have the plug, keep in mind that you're going to have something much larger up your ass later."

"That's fair," I chuckle. "Okay, hurry up, we're going to be late."

I attempt to take the remote from Devon, but she clutches it to her chest. Her father gets a closer look, and when his eyes meet mine, a swirl of fear and humor dance in them. Based on the stories I've heard from Ileah after one too many glasses of wine, he likely knows precisely what this remote goes to, or at least that it is paired to an item inside someone. I'm just thankful it's not me.

With Devon unwilling to relinquish the remote, I return to Alex, who is doing his best to remain upright, and insist, "Go to the bathroom and remove it."

"No, I can take it," he grits out.

"Alex, this is not the time." I never use his real name unless I'm angry or if I'm coming—which is sometimes at the same time. The only one close enough to overhear is Ileah's husband, who is privy to our unique situation. "If I can't get the remote from her, it's only going to get worse..."

If the look on his face is any indication, it absolutely got worse.

Ileah looks back at us in the alcove; we're likely making a scene. I'm ruining this for her, so I whisper-shout to Alex, "Go."

Thankfully, he listens and rushes off the stage. Two minutes later, he returns. "Fuck, that was a close one."

"No more fun and games," I huff. "You're going to be First Gentleman."

"The offer still stands to be your personal chair behind the Resolute desk," he quips beside my ear, his warm breath tickling my neck. My thighs clench at the thought, heightened by his soft kiss to my shoulder. "Shall I use my own remote while you're out there?"

"You two are worse than when my dogs are in heat," Ileah's husband growls. "Give me the damn remote."

There's a silent standoff, but Alex finally pulls it from his pocket and removes the small battery before handing it to him. He gives it to Devon, who is elated by this turn of events. "Now, go out there and be your brilliant self, princess."

"For the record, I thought you were brilliant first," I retort and Alex grumbles, making me laugh.

Our attention returns to Ileah as she wraps up her speech with, "She's a bridge that brings together all Americans," and beams, "So, it is my pleasure to introduce to you *your* President-Elect of the United States of America, Jaclyn Taylor."

BONUS EPILOGUE
ILEAH - THE GALA

Tonight was incredible. Between the beautiful decor Jaclyn coordinated, the lively music, and watching the bachelors auctioned off to women with entirely too much money, I don't remember the last time I had this much fun at a gala.

Settled in bed with Tim fast asleep, I count the minutes until it's 2 a.m. In thirty, my husband's political future will be secure. The Gallaghers didn't give me the details other than it would be solved by two this morning—the less I know, the better. Exhausted from the night, I finally close my eyes, giddy that Tim will have another term in the Senate.

Several minutes later, I'm half asleep when there's a loud click of the door unlocking with a key card. My eyes flutter open, and I mumble to Tim, "Everything okay?"

He doesn't answer. Instead, there's a strange gurgling sound. I sit up and turn on a light, but it doesn't work.

The alarm clock is blinking 12:00; there must've been a power outage. Using the flashlight on my phone, I find Tim next to me, hand on his neck, choking on his own blood.

"Tim!" I shriek, tossing my phone aside, even if it's the only light illuminating the room. His face is cast in shadows as my hands instinctively reach for his throat to keep him from bleeding out. I'm unable to stop the crimson syrup from spilling from him. "I'll get help." Before I can reach for my phone again, his watery breath ceases. "No! Stay with me, baby!"

I press my ear to his chest.

Nothing.

Check his pulse.

Also, nothing.

"Don't you dare die on me." Placing one palm over the other, I shove my hands against his chest to the rhythm of "Staying Alive" by the Bee Gees. I continue chest compressions for over a minute, more blood gushing from his neck.

Tears fall as he remains breathless. I pick up the hotel to dial 911, but the line is dead. My cell phone has no reception. I attempt to use the WiFi; also out.

Sliding off the bed, my fight-or-flight response finally does what's supposed to; the fight outweighing the flight. Someone sliced my husband's throat, but I never heard the door open a second time. Whoever did this could still be here.

I may be next.

As I take a quick survey of the room, the sharpest item in here is a plastic spork. Then, I spot the two champagne flutes from earlier. I snatch one and smash it against the table. There are four sharp peaks; if I aim properly, I can do enough damage to get away.

There's a small rustle in the closet, confirmation that they are still here.

My options are slim:

1. Make a run for it and risk whoever is in there catching me first.
2. Murder this motherfucker and call someone to clean it up.

I have no desire to die tonight, so option two it is.

Keeping my back flush with the wall next to the closet, I'll wait him, or her, out. My hands shake, the champagne flute raised next to my head, ready to attack. They likely assume I'm still in here, so I open and close the bathroom door, hoping they'll believe I've fled, then return to my spot on the wall.

If this is how I die, I'll go down swinging.

My heart stops, sucking in a breath when the air conditioning roars to life and the lamp on the bedside table turns on. I wait several minutes and stifle a scream when the closet door opens. Still poised to attack whoever is in there, the moment they come into view, I jab the broken flute into their neck, effortlessly slicing through their flesh. Blood spurts from the puncture as they crumple to the ground, grasping the glass and pulling it from the wound. There's a vase with faux flowers sitting on the table. I run for it and launch it at their head. My aim is perfect, striking them in the temple, and they fall flat, lying lifeless on the ground.

Looking back at my husband, his face is now white, and my heart plummets. This wasn't a random hotel break in. Whoever this man on the floor is, he planned it. He had access to a key card—or at least found a way to have a universal one made.

Could it be one of Tim's opponents?

Rage fills me, and not giving a fuck that I'm barefoot, I stomp once on his neck. It crunches beneath my heel, and the satisfaction momentarily eases my anger.

"That's for killing my husband." I stomp a second time, more blood seeping from his neck and mouth. "And that's for thinking you can fuck with a Vasileiou."

With everything that's happened, there's only one person I could call about this who would be able to help me. Unfortunately, I'd rather join this asshole on the ground in a bloody death than call him. I settle for his brother instead. The phone rings twice, and he picks up.

Without giving him a chance to say 'hello,' I growl, "I need a cleaner. Right fucking now."

LOVED ARRANGED VACANCY?

I hope you loved reading Jaclyn's story as much as I loved writing it!

Wherever you feel most comfortable, please consider leaving a review on Goodreads, Amazon, or social media! Your honest review means the world to me.

To keep up with all of my upcoming releases, be sure to follow me over on Amazon!

xoxo,
Irene

P.S. As you may have guessed, Ileah's story is up next in Absolute Majority!

ACKNOWLEDGMENTS

Thank you so much to my amazing readers who took a chance on this book! I know it's unlike anything I've ever written, and I hope you enjoyed it all the same.

To my fabulous alpha readers, Alex and Alicia — thank you for being on this journey with me and making sure Jaclyn's story wasn't absolute trash. I couldn't have done it without you

To my incredible beta readers, Amanda, Megan, and Jasmine — I'm so grateful for you three reading this book before I sent it out into the world! I appreciate your encouragement so much!

To my ARC readers, thank you for being so supportive and reading my silly little political romance I came up with while drunk and talking with my work-wife. I appreciate you taking the chance on me.

Huge thank you to Katie and Kendra from Spice Me Up Editing for making sure this novella was absolutely perfect! You ladies are absolute queens!

And finally, to my friends and family, thank you for loving me as the hot mess that I am.

ABOUT IRENE

Irene Bahrd is a feisty Capricorn and one of the most avid readers you will ever meet. Her favorite genres to read or write include romantic comedies, political romance, romantasy, and the occasional contemporary or dark romance.

She started her writing journey as a dare from a friend, after recounting dating stories from her early twenties. They inspired her to write spicy romantic comedies and parodies that feature a variety of book boyfriends—though most are cinnamon roll golden retrievers. Many of her stories contain LGBTQIA+, disabled, and neurodivergent characters.

Irene can be found on Instagram and TikTok under @irenebahrdauthor

Also by Irene Bahrd

Love & Politics Series

Arranged Vacancy

Absolute Majority

Accepted Precedent

Love at all Cost Series

A Voice Without Reason

Not Her Villain

Maybe in Fifty (*Prequel Novella to Unexpectedly Ruined*)

Unexpectedly Ruined

Sip Happens (*Novella*)

Top Shelf Romances Series

Mine with Extra Lime

Falling the Old Fashioned Way

Royally on the Rocks

Trouble with a Twist

Top Shelf Novellas

Wine About It

Rosé to the Occasion

Mule Tide Cheer

Sapphire Lake Series

Never Yours

Always Heated

Needing to Score Series

Kick Out of It

There is No Try

One Goal in Mind

Ready to Snap

Stand Alone ErotiComs

Flexible Standards

Royally Cuffed

Hard to Swallow

Holiday ErotiCom Novella Series

Merry in Spite

ForNever Mine

Summer of the Switch

Haunted Happenstance

Save a Horse

Standalone Romantic Parodies

Divorce of Convenience

Treble

Expect the Unexpected Parody Novella Duet

Undeclared Heir

Undecided Heiress

Pelligini Crime Daddies Parody Novella Duet

Running from the Garden with Eden

Not My Bodyguard's Keeper

www.ingramcontent.com/pod-product-compliance
Lightning Source LLC
Chambersburg PA
CBHW072022020726
47501CB00006B/1905